SO-ABD-916

THE WALL

THE BRYANT LIBRARY
PAPER MILL ROAD
LYN, NY 11576-2193

DEANNA MADDEN

Copyright © 2016 Deanna Madden

All rights reserved.

ISBN-10: 1535173823
ISBN-13: 978-1535173827

Cover design by SelfPubBookCovers.com/rgporter

Flying Dutchman Press

2016

All characters in this novel are fictional. Any resemblance to real
persons is coincidental.

For those who have lost their lives to the AIDS epidemic, those who have survived it, and those fighting to end it.

No Man is an island entire of itself;
Every man is a piece of the continent, a part of the main. . .

—*John Donne*

CHAPTER 1

Sometimes something happens that lifts my heart and gives me hope all could still be well. That's what it's like when the plane flies over. I'm on playground duty when I see it glinting in the sunlight and hear the familiar drone. All the children stop what they are doing and turn their faces up to the hot blue sky. The plane slowly descends toward the South Zone, where the airport lies. It's the first in a week, and I feel as thrilled as if rain has fallen. It's a good sign. It means supplies are still getting through. For a little longer, we are safe.

It's so hot again today. I hate to think what it must be like on the other side of the wall. Their power went off two weeks ago. Without electricity, people in the South Zone have no air-conditioning or fans. Even on our side everyone is grumbling about the heat. Roberta thinks we shouldn't have to do playground duty when it's so hot. Better to stay inside and continue classes. But the children don't seem to mind. In spite of the heat they are eager for recess and disappointed when it ends. To see them on the playground, shouting, running,

1

jumping rope, and playing ball, you wouldn't know their world has fallen apart. They might be children anywhere, anytime. Or at least most of them might be. There are always a few hanging back on the fringes, orphans feeling strange in their new surroundings, still mourning the loss of fathers and mothers, like Mary, the little Havasupai girl who stands by the chain-link fence watching the other children but making no effort to join in their games. She has been in my class for one week. We don't know her last name. Her file says she speaks English, but so far she hasn't uttered more than a few words. I don't push her. When she's ready, she'll talk.

As the plane disappears, a scuffle breaks out on the playground between Juan and Eric, two second graders. As soon as I see them, I start running. Juan has his fists raised, ready to fight. Eric is down on his knees, teeth bared, snapping at Juan like a dog. The other children are shouting and screaming. Eric is a biter, and I'm afraid he might sink his teeth into Juan before I can stop him. I charge into the circle of children, grab Juan by the shoulder, and push him behind me. I face Eric, who is still on his knees with his teeth bared. For a horrifying second I realize he could bite me. As easy as that, I could be infected with the virus. But of course he isn't infected. They have all been tested. Yes, they have been tested, says a little voice in my brain, yet you can never be sure who has it. I force myself to reach for him in spite of my fear, to grip his thin shoulder and pull him to his feet. He's one of my students and I'm responsible for him.

"Stop this right now," I tell him. "You know the rules. No fighting on the playground."

He pulls sullenly away from my hand. "He started it."

2

"I don't care who started it. There's to be no fighting."

He glares at Juan, and Juan glares back at him. Then the bell rings. The other children immediately lose interest in the fight and surge toward the door. Juan and Eric are gone before I can stop them. I glance at the windows of Strickland's office, and sure enough, he's there. I can see the gleam of his glasses. He must have seen the playground fight. Just my luck. He has a knack for being around when anything goes wrong, like a sort of sixth sense. I think he gets some kind of perverse pleasure from catching one of us at a disadvantage. Well, unfortunately for me he has caught me and that gives him an excuse to call me in. I bet that made his day.

Sure enough, I have hardly stepped into the building when Mrs. Stevenson scurries up to say I'm wanted in the office. She gives me a look of sympathy. I don't blame her. It isn't her fault she has to act as his messenger. I like Mrs. Stevenson. She always has a kind word for everybody. I don't know how she can stand working under a tyrant like Strickland. I suppose, like the rest of us, she needs a paycheck and so she puts up with the crap that goes with it.

It's my second time in a week to be summoned to the office. As usual, Strickland is sitting behind his desk and pretends to be so wrapped up in his work that he lets me stand there a few minutes before he deigns to notice me. I glance at the security monitors mounted on the wall facing his desk. They display all of the classrooms, the cafeteria with its long tables, Mrs. Stevenson at her desk in the outer office, the auditorium, the library, the corridor, the sunbaked grounds. Every trip to his office reminds us that he's watching us like Big Brother, waiting for us to make a mistake. His beady eyes behind his glasses remind me of a rattlesnake I saw when I first came to the Southwest seven years ago. The city wasn't yet closed then and my college science class took a hiking trip into the desert. Our guide, a young Navajo, pointed out a rattlesnake coiled and ready to strike. We all looked at it, keeping a safe distance between us and the snake while the guide stood by with a stick. That's what Strickland reminds me of, a rattlesnake sitting behind his desk looking as if he's about to strike. You can almost hear the rattle.

While I wait, he runs one hand over his bald head, as if smoothing the hair that isn't there.

"I saw what happened on the playground," he says, not looking up.

"It won't happen again," I assure him.

"Those were your students, weren't they?"

Yes, they were my students. He knows that.

Now he looks up. "You have to control the children, Miss Davis. You understand that, don't you? That kind of behavior can't be tolerated."

"Children their age sometimes don't stop to think," I tell him, for all the good it will do.

"They must think," he says coldly, beady eyes fixed on me. "We're here to teach them to think." He taps an index finger against his temple. "The survival of the human race may depend on their ability to think. If they fight, someone may bleed. It's a matter of life and death."

"I know that."

I also know it would be pointless to argue with him. Better to say as little as possible and get this interview over with faster. I don't really see how I can stop Juan and Eric from fighting, but I know I'll have to talk to them, especially Eric, who has already bitten one student. If he bites another, Strickland may decide he's too much of a risk, and if he gets expelled, where will he go?

"These are difficult times for us all." Strickland shifts his gaze from me to the windows that look out on the dusty playground. "I've often wondered what it's like, growing up in times like these. It's so different from when I was young."

Different from when any of us were young, I could say but don't.

"Miss Davis, do you have a boyfriend?" he asks abruptly, his eyes swiveling to me again.

I want to tell him it's none of his business, but of course I can't, not if I want to keep my job. No, I don't have a boyfriend.

"It must be hard—a pretty young woman like you."

I clench my teeth, determined not to let him get to me.

"May I go now?" Without waiting for an answer, I turn and head for the door. A rattlesnake can't hurt you if you are out of range. That's what the guide told us that day.

"It's a shame," Strickland says behind me. "No one is safe from the virus, not even pretty young women."

I pretend I haven't heard and keep going. Someday he's going to go too far, and I'll tell him what I think of him, but this isn't that day. What a jerk! As if I need him to tell me I'm not safe from the virus. No one is safe from the virus. It's everywhere around us. You can't watch TV without seeing it in the news, on commercials, in the sit-coms and the dramas. You can't pick up a newspaper without reading about it. You can't have a conversation without someone mentioning it. But I'm not going to let him goad me into saying something I'll regret later. I don't want to lose my job at the school. My students need me, and I need them. They are my family, the only family I have now. A bully like Strickland is not going to take that away from me.

I have already lost so much. At night I dream about people who are gone. I dream about friends who have died. I dream about my family. In my dreams they are still alive. My dreams are crowded with people, and then I wake to a world which every day seems a little emptier and lonelier.

CHAPTER 2

The North Zone seems like a city mysteriously abandoned by half its population. Everywhere you see the signs. There is less traffic than there was in the past. There are fewer cars, of course, because not many people can afford to drive them now that gas costs so much. Most people commute by bus or ride motorcycles or mopeds or bikes. The faster vehicles use the speed lane, which leaves the other lanes for the rest of us. When I first came to the city seven years ago, the streets and freeways were jammed with rush hour traffic when I got off work. No more. And it's almost eerily quiet, except for the occasional police car or ambulance racing by with its siren wailing. Most of the buildings I pass now are deserted-looking and the storefronts boarded up. So many places have gone out of business. The only thing that hasn't changed is the big billboard of a smiling woman with the message 'Be Safe, Not Sorry.' Sometimes I imagine her smiling down on an empty street after all of us are gone. I wonder what the infected workers think when they pass her. Was she deliberately placed there so that they will see her just before the wall comes into view? Was she intended to be a rebuke as well as a warning?

I was eighteen years old when I left my hometown in the Midwest. I have lived here for seven years now. I suppose it's as good a place as another to be during these uncertain times. You can't really blame the people who live here for building the wall. Cities which did not try to separate the healthy from the sick have become violent and terrible places to live.

Here there has not been a lot of violence because we have the wall. Topped by high-voltage wires, the wall stretches across the city. Where it stops for a street or highway, there are surveillance cameras and armed guards at sentry posts. Built five years ago, it separates the north part of the city from the south, dividing the city into the North Zone and the South Zone. Before it was built, the northern part of the city was the more prosperous half with miles of suburbs where the affluent and middle-class lived. The southern part was dirtier, crime-ridden, an eye-sore where the poor lived in rundown neighborhoods. Now those who test positive must live in the South Zone. They have no choice. The North Zone sends them food, clothing, and medicine. They have their own schools, their own police, their own churches, and hospitals for their sick. Those who still show no symptoms can even work at jobs on this side of the wall during the day, provided they wear the regulation red armband.

Even though I pass the wall every day, it still makes me feel uncomfortable. You would think I'd be used to it, but I'm not. It has more graffiti now than when I first started teaching at the State School fresh out of college three years ago, although I can't imagine when anyone has the opportunity to scrawl graffiti on it since there are always guards around as well as security cameras. At the checkpoint bicyclists and pedestrians with red armbands wait in line in the scorching heat to be allowed to return to the South Zone.

So far there's enough food, but that's because there are fewer of us to buy it. I usually stop at Safeway on my way home. The shelves are no longer well stocked nor the aisles crowded with shoppers. Fresh produce is scarcer than it used to be, and what there is, is expensive. I have learned to eat simply and rely on canned food. Besides, since I don't have a car, I'm limited by what I can fit in my backpack.

Today a new girl mans the checkout counter, a sullen teenager with wild red hair, lots of eye makeup, a nose ring, and a red armband. Usually Phyllis checks me out. I feel like I know her because I've been shopping here for so long. She always has a friendly smile and asks me how I'm doing. I know her name from her name tag. The new girl's tag says her name is Audrey.

"Where's Phyllis?" I ask as Audrey rings up my groceries.

As soon as the words are out, I wish I hadn't asked. They just slipped out. I should have known better. If someone disappears, you don't ask. You pretend not to notice. Audrey hands me back my debit card and shrugs. She doesn't look sick, but then workers don't. That comes later.

By the time I get back to the Glenview Tower, I'm feeling mildly depressed. It hasn't been a good day. There was the fight on the playground, Strickland calling me into his office to reprimand me, and then Phyllis missing. I don't really know Phyllis, but I feel upset by her disappearance all the same. I tell myself perhaps she just has a cold or the flu. Perhaps there's some perfectly normal explanation for why she wasn't there today. But I don't believe it. People disappear every day. So many have disappeared. You just can't get attached. It only leads to heartache.

I have just finished chaining my bike in the parking garage and am walking toward the back entrance of the building when I hear a meow. A black and white cat steps from behind a concrete divider and looks up at me with soulful eyes. She meows as if she knows me, so I kneel and pet her. She has lovely fur, soft as silk.

"Who do you belong to?" I ask. She keeps meowing. Probably hungry. "I can't take you in," I tell her. "No pets permitted." I wonder if she belongs to someone in the building. (Not everyone obeys the rules.) Or used to belong to someone. Maybe her owner was banished to the South Zone. There are getting to be a lot of stray cats and dogs about whose owners have been sent to the South Zone. She meows again. I wonder if I let her in, would the security cameras spot her? If they did, I'd be in trouble. So would the cat, for that matter.

"You can't come in. It's against the rules."

She looks up at me and meows again. Then she rubs against my legs. How do you argue with a cat? It's a stupid rule anyway. And what will they do if they catch her? Probably just put her outside again. She would be no worse off for being caught. I unlock the door with my key card, and as soon as it opens of course the cat streaks in. Now I ask you, is that my fault? I can always say I didn't notice her. Hopefully the security guards in the lobby aren't watching their monitors closely. With any luck they are reading the newspaper or doing a crossword. I press the elevator button, but as usual the elevator takes forever to arrive. All the time the cat keeps looking up at me and meowing while I try to ignore her. When the doors finally open, I'm relieved to see the elevator is empty. So far, so good. The cat rides up to the fifteenth floor with me.

"This is only temporary," I warn when we get off. "I want you to understand that." I figure even cats need to learn they shouldn't get attached in times like these. In answer she merely meows again, and when I open the door to my apartment, she walks in as if she owns the place. I know right then I'm going to regret this. But now that it's done, I might as well feed her. If a security guard is on the way up, at least she can get a little nourishment in her before being kicked out again.

I open a can of tuna and slosh some milk into a saucer. While the cat is busy with these, I take Mrs. Franklin's supplies down the hall to her. The first thing I do each day when I get home is check on her. Mrs. Franklin is in her seventies and lives at the end of my hall. She has a son in Los Angeles, but she hasn't heard from him in a year. Probably he's dead, although we never say that. She has no way of getting to a grocery store since she can't ride a bike and walks with a cane, so I buy food for her and whatever else she needs. Someone has to.

Because of our arrangement, I have a key card to let myself into her apartment. Today Mrs. Franklin is sitting in front of her television as usual when I arrive. The late afternoon sun streams in through the sliding glass doors and falls on the shelves of small Hopi Indian dolls and rocks collected with her husband. She sits in her armchair looking like an ancient priestess with her leathery wrinkled skin and her snow white hair. Around her neck she wears the turquoise necklace which her husband gave her on their fortieth anniversary and which I have never seen her without. I suspect she even wears it in her sleep. On the wall above her hangs another of her prized possessions, a Navajo rug she has had for years. She is surrounded by furniture as old and worn out as herself, including the television, which must be at least twenty years old and which I keep hoping won't break down because there's no way we can replace it.

"There you are, Sarah," she says. "I knew you'd be along soon."

"Anything in the news?" I go into her small kitchen and start putting away her groceries. I always ask her if there's any news. She never leaves her apartment, and yet she knows more about what's going on in the world than I do because she watches TV all day long.

"Did you hear about the plane that flew from Beijing to Tokyo?" she asks me.

No, I haven't. "What about it?"

"Everyone on it was infected. Tokyo complained. They wanted it to turn around and fly back."

"Did it?" I'm curious in spite of myself. We've all heard so many news stories like this that it's hard to feel shocked. I almost never listen to news anymore. I don't see the point. If it's bad, it depresses me, and if it's good, I don't believe it. But unlike me, Mrs. Franklin never seems to lose her conviction that everything will work out.

"No, it couldn't go back. The people on the plane said they'd be killed."

They were probably right. "So Tokyo will let them stay?"

"I don't think they had decided. But what other choice do they have?"

I sigh. They could send the people back to die, but I don't say that aloud. That was the choice they had. I hoped they didn't do that, but I knew they might. Not that it mattered in the long run. In the long run the people who were infected would all die anyway, but at least if they were allowed to stay in Japan they would have a little more time. That was the best they could hope for.

"The electricity is still off in the South Zone," I tell her. I think this is something she should know. Her apartment doesn't face toward the wall, like mine does, and the local news seems to be ignoring the power outage. No surprise there. We are all encouraged to keep up the pretense that all is well when day by day the situation grows bleaker. I no longer believe the news reports that the virus is under control. Daily we are assured by the news media that as long as we behave like responsible citizens and observe all the emergency restrictions, we will be safe. The authorities insist that we are dealing with this unprecedented health crisis in the most efficient way possible. The number of cases detected daily is falling, or so they claim. And here in the U.S. our manner of dealing with the infected is humane compared to places like China, where people testing positive are sent directly to euthanasia centers. The reports of violence in New York and Los Angeles have ceased. I don't know if the violence has stopped or if the news media has just stopped telling us about it. I suspect they have just stopped telling us about it.

"I'm sure it's just temporary," she says, ever the optimist.

"You're probably right," I agree, because what would be

the point of upsetting her? I wish I could share her optimism, but I don't. What if their electricity doesn't come back on? In fact, what if we lose ours too? And what if the wall can't keep out the violence brewing in the South Zone? Will we be safe in the Glenview Tower, fifteen floors up? Will anywhere be safe? I try to push these negative thoughts away. Worrying won't do any good. I really have to learn to stop worrying so much. And that makes me remember something else I've been trying not to think about all day. Tomorrow is Saturday and I'm due for a blood test. One of my least favorite things in all the world.

"What's wrong?" she asks.

"Oh, it's nothing." Our eyes meet and I look away. She's actually a very sharp old lady. I might as well tell her. I take a deep breath and try to sound casual. "I have to go for my six-months' blood test tomorrow."

She doesn't say anything right away. When I look at her again, she gives me an encouraging smile. "I'm sure it'll be just fine."

She's only an old woman who can't even take care of herself, but all the same, sometimes she can comfort me like my grandmother did when I was a child. I turn away so she won't see tears in my eyes and busy myself putting away the rest of her groceries.

CHAPTER 3

As long as I can remember, I have hated hospitals and done my best to avoid them. However, since the blood test became required by law, I have dutifully shown up every six months at the State Hospital. The building itself does nothing to calm my anxiety. It's like an armed fortress, surrounded by barricades and wire fences, with armed security guards standing at the entrance. Every time I pass through those glass doors, I must gather up my courage and steel myself for the ordeal like a test by fire. And yet once inside, I'm surprised by how tranquil the building seems. After the heat outdoors, it's like stepping into a cool underwater chamber. Even sounds seem muted. A soothing voice is paging a doctor over the intercom. I don't need to ask directions. I've done this enough times to know where to go. I just follow the big yellow arrows painted on the tile floor to the blood lab in the back of the building.

When I go up to the counter of the lab to check in, I notice the young Mexican receptionist is wearing a red armband. She barely glances at me but goes on talking on her headset in Spanish while she checks my name off. It's a small room and most of the chairs are occupied. A large TV screen mounted on the wall shows a game show in progress. I sit down in one of the few remaining unoccupied chairs. Beside me a well-dressed woman, maybe in her mid-thirties, has a magazine open in her lap and is idly flipping the pages with manicured nails.

"You wouldn't think they'd have them working here," she says in a low voice, shooting a look of disapproval at the Mexican girl with the red armband.

I wonder if I should get up and move to another chair. And why shouldn't they be working here? Does she think she's going to get the virus just by breathing the same air? I'm tempted to say something of this sort but restrain myself. It wouldn't be polite.

Some people in the North Zone would like to ban workers from the South Zone altogether. There have been impassioned debates on TV. They argue that we have a right and a duty to protect ourselves from contamination, and others argue that the infected workers pose no real threat to us, so long as we all obey the new laws. I believe infected workers will continue to be allowed to cross the wall. Not just because it's humane to allow them, but because we need them. The North Zone carefully regulates their numbers, for fear they might rise up against us, but if we attempt to ban them all beyond the wall, who will keep the city running? There aren't enough of us anymore.

"I expect they're short on staff, just like everyone else," I respond.

She is wearing a wedding ring I notice, which means she

probably has a family to go home to. I know I shouldn't look at women's fingers to see who's wearing a wedding ring. It's getting to be a bad habit of mine. Besides, her whole family could be dead and she still might wear her ring. A little diamond on the ring finger of her left hand means nothing at all. All the same, I can't keep myself from asking the question. So much for self-control.

"Do you have children?" I ask in the sunniest voice I can muster and smile brightly. I just hope she won't say they are dead. But if she does, it will serve me right for being so nosy.

To my relief she smiles back. Now she looks younger and less anxious. She leans toward me confidentially and speaks in a low voice, all in a rush, as if she was just waiting to be asked. "A boy and a girl. Eight and six. My son's good at math. He takes after his father—my husband's an engineer—and my daughter is musical. She's learning to play the piano." Obviously she likes to talk about her family. Having gotten her started, I wonder if I can get her to stop. I feel my smile stretching thin as she tells me about her children's seemingly endless accomplishments. Well, I have only myself to blame. I asked, didn't I?

Then she whips out a phone and starts flipping through family photos, ending with one of the whole family—mother, father, daughter, son—all smiling at the camera against a background of blue sky and squinting a little in the sunlight. Even though I feel a pang of envy, I find it comforting to know there are still families like that. My work at the State School for Homeless Children sometimes makes me forget there are still real families out there.

She finally breaks off her stream of patter and glances

nervously at her phone. "It's been forty-five minutes. I don't understand what's taking so long."

"They're probably understaffed," I say again.

Just then a young male orderly sticks his head out of the swinging doors and calls my name. I stand up quickly and follow him. He too wears a red armband. Of course he looks perfectly healthy. Cheerful too. He's whistling as he leads me to a small cubicle equipped with two stools and little else. You wouldn't think he had a care in the world. At any rate he doesn't seem to be bothered by the fact that he's going to die in the foreseeable future. I'm sure if I had the virus, I wouldn't be nearly so cheerful about it.

When I'm seated, he reaches for my left hand. This is the moment I've been dreading. I jerk back involuntarily.

"Sorry." I take a deep breath and hold out my hand. I can do this I tell myself.

He sits there with the needle poised, regarding me. He has hazel eyes and reminds me of boys in the Midwest I went to high school with. "You think I'm going to infect you, is that it?"

I try to concentrate on his eyes and not look at the needle. I realize he's waiting for an answer. "No, I'm sorry, I couldn't help it. It's nothing to do with you."

"You think I might deliberately give you the virus, don't you?"

"No, of course not." I wish he would just get it over with. I really don't want to explain.

But he isn't ready to let it go. "When you see this red armband, you think—"

"I hate needles, all right?" My voice is louder than I intended. I bite my lip.

He looks at me blankly. Hasn't he ever met anyone who hates needles?

"I faint at the sight of blood," I explain, risking humiliation. "Especially my own." I would have preferred to keep this little flaw of mine private, but I don't want him to think I flinched because he has the virus.

He looks at the syringe and then at me, as if trying to understand. Then he starts laughing, although I don't see what's so funny. He laughs so hard he has to wipe the tears from his eyes. I begin to think he's never going to stop. I wonder if I should pummel him on the back like you do when someone is choking. Finally he gets himself under control, but just barely.

"Maybe you shouldn't watch," he suggests magnanimously.

As if I ever had any intention of watching. I nod, clench my teeth, and close my eyes tightly. The needle pricks my finger. I tell myself I must not faint. It would be too embarrassing. Especially after the way he laughed. I can just see myself keeled over on the floor while he bends double laughing.

After he has his samples, which I am careful not to look at, he gives me a piece of gauze to press against my finger to stop the bleeding.

"So you faint at the sight of blood," he says, smiling broadly. I can imagine how he'll enjoy telling the other orderlies later. The story will be repeated over and over. I'll be famous as the young woman who couldn't bear to be pricked by a needle. Sleeping Beauty, move over.

"It will be about forty-five minutes," he says, still grinning.

When I get back to the waiting room, the woman with the wedding ring is gone. I pick up the magazine she left behind and try to read. I don't want to spend the next forty-five minutes worrying about the results of the test. I run little risk. Still, there are always horror stories. People infected by their dentists. People infected by crazed people who wanted revenge. People who have no idea how they were infected. And then I've heard the tests are not one hundred percent accurate. Sometimes they make mistakes. Sometimes there are false positives.

I turn the pages of the magazine listlessly. It seems to be almost entirely ads. The faces of attractive young men and women smile back at me, gleaming white teeth and perfect tans, their bodies sleek and healthy. To look at them, you wouldn't know there was an epidemic. They look as if they exist in a world where no one wears a red armband.

I'm skimming an article about nutrition when I hear a scream. There are about fifteen of us in the waiting room, and the scream sends a shock wave through us. We all know what it means. Someone has tested positive. A minute later a woman bursts through the swinging doors. It's the woman with the wedding ring. She looks around wildly and her eyes fix on me. "Help me!" she cries. Before she can say anything else, a male orderly lunges through the door behind her and tackles her. She struggles to free herself, but he's on top of her shouting for help.

The doors swing open again and I see the young orderly with the red armband who took my blood. He's carrying a hypodermic. At sight of it the woman struggles even harder. I don't blame her.

"Oh, please let me go," she pleads. "It's a mistake."

I look away, unable to watch.

"Jones! Hurry up!" the first orderly shouts.

"I'm married," the woman insists. "It's not possible. It's a mistake."

The first orderly is swearing. Jones manages to administer the hypodermic.

It's several minutes before she is subdued enough for them to carry her away. After they are gone, we all just sit there avoiding each other's eyes. I wonder if the others feel as guilty as I do. Not one of us raised a finger to help her. We sat by like sheep and did nothing.

My hands are shaking. I give up trying to read the magazine and fling it down on the end table. I wonder if she will have a chance to see her husband and her children before she is sent across the wall. I've heard that sometimes people just disappear. Their families make inquiries, but no one seems to know what happened to them. Will it be like that for her?

After what seems like an eternity but probably is only twenty minutes, the Mexican girl at the desk calls my name again. "You can go in now." She doesn't smile; her attention is already focused elsewhere. I'm just another patient. It's nothing to her whether I test positive or negative. Maybe that's what wearing the red armband does to people—makes them indifferent to the fate of others, especially strangers. I take a deep breath and walk through the swinging doors, heading for the same cubicle I was in before. My orderly with the red armband is there looking at a file and drinking a can of soda as if nothing happened.

"You're okay," he says without looking up. "You can go." He waves his hand toward the door.

I feel a wave of relief. I know I should just turn and leave but I don't.

"What about that woman?" I ask him. For once I'm determined not to keep quiet. After all, she looked directly at me when she cried out for help. She asked *me* for help.

"What woman?"

"The one who tested positive."

Now he looks up. I have caught his attention. "Do you know her? Is she a friend of yours?"

"No. I've never seen her before."

"She'll be okay," he says, losing interest again. "Don't worry about it."

"She won't be okay," I say, unwilling to be dismissed so easily. "Not if she has the virus."

"Hey, I don't make the rules."

I feel a surge of anger, but I know anger will get me nowhere. I want to do something for the woman. She begged for help. Obviously no one else is going to help her, certainly not this orderly named Jones who only knows how to stick needles into people. "Well, could you tell me her name?" I ask, holding my anger in check. If I know her name, I can call her family. I can tell them what happened to her. It isn't much but at least it's something.

"Sorry. We aren't allowed to give out patients' names."

Of course he isn't.

"Doesn't it even bother you?" I ask, thoroughly exasperated by his apparent lack of concern.

"Yeah, it bothers me," he says, looking up again, meeting my eyes. "I just can't do anything about it. Neither can you. Now get out of here before you get into trouble."

He turns his back on me, as if that's the end of it. I wonder how he can be so callous. He has the virus himself and yet he lacks compassion for someone else's suffering. She just found out she has the virus. Her whole world has been turned upside down. Doesn't he understand that?

I storm out of the hospital and pedal my bike furiously through the half-deserted streets. Instead of feeling relief that I passed the blood test, I feel only anger. In my mind I keep seeing the frightened look on the woman's face. This alternates with the face of the orderly Jones. Why didn't he help her? The other orderly was to blame too of course, but Jones wears a red armband. He knows what it's like to be infected. At the very least he ought to have refused to help subdue her. Of course, if he had, he'd probably lose his job. And no doubt he sees people every day who test positive. He's probably used to it. Why does it bother me so much anyway? Is it because of the woman or is it because of Jones? She was a total stranger, and I didn't even like her very much. In a way there was a cruel sort of justice about her fate. I doubt she would have made that comment about the Mexican girl at the check-in desk if she had known she was about to be diagnosed with the virus herself. Still, as a punishment it was far too harsh for her offense.

And what of Jones with his hazel eyes and boyish grin? Admit it, I tell myself, you were attracted to him. You felt a twinge of regret about the red armband—and not just because it meant he had the virus, but because it meant you must not allow yourself to feel attracted to him. And why should it bother me anyway? Haven't I resigned myself to the fact that I'll probably never fall in love, never get married, and never have a family? The chance of any of those things happening is fairly remote. Sometimes it seems as if there are no young men left. The great majority of them, I conclude in my darker moments, recklessly exposed themselves to the virus, just as they drove cars too fast and jumped out of planes for the thrill of it. Why couldn't they have been a little more cautious?

I need someone to talk to, so I ride to Roberta's apartment instead of going back to the Glenview Tower. Roberta lives with her brother Victor and his wife in a low-rise apartment building about twenty minutes from the school. Their place is always noisy and full of life. Often friends are visiting. Mexican music blares through the apartment, and people are shouting and laughing. I envy the way they have each other and the way they can carry on as if all around us people aren't getting sick and dying.

Victor answers the door and flashes me a smile of perfect white teeth. The TV is going in the background. "Sarah," he says, "hey, you're just in time to settle an argument. Who played Che Guevara in the movie? You know the movie?"

I shake my head. "I don't think I saw it."

"No kidding? I thought everybody saw that movie. Hey, you know what? We got to rent the DVD. You got to come over and we'll all watch it."

"Okay," I say. "You rent it, and I'll bring the popcorn."

"Hey, Sarah," Roberta calls from across the room, where she's folding laundry on the sofa. "What's up? You look like someone died." She claps her hand over her mouth. "Oh, my god, I can't believe I said that."

"It's all right," I say, smiling wanly. "No one died."

"She doesn't know who played Che Guevara," Victor says.

"Yeah, I heard. Sarah, how about we go for a run? You look like you need a good run."

"You have to lend me clothes. I'm not dressed for it."

"Sure. I've got something."

I borrow a jogging outfit and ten minutes later we set off in spite of the midday heat. We run on the sidewalks, our shoes pounding a steady rhythm. She was right. It feels good to run. It's just what I need. I try not to think about what happened at the hospital. By the time we've gone six blocks, I'm sweating and out of breath. I stop to let myself recover. Roberta takes a swig from her water bottle and hands it to me.

"You ought to run more," she says. "You need to keep in shape." She runs every day and works out at a gym several times a week. Like so many others, she thinks if she's in great physical condition, she can't catch the virus, which of course isn't true.

"I'll be all right," I say. "Just give me a minute to catch my breath."

"So what's bothering you?"

I tell her about the woman at the hospital.

"Her husband probably gave it to her. They'll check him of course."

"But they didn't have to treat her like that." I feel like she missed the point.

"In New York or LA they'd probably just shoot her." Roberta stretches her arms up, then out. Then does a couple of lunges.

"I don't see why she has to be taken away from her family. What would it hurt to let her stay with them?"

She shrugs. "People are scared. You know that. They don't

want to catch it. They don't want to die. Can you blame them? Come on, let's go a little farther."

We cut through a small park, where we stop again in the shade of a tree. Not far from us, a man is lying on a bench near a trash barrel. I know we should just ignore him, but I can't.

"Maybe he's sick. We should check."

Roberta puts a hand on my arm. "You know it's not safe."

"I'm tired of worrying about what's safe." I start walking toward the man. Perhaps he's had an attack of some sort. Perhaps he's suffering from heat exhaustion or dehydration. All the same I stop a few feet away.

"Are you all right?"

He doesn't move. Maybe he's sleeping. But this isn't a good place to sleep. Somebody walking or running through the park might report him. It's a law now—suspected vagrants are to be reported.

"Excuse me." I reach out and touch his shoulder.

I can feel the bone of his shoulder through his shirt. He opens his eyes and blinks up at me. Pale blue eyes with white eyelashes.

"Are you all right?" I ask again.

He's so thin, eyes sunken and vacant. He looks as if he's dying. Why is he here? Why isn't he on the other side of the wall?

He smiles at me and holds out his hand. It's skeletal. With effort I force myself to touch it. I feel the bones of his hand against my own and hear a siren in the distance.

Roberta pulls me away. "We have to get out of here."

"What about him?" I look back over my shoulder.

The siren is growing louder. Out of the corner of my eye I see a police car veer into the park, blue light flashing.

"We can't do anything. It's already too late." She breaks into a run, and after a second's hesitation, I run after her.

As we emerge from the park, we hear gunfire behind us.

"Why are they shooting?" My eyes blur with tears.

"Don't stop," Roberta says. "You want them to shoot at us too?"

CHAPTER 4

We are doing sums when the alarm goes off. My students look up at me to see what they should do.

"All right. You know where to go," I say. "No talking. No pushing. Follow Lydia."

Lydia Hogue is my teaching assistant, an LA transplant, tall, regal, African-American, eighteen years old, unflappable, a natural at corralling second-graders.

Excited by the break from their routine, they spring into action, surging toward the door to follow her out of the room. We have weekly emergency drills now, and the children look on them as a way to get out of schoolwork. The number of drills has increased because everyone is worried about what will happen if the violence of the South Zone crosses the wall. No one knows how much longer our police can keep out the wild gangs that attack the wall each night. Even with the emergency draft, there are not enough men and women to police the city anymore.

As the last students file out of the room, I notice Mary still sitting at her desk, her black braid dangling down her back, her black eyes watching me.

"Mary, hurry," I urge.

She doesn't move.

It's only a drill, but every drill has to be taken seriously so the children will know what to do in a real emergency. And I'm supposed to stay with my class.

There's no time to lose. I lean down beside her and look straight into her eyes. "You can't stay here. You must go with the others."

Still she doesn't move.

"Don't you understand?" I ask. "When the alarm goes off, we must all go to safety." Not for the first time, I wonder if her file could be wrong. Perhaps she understands very little English. I have never heard her speak more than a few words. When students read aloud, I always have to skip her because she won't do it. She just looks at me with those impenetrable eyes. I have no idea what's going through her mind. On impulse I hold out my hand. She hesitates, then takes it. "Run with me," I say. She nods. And so we run hand in hand out of the classroom, down the now deserted hall, and out through the doors to the playground, where all the other classes wait, lined up, teachers attempting to keep their students under control.

As usual, Strickland is standing just outside the door, stopwatch in hand.

"You're the last, Miss Davis," he says sternly. "You must do better than that."

"I'm sorry," I murmur.

"And who is this?" He scowls down at Mary, who shrinks a little closer to me and stares at the ground.

"Mary. She's new. She didn't understand what to do."

"Well, perhaps you'd better enlighten her before our next drill."

"I will." I hold tight to her hand and head to where my class is lined up against the fence, with Lydia threatening the troublemakers with detention if they don't behave.

Roberta stands nearby with her third graders. "Hey, girl, you trying to get yourself fired?" she says in a low voice when I pass her.

"Looks that way, doesn't it?" I mutter.

When we get to my class, I release Mary's hand and turn my attention to the other students. Lydia still has them under control, but they are starting to get restless now that the excitement is over.

"What happened?" Lydia asks too low for the nearest students to hear.

"Mary didn't know what to do. Maybe she hasn't been through a drill before."

"Well, she'll get plenty of practice here. What about old Strychnine?"

I look back and to my relief Strickland isn't still watching me. One of the new young teachers has caught his attention and is getting a scolding for some minor infraction like chewing gum or wearing open-toed shoes. I'm off the hook for now.

I hope that will be the end of it, but of course it isn't. We march back inside and the children hardly have time to resume their lesson when Mrs. Stevenson's motherly voice drifts across the intercom: "Will Mary in Miss Davis's class please report to the principal's office."

All heads turn to look at Mary. She keeps her eyes on her book.

"Keep working," I tell my class and their heads bow reluctantly over their books again. I walk over to Mary. "You have to go to the office," I tell her.

She looks at a spot on the floor. I'm sure she understands me. She probably understood the intercom message too.

"You have to," I insist as gently as I can.

This time she raises her eyes and meets mine. "Please don't make me go, Miss Davis," she whispers. Since I have hardly heard her speak so far, this seems like progress. Evidently she can speak English when she wants to.

I try to reassure her. "It'll be okay."

"I'm afraid."

"Afraid of what?"

"Mr. Strickland."

"You shouldn't be. Listen, I'll go with you. We'll go together. Okay?" I offer my hand again, remembering that it worked during the fire drill.

After a slight hesitation, she takes it for the second time today.

Strickland is glowering at his computer when we enter his office. Behind him the monitors show what is happening in each classroom. Bill Myers' fifth graders are watching a film about lions. Two students in Roberta's class are writing on the blackboard. In my classroom Lydia is walking up and down the aisles, stopping from time to time to look more closely at a

31

student's paper. I can always depend on Lydia to keep the class under control. She's a good assistant, and I'm lucky to have her.

"Miss Davis, I don't remember asking you to come to my office," Strickland says, frowning at me over the top of his glasses.

"Mary is shy."

"So shy that she can't come here by herself?" He raises an eyebrow.

"I thought I could help."

Mary holds tightly to my hand. I'm not about to abandon her to Strickland.

"She ought to be able to come to the office by herself when she's called." He glares at me, but I hold my ground. "I only want to ask her a few questions." He looks hard at Mary. "You don't mind if I ask you a few questions, do you?" She presses even closer to me. "There. See. No problem. How old are you, Mary?"

She looks down at the floor. "Eight," she says so softly I wonder if he heard her.

He picks up a pen and taps it on his desk, as if still waiting for the answer. I could repeat it, but that would probably make matters worse.

"And do you like it here at our school?"

She glances up at me uncertainly. If he keeps this up, she will be so intimidated she'll say nothing at all.

"It's all so new for her," I explain. "She needs time to adjust. She's only been here a week."

"Let her answer for herself," Strickland commands. "She can speak English, can't she?"

"Of course she can." If Mary can't speak English, he might use that as an excuse to get rid of her.

"Then let her speak."

I clench my teeth and hope she will answer his questions.

"Well, Mary, do you like it here?"

"I don't know," she says in a barely audible voice.

He leans back in his chair and runs his hand over the dome of his bald head. "I ask because there's a bus taking some of your people to a reservation near Tucson and we've become so crowded now that we can hardly take care of all our students. I thought you might fit in better there."

It seems I was right to suspect his intentions.

"Please give her a little more time," I urge. I don't want him to send her to a reservation. The reservations have become terrible places of starvation and sickness with the spread of the epidemic. Children from them have been sent to the city in an attempt to save them from it.

"Mary would be with her own people," he says.

"They're not her people. Mary is Havasupai."

Last week I looked the Havasupai up on the Internet to see if I could find out more about them. There wasn't much, but I did find two color photos—one of a waterfall dropping from a canyon wall to a pool of blue water below (Havasu Falls, according to the caption); the other of the village of Supai, nestled in the canyon with rocks towering above it against a blue sky with white clouds drifting by. It's a remote spot. According to the article, you can only get there by going down a steep trail into the canyon. Apparently people used to be able to go down by mule or horseback for a price, but I imagine with the way things are now, it's probably completely cut off. Poor kid, so far from home.

"They're Indians," he says coldly. "That's what matters.

Well, Mary, what do you say? Would you like to go to the reservation and be with your own people?"

She looks up at me again. "I'd like to stay with you," she whispers.

"Speak up," Strickland snaps. "No one's going to bite you."

"She says she would like to stay at the school."

He gives me a warning look.

"But if you aren't happy here— No, I think we'd better send you to the reservation."

I can't stay silent and let this happen. "Please. Let her stay." I don't like to ask him for anything, but this is not for me. This is for a little girl who can't speak for herself. I'll swallow my pride if I need to. I can't let him send her to a reservation.

"We have too many students now," he says, waving vaguely at the monitors. "It isn't practical."

I tell myself not to lose my temper, try to appeal to his better instincts, if he has any. "We have to save as many of the children as we can. The future depends on them."

But I might as well try to argue with a block of concrete.

"I decide what's best for the school, Miss Davis," he says. "And my mind is already made up. She doesn't belong here. She belongs with her people."

Mary looks up at me with anxious eyes. I squeeze her hand. I want to reassure her, but in fact what can I do? If Strickland decides to send her away, I can't stop him. I'm only a teacher, not the one in charge.

"Of course we might work out something," he says. "A sort of compromise. It depends on how badly you want Mary to stay." He clicks his pen open, then closed. "Think about it."

I don't ask him what sort of compromise he has in mind. Whatever it is, I won't like it. I'll get Mary out of here and then think what to do. "Come on, Mary," I say and lead her out of the room. I'm so angry I barely nod at Mrs. Stevenson as we go through the outer office. I don't trust myself to speak.

"Miss Davis, please don't let him send me away," Mary pleads as we walk back down the corridor.

"Everything will be okay," I assure her, trying to sound more confident than I feel. I wonder if there is really a bus going to Tucson. Could a bus get through? Would Mary be safer there than at the school? It's true the school is overcrowded, but getting rid of one second grader won't change that. No, Strickland plans to use Mary to get at me. When he saw her with me at the drill, he guessed I took a special interest in her and decided to use it against me. Poor Mary. She has gotten us both into more trouble than she knows by not jumping up from her seat when the alarm went off. If I don't cooperate with him, what will happen to her?

"Couldn't I live with you, Miss Davis?" Mary asks, looking up at me. "I wouldn't be any trouble."

I look down at her anxious face. I'm glad she's speaking now. At least that's one good thing that has come out of this. I know I should be careful what I say. I don't want her to stop talking again. I have no idea what she has been through, but I know it's important for her to trust me enough to open up.

"I'm sorry," I tell her. "You can't live with me. It's against school regulations."

"I wouldn't eat much," she says. "I could sleep on the floor."

I want to hug her and promise that everything will be okay. We are outside the classroom door, and I can hear the children's voices reciting addition tables in unison.

"I know you're lonely and you miss your family and everything seems strange. But you must be brave. All of us must be brave. And we mustn't lose hope. Do you understand?"

She nods.

"Good." I reach for the door handle.

I don't know how I'll persuade Strickland not to send her away, but somehow I have to. I can't let her be sent to a reservation, where she will surely die.

CHAPTER 5

"They say things are getting worse on the other side of the wall."

Lydia has stayed after classes are done for the day to help me mount the students' artwork on the bulletin boards. My mind isn't really on our conversation; it's on Mary and Strickland's threat to send her to a reservation. All day I have been trying to think what I can do to help Mary. I didn't tell Lydia about Strickland's threat. After all, it isn't her problem.

"It's got to be bad with the power off," I remark automatically.

The drawing I'm taping up just caught my attention. Ramon Martinez has scribbled over a number of stick figures in his drawing with heavy black crayon. I make a mental note to refer him to the school psychologist. Heavy black crayon scribbles are always a bad sign.

"I hear they don't even give people funerals anymore. They just dump their bodies in pits or burn them. Do you think that's true?"

"Might be," I agree absently.

"You think they'll ever find a cure?"

"Maybe."

I tape up a drawing of three small smiling people and a huge sun that occupies most of the sky. At least there are no black scribbles on this one.

"I don't know. They've been saying that a long time now. What if they don't? What if they never find a cure?"

A hint of despair in her voice finally makes me turn and look at her. To my surprise, she has tears in her eyes. "What is it?" I ask her. "What's wrong?"

She begins to cry. "I don't want to be thrown in a pit with a lot of other corpses when I die, just thrown away like a piece of garbage, or burned."

I don't know what to say. What brought this on? Does she think she has the virus? Surely we wouldn't be standing here talking so normally if she thinks that, but clearly something has upset her. I've never seen her cry before. She's usually so practical and strong. I wonder if someone she knows has contracted the virus. I don't think she has any family. She just graduated from high school a couple of months ago. If it weren't for the epidemic, she would be in college, but as it is, she needs the money, so she's working as a teaching assistant. She's a fast learner and good with kids. I don't know how I got along before I had her to help me. But the truth is I don't know her very well. We don't talk about our private lives. She has never volunteered much information, and I don't like to pry. Besides, if I ask her about her private life, she'll expect me to open up about mine, and I don't want to do that. I don't have much of a private life, and I don't want to talk about the past, which is best forgotten. But Lydia stands there crying, and I can't just pretend I don't notice.

"Is there anything I can do?" I ask.

"Yeah, can we talk? I need some advice, and I don't know who else I can ask."

"Of course."

"But not here." She glances meaningfully at the surveillance camera mounted above our heads. "Somewhere else. Somewhere private."

I can't think of any place except my apartment. I seldom invite anyone there, not even Roberta. My apartment is my retreat, my shelter from the rest of the world, where I can close the door and forget about the epidemic. But I can't think of any place else private. Certainly a Starbucks or a McDonald's wouldn't be private. My apartment seems the only alternative.

"Would you like to come to my place for dinner? I could make a salad and some spaghetti."

"Yeah, that would be good," she says, wiping her tears away with her fingers. "Thank you."

So Lydia rides home with me after we finish mounting the students' artwork, and since returning to the school by bike after dark would be dangerous, we agree she will spend the night at my apartment. As we get farther and farther from the school, she begins to relax and smile more. Maybe she is just stressed out by school, I tell myself, unable to imagine what advice she thinks I can give her.

We stop at the supermarket, where I'm able to buy more groceries than usual since Lydia has a backpack to help carry them in. Young Audrey of the red armband and heavy eye makeup is on duty again. No sign of Phyllis. This time I don't ask.

Fifteen minutes later we park our bikes in the garage of the Glenview Tower. I take Lydia up to the lobby security desk to register her before we go up to my apartment. We aren't supposed to have guests without registering them first. Management wants to know who is on the premises. It's all part of the tightened security you find everywhere since the epidemic has gotten so bad. I would have preferred to skip the requirement, which I don't agree with. As far as I'm concerned, it's no one else's business who I allow to sleep over. However, I don't want to get into trouble so I follow the rules.

Two security guards are on duty when we go down, a short man with a mustache who is reading a newspaper from which he glances up occasionally at the security monitors, and a tall bored-looking man who is in charge of registering guests. The tall man looks at Lydia suspiciously and then at the name she has just written in the register.

"Lydia Hogue," he says with a contemptuous snort. "What sort of name's that?"

"It's my name, R. Lipski," she says, reading his off his name tag. "What sort of name is yours?" Lydia is young but she can hold her own against just about anyone. Did I mention that she's from LA?

"Polish, for your information," he says stiffly. He looks down at the register again. "Hey, I can't read your address. You'll have to write it again. You have to write it so as we can read it. If I can't read it, how can I check it?"

"Oh, for Pete's sake," mutters Lydia. "Give me the pen."

She prints it in block capitals. "Can you read it now? Or didn't you learn how to read?"

R. Lipski looks at her with dislike. "You just watch it if you know what's good for you."

I think I'd better intervene at this point and get Lydia away from the guard before either of them says anything else.

"Come on," I say, nudging her elbow. "I want you to meet someone."

We ride up to the fifteenth floor and I lead the way to Mrs. Franklin's apartment, which is just down the hall from mine. I know how much my elderly neighbor enjoys meeting someone new. Since she can't go out, the only people she meets are those who come to her, and since I seldom bring anyone home, I'm nearly her only visitor.

We find her in her little kitchen. She has just finished washing up after a meager dinner. A lone plate and upturned cup stand neatly in the dish rack beside a small pan.

"Soup again?" I say. She practically lives off cans of soup in spite of my best efforts to get her to vary her diet.

"What's wrong with soup?" she says, reaching for her cane. "I don't need much."

I introduce Lydia to her and start putting away the groceries we have brought for her. When I finish, we go into the living room and I help settle her in her favorite armchair.

"Lydia's my teaching assistant," I explain as I sit down beside Lydia on the faded sofa.

"Aren't you awfully young to be a teaching assistant?" she asks.

"I'm eighteen," Lydia says.

"You look more like a student than a teacher."

"I'm not a teacher yet. Just an assistant. It's sort of like being an understudy."

"But you hardly look old enough to be out of high school."

"They're talking about training sixteen and seventeen-year-olds starting next year," I tell her. "Because of the teacher shortage."

"Teachers, police, doctors—there's a people shortage if you ask me."

"Well, there's no shortage of kids yet," Lydia says. "There are plenty of those." Her eyes roam around the room, taking in the Navajo rug on the wall and the shelves of Hopi dolls and the rock collection. "You have some pretty cool stuff. Is all of this yours?"

"It's the accumulation of a lifetime."

I can tell she's pleased Lydia has noticed. She's very proud of her collections and seldom gets to show them off.

"Is that turquoise?" Lydia asks, her eye caught by the necklace Mrs. Franklin is wearing.

"It's Navajo. It was a gift from my husband." She touches the turquoise necklace at her throat.

"It's gorgeous."

"Go in the next room and open the top drawer of the dresser and see if you can find a little box."

Lydia gives me a quizzical look, then goes into the other room.

"She seems like a very capable young woman," Mrs. Franklin remarks in a low voice.

"She is. But you don't have to—"

"Did you find it?"

42

"There are a lot of little boxes in here. Which one do you want?"

"Oh, any of them will do."

I roll my eyes. Mrs. Franklin pretends not to notice.

Lydia returns with a little ivory colored box. "How about this one?"

"Yes, that one's fine. Go ahead, open it."

Lydia lifts off the lid and tilts the little box for us to see. Nestled inside is a small irregular-shaped polished black stone on a fragile silver chain.

"That's black onyx," Mrs. Franklin says. "I found it in a gift shop not long after my son was born. I liked the feel of it between my fingers and so I had it put on a chain. They say black onyx protects the person who wears it, although I've never put much stock in things like that."

"It's beautiful."

"I want you to have it."

"Me? Oh, I couldn't."

"Nonsense. I'm getting old. I don't know what's going to happen to all my pretty things when I die."

Lydia glances at me uncertainly. "Why don't you give it to Sarah?"

"I already tried and she wouldn't take it."

This is true. She gave me several pieces of jewelry before I threatened not to bring her any more groceries if she didn't stop. But if she wants to give her black onyx to Lydia, I won't stand in her way. She has a right to give her things away.

"Go on," I tell Lydia. "She wants you to have it."

"If you're sure. . . ." Lydia looks doubtfully at the onyx in her hand.

"I'm sure," says Mrs. Franklin firmly. "You can give it to your daughter one day. Now put it on and let's see how it looks."

"Maybe I should give it back," Lydia says later as we sit on my balcony. She has said this at least half a dozen times and I have assured her each time that it really isn't necessary so now I simply let it pass.

The cat is curled up in my lap, eyes closed. Her fur feels silky under my hand. Overhead the sky is full of stars. It's a hot night once again and the faint smell of smoke hangs in the air. From time to time we can hear the crackle of gunfire and the wail of police sirens. Out there, where the lights end, is the wall. There is only blackness, except for the fires which burn like torches in the dark. Watching them makes me think about my sister Laura. Once when she was ten and I was twelve she told me she had a fear of fire. She said sometimes she dreamed about fires when she had bad dreams at night. I've wondered since if that was a sort of premonition. My fear was of bridges, especially ones like the truss bridge on the highway a few miles north of my hometown. Crossing it in a car was like riding through a large iron cage and I could look down and see the narrow muddy river flowing below. Our tires whined when we went over it. It wasn't a long bridge, but I always held my breath until we got safely to the other side. I'm not sure what frightened me about the bridge. That it would break? That we would fall into the water and drown? Well, there are no rivers here—and no bridges either. However, there are fires. I think it must be terrible to die in the way you most fear.

"What do you suppose it's like over there?" Lydia asks.

"I don't know." Beneath my hand the cat purrs contentedly. I wonder if she misses her owner. She acts as if she has always lived with me. I think it must be nice to be a cat if it means letting go of the past so easily.

"Jeff says the police may not be able to keep infecteds on the other side of the wall much longer. He ought to know. He's on the police force."

During dinner she mentioned her boyfriend Jeff at least half a dozen times. I wonder if he's what she wants advice about. Maybe she's having boyfriend problems. If that's it, I doubt I'll be much help. The time of boyfriends seems far behind me. You couldn't really say I've had a boyfriend since Rick, which was seven years ago. I haven't really had a boyfriend since. When I first came here I just wasn't interested, although sometimes I went out with guys I met. Later there just didn't seem to be many around. The ones who were still uninfected all seemed to have something wrong with them. Or maybe as Emily, my youngest sister, used to say, I was too picky. At any rate, I waited throughout dinner for Lydia to bring up whatever it is she wants to talk about and she never did. I'm beginning to wonder if maybe she's just lonely and wants someone to talk to. But if that's it, why not talk to her boyfriend?

"I didn't know who else to turn to," she says now, as if her thoughts are running in the same track as mine. She's staring out at the black void of the South Zone, where the fires burn.

I wait, knowing that when she is ready she will tell me.

"You'll probably think I'm terrible."

"Why would I think that?"

She shakes her head. "I told you about Jeff."

So this is about her boyfriend after all. I wait for her to continue.

She takes a deep breath. "Sarah, I'm pregnant."

It isn't what I was expecting. I don't know what to say. Why is she telling me this? Surely there's someone else she could talk to about it, one of the other assistants, or another teacher. Why does she think I might know anything about it? I know even less about pregnancy than I do about boyfriends. But there it is. She expects me to say something, so I say the only thing I can think of.

"Are you sure?" I know. Totally inadequate.

She nods. "I hoped I was wrong, but I've tested myself three times now. I'm pregnant all right."

I reach out and take her hand. If the authorities find out, she could be arrested and jailed for breaking the emergency law against sex outside of marriage. I'm surprised she trusts me enough to tell me. I'm not sure I'd trust anybody if I were her.

"I haven't told Jeff." She bites her lip.

"But you're going to tell him, aren't you?" Surely she wouldn't keep something like this to herself? If it happened to me, I feel fairly certain my boyfriend would be the first person I'd tell. Then again, given the way things are now, maybe not. Maybe she doesn't trust him because he's a policeman.

"He can't marry me." Her voice wobbles. "His parents don't approve of me."

I look at her. "Why not?" I can't imagine anyone not approving of Lydia. She's attractive, smart, hardworking, capable—one of the best teaching assistants ever assigned to me. She's great with children.

"They're white."

It hangs there in the air between us.

"What about Jeff?"

"He's white too."

"I don't mean that. I mean, how does he feel about you?"

"He says he loves me."

"And you?"

Lydia sighs and nods. "Yeah, I love him, the big jerk."

"Then you should tell him."

Behind us, in the living room, my phone rings.

"Ignore it," I say. "It's probably a wrong number."

"How do you know that? Maybe you should answer it."

I could tell her I've been receiving calls from someone who refuses to talk after I answer and that I suspect it's Strickland. I have no idea what he wants, but I'm pretty sure it's him. Lydia is watching me, and I don't want to explain so I scoot the cat off my lap and reluctantly go inside to answer it. When I pick up the phone, I expect to hear silence, or worse, heavy breathing. Instead I hear a male voice I don't recognize.

"Sarah Davis?"

"Yes," I say cautiously.

"My name is Jones. Martin Jones. I did your blood test."

The orderly with the red armband. Why is he calling me? I grip the phone tighter and feel a sinking sensation in the pit of my stomach. Was there something wrong with my blood test after all?

"No, nothing's wrong. Do you remember the woman you wanted to know about?"

I'm so relieved there's nothing wrong with my blood test that it takes me a few seconds to remember. "The woman who tested positive?"

"That's right. I have her name—if you still want it."

"All right." I reach for a pen and my memo pad. "What is it?"

"I can't tell you on the phone. I'm taking a risk giving it to you at all. If you want it, you have to come down for it. I'm in your parking garage."

I take a deep breath. He's in my parking garage? Why? And what makes him think I'll come down? I know nothing about him. He's a complete stranger, and he's infected with the virus. What if he attacks me? Never mind that he could get the death penalty. Punishment holds little threat for people who know they are going to die anyway—which is why the wall was built in the first place.

"Well?" he says. "It makes no difference to me, although I wouldn't have bothered to ride over here if I'd known you weren't serious."

It occurs to me that I'm not showing proper appreciation for the trouble he has gone to. Besides, I was serious. "All right, I'll come down," I say, as if there is nothing unusual about receiving visits from strangers in the parking garage after dark. I push the end call button. And then it hits me. What's he doing on this side of the wall past curfew? Infected workers are supposed to return to the South Zone before dark. He shouldn't be here.

I go back out on the balcony, where Lydia is still sitting in one of my patio chairs, staring pensively at the South Zone. "I have to go downstairs," I tell her.

"What's up?"

"Someone wants to talk to me. I'll only be a few minutes."

And then I leave her before she can ask any questions.

CHAPTER 6

Even though I really don't believe Martin Jones is dangerous, I don't want to go down to meet him without some kind of weapon. I don't believe in taking unnecessary risks. So I go to the kitchen, find a paring knife, and tuck it into the pocket of my jeans.

When I turn around, Lydia is watching me from the doorway. "Okay, what's wrong?"

"I told you. I have to go downstairs. There's someone I have to talk to."

"With a knife?" She raises an eyebrow.

"I don't know him very well."

"You want me to come along?"

I hesitate. Of course it would be safer to take Lydia with me, but then I'll have to explain to her who Martin Jones is and about the woman at the clinic. I have a feeling she'll disapprove of him if I tell her that story, and besides it would take too much time. He's waiting for me to come down.

"Don't you have a gun? You expect to defend yourself

with a little bitty knife? Whoever's down there will probably laugh. I know I would."

"I'll be okay. Don't worry."

"If you're not back here in five minutes, I'm calling security." She looks like she means it.

I sigh and glance at my watch. All right. So I have five minutes to take care of this.

As I ride down the elevator, I wonder again why Martin Jones is violating his curfew by being on this side of the wall after dark. I pat the pocket of my jeans to reassure myself that my knife is there.

Within minutes the elevator takes me down to ground level. I step out warily into the parking garage. It looks deserted—just bikes, motorcycles, mopeds, and a few cars. In spite of the safety lights, it's shadowy and vaguely sinister.

"Over here," he calls.

"Where?" I don't see him and that makes me nervous.

"Over here," he calls again.

I take a few steps in the direction of his voice, my right hand ready to whip out the knife. My better judgment tells me to turn around and go back in while I still can. I don't like this.

"Where are you?" I call out.

Then I spot him sitting in the shadow of a concrete pillar, slumped against it. He's wearing a black T-shirt and jeans, not his white lab coat. I look around uneasily, wondering if it's some kind of trap. What if he isn't alone?

He must have guessed what I'm thinking. "There's nobody else. Just me. Sorry, I can't get up right now. I had a little accident."

As I move closer, I notice his red armband is missing. If

he's caught without it, he could lose his job and be thrown in jail.

"I know you could call security and have me arrested, but I'm hoping you won't."

"Why shouldn't I?" I ask, stopping a few yards away.

"Look, I need your help. Like I said, I had an accident."

"What kind of accident?"

"I fell off my bike."

I don't believe him. He doesn't strike me as the type to fall off a bike. "I could call for an ambulance," I offer, still keeping a safe distance between us.

"And I'll be arrested. I'm not supposed to be on this side of the wall after dark." He sounds a little out of breath, like he's been running.

"What do you want me to do?"

"I need a place to stay. Just for tonight."

It's a lot to ask of a complete stranger, but maybe he doesn't know anyone else he can turn to. I look at him sitting there. He doesn't look dangerous. Besides, Lydia is upstairs. If I take him up to my apartment, at least I won't be alone with him.

"Can you walk?"

"If you help me."

A little voice in my head is telling me not to be an idiot—just walk away. But I can't.

When I offer him my hand, he grins, or maybe it's a grimace. Taking it, he pulls himself rather clumsily to his feet. That's when I see his left arm is injured. It hangs uselessly at his side. So he was telling the truth about being hurt. He puts his right arm around my shoulders and leans on me for support. He's a head taller than me and heavier than I expected. I wonder how I'm going to explain this to Lydia.

"There's a surveillance camera inside," I warn.

"I figured there would be. Can you grab my backpack? I don't want it to get stolen."

When I pick up his backpack, I'm surprised how light it is. It feels empty. We don't talk as we stagger to the door. I let us in with my key card and feel relieved to see the entry is deserted. Ignoring the security camera, I steer him to the elevator. Maybe security will think he's a drunk friend.

We're riding up the elevator when I notice he's bleeding. Oh, great. This has got to be one of the dumbest things I've ever done. I know nothing about this guy except that he's infected. Why am I taking him up to my apartment? But it's too late now to change my mind. I just hope I don't have any cuts. All it takes is a small open cut and I could have the virus too.

"Why did you come here?" I ask as we step out of the elevator on the fifteenth floor. I look to right and left and feel relieved when I see the hall is empty.

"I had your address," he says in a tight voice.

"Are you in pain?"

"A little."

I have a feeling it's more than a little.

Lydia looks up in surprise when she sees Martin with his arm draped around my shoulders, leaning heavily on me.

"He fell off his bike," I say, trying to sound like it's no big deal as I ease him down on the sofa. "He's hurt."

"I can see that. I'll find some towels." She heads for the bathroom with her usual quick efficiency. I'm grateful she didn't ask any questions.

Now that we are safely in my apartment, I look at his shoulder and feel sick at what I see. There's so much blood. It isn't a little wound. This is major. I have visions of him bleeding to death on my sofa.

"You okay?" Lydia asks me, returning with towels.

I nod, but I think I might throw up.

"She faints at the sight of blood," Lydia says matter-of-factly. She knows that because once when one of the children fell down and bloodied a knee and I took him to the infirmary, I passed out.

"I know," Martin says with a wan grin. "She's got a thing about needles too."

I can't believe they are bonding over my squeamishness about blood.

"Mmm. Better cut off the arm of that T-shirt and see how bad it is," Lydia says. She acts as if she has seen men bleeding to death dozens of times. "You got a knife or scissors or something?"

I remember the knife in my jeans pocket and pull it out. My hands are shaking as I rip the shoulder of his black T-shirt and expose the wound. Oh, my god. I think I'm going to be sick.

"You want me to do it?" Lydia asks.

I shake my head and grit my teeth. I can do this. If I get infected, it's my own fault for having helped him. That will teach me not to trust strangers.

She hands me a wet washcloth to wipe away the blood. There's a small hole from which the blood keeps flowing.

Lydia takes a step back, frowning. "What kind of accident were you in? That's a bullet hole."

I wonder how she knows what a bullet hole looks like, but it doesn't seem like the time to ask.

"Is it?" Martin twists his head as if to look. "You sure?"

"I'm sure."

For a while no one says anything while Lydia and I press wet towels on the wound and sop up blood until finally it looks as if the bleeding has stopped. My hands are still shaking as I reach down to pet the cat, which is rubbing against my ankles demanding attention.

"Who shot you?" I ask Martin.

"The police were shooting at someone and I got in the way."

"Sure," Lydia says. "You expect us to believe that? They were shooting at *you*."

The doorbell rings, and we all look at each other.

"The police?" Lydia whispers. "Do you think they followed him here?"

It rings again, and then someone raps loudly on the door. I glance uncertainly at Martin.

"Better answer it. You don't want them to break down the door."

I answer at the third ring. When I open the door, a security guard is standing there. It's the short man with the mustache who was sitting at the front desk when Lydia signed in.

"We have a report of an unregistered person being admitted to this apartment," he says, trying to look past me into the room. I open the door no farther than necessary so he can't see Martin stretched out on the sofa.

"You must mean my cousin. I was just about to come down and register him."

"You have *two* guests?"

"That's right." I keep a firm hold on the door.

He looks at me skeptically.

"Is it against the rules?" I ask, lifting my chin.

I don't know what I'll do if he demands to come in. One look at Martin and he'll know something is wrong. He's bound to call the police.

"No, not if you register him," he says grudgingly and holds out his clipboard.

I hesitate a fraction of a second, then write Michael Johnson, 1861 Roadrunner Road. Hopefully he won't check. I give him a friendly smile as I hand back the clipboard. He just scowls.

"Thanks," Martin says after I close the door.

"Tell me you gave him a fake name," Lydia says.

"I did."

"What do we tell the police if they show up?"

"I don't think they'll track me here," Martin says. "It was dark."

"Let's hope you're right." She leans down to pick up his backpack, which is lying by the door.

"Hey, what are you doing?"

"Moving it."

"Just bring it over here by me."

She looks at the black backpack and pokes it. "What's in it?"

"Personal belongings."

"Is that so?" She starts to unzip it, and Martin struggles to his feet.

"Don't!" I cry out, afraid his shoulder will start bleeding

55

again. I take the backpack from Lydia and give it to him. Clutching it to his chest, he sinks back down on the sofa. Whatever is in it is important to him.

"Look, you need a doctor," I tell him.

He shakes his head stubbornly. "No. No doctor."

"But you have a bullet in you. You can't just leave it there."

"A doctor would report me."

"But if you're innocent—"

"He's not," Lydia says flatly. "Isn't that obvious?"

He glances at her, then back at me. "I came here because I thought you'd help me."

I groan. Do I have a sign plastered on me that says 'easy mark'?

"Do you know how much trouble she could get in just by your being here?" Lydia demands. "Did you think about that when you came here? And how exactly do you two know each other?"

His eyes flick to mine. "Maybe you should look in my bag." He fumbles at the zipper, trying not to move his injured shoulder.

I lean forward and unzip it for him. Then I look inside. It's packed with lots of small plastic pill vials. That's why it was so light.

"Those are badly needed in the South Zone to fight the virus," he explains.

"You stole them," Lydia says.

He looks at her. "You're right. I stole them. And this isn't the first time. And if I can help it, it's not going to be the last. Don't you understand? People are dying."

"Don't your hospitals have drugs?" I ask.

Lydia shoots me a funny look. I forgot she doesn't know he lives in the South Zone.

"Not nearly enough," Martin says. "And every day more people are sent across the wall. Our doctors have to make hard choices about who gets the drugs. People steal them. They even kill for them. You wouldn't believe how bad it is."

"Can't you explain that to the police or city hall or someone?" I say. "Can't you ask for more help?"

"Don't you think we have? We've begged for help. They say they need the drugs on this side. They keep telling us to wait. Meanwhile people are dying."

"So the police were shooting at you because you stole those drugs?" Lydia says.

"Yes." His eyes meet mine. "I'm sorry. If you want me to leave, I will. I didn't know where else to go. I can't cross the wall with a bullet in my shoulder. I'm bound to get arrested."

"And if they find you here," Lydia says, "what happens to Sarah? You thought about that?"

I lay my hand on her arm. "It's okay."

"Okay? What happens if security checks out the phony name you wrote down for him? What then?"

"I'll tell them I made a mistake."

"I don't like it." She walks toward the bathroom.

"Where are you going?"

"I'm going to find a sink and wash my hands. And maybe you should too."

"I'm sorry," Martin says when she's gone. "I didn't mean to make trouble for you."

"That's okay," I say. "Don't mind Lydia. She's just trying to look out for me."

"You don't think she'll turn me in, do you?"

"No, don't worry about it. No one's going to turn you in."

Suddenly I feel tired. It's been a long day. Usually I spend my evenings by myself watching a little TV, listening to music, reading a book, or doing a crossword puzzle. I didn't expect to have Lydia come home with me, and I certainly didn't expect Martin to show up. When he took my blood at the hospital on Saturday, I had no idea we would meet again. I remember how angry I felt at him when I left the hospital. I blamed him for helping to subdue the woman with the wedding ring.

"That woman—the one at the hospital the day I was there…."

"What about her?"

"Tonight when you called me you said you'd give me her name. Was that just a trick to get me to come down?"

"Would you have come down if I'd told you the truth?"

"Probably not," I admit.

"I could tell you her name, but what good would it do? You can't do anything to help her. By now she's on the other side of the wall."

I wonder if he's telling the truth. Does he really know her name? I want to trust him, but maybe Lydia is right. Maybe he isn't someone I should trust. I don't really know him.

"What's her name?" I ask.

"Teresa Lundquist." He looks at me evenly with those hazel eyes. So he knows her name, but I want more proof.

"Do you know her number?"

"No, but it's probably in the phone book."

I open the bottom of the stand beside me, take out the phone book, and begin to search for the name.

"You're going to call *now*?"

"Why not?"

"What will you tell them? They already know. The hospital will have called them."

"I don't care."

"They may not appreciate it."

The more he tries to dissuade me, the more determined I become. It's not just because of the woman's cry for help that day. I have to know if he's telling the truth. I have to know if I can trust him.

There are three Lundquists listed. I try the first. The phone rings a few times and a child's voice answers, a little girl. *My daughter is musical*, she said. *She's learning to play the piano.* I don't know what to say.

Then a man's voice comes on. He must have taken the phone away from the little girl. "Yes?" he says sharply.

What do you say to a man whose wife has just been sent across the wall? Suddenly I think this was a bad idea. But he's on the phone now. I have to say something.

"Mr. Lundquist?"

"Yes?"

I take a deep breath and plunge in. "I was at the hospital on Saturday when your wife was there. I just wanted. . . ."

"Who is this?" he demands.

I hesitate. "It doesn't matter who I am. I just want you to know—"

"You must have the wrong number."

"Is your wife Teresa Lundquist?" I ask quickly, afraid he's going to hang up.

"That's right." He sounds stiff, suspicious.

"She tested positive last weekend at the State Hospital when I was there."

A pause. "I don't know what kind of sick joke this is. If you call this number again, I'll report you to the police. There's nothing wrong with my wife."

"I'm sorry. Could I please speak with her?" Maybe this is not the right Lundquist, but I have a feeling it is.

"My wife isn't here right now," the man says in a tight voice. "She's visiting her sister. Now don't bother us again or I'll call the police." He breaks the connection and leaves me with a dial tone buzzing in my ear.

"I tried to warn you," Martin says.

"He wouldn't admit his wife tested positive."

"He's scared. He knows he could be next."

"They have two kids. A boy and a girl." In my mind I see again the family photo of all four smiling against a background of blue sky. *My son's good at math . . . My daughter is musical.*

"The kids will probably be okay."

I shake my head. "They won't be okay. I see kids every day at school. You take away their parents and they aren't okay."

"Maybe they have a relative who can take them in. An aunt or an uncle."

How can he be so matter-of-fact? Doesn't he have any feelings? Doesn't he understand?

"Don't you see how everyone's disappearing?"

"Of course I see it. I live in the South Zone."

Now I feel guilty. It isn't his fault things are the way they are. Living in the South Zone, he sees much worse every day than I do.

"I'm sorry. I didn't think."

"Forget it. People with electricity don't have to think. It's one of the advantages." He gives me that boyish grin that takes the edge off the implied criticism.

I like Martin. Even if he is infected. Even if he helped subdue the woman at the hospital. Maybe I shouldn't, but I do.

And he's right. Things *are* falling apart all around us, but the lamp on my stand casts a circle of light around us and we are surrounded by cool air provided by the central air system. Things could be worse. A lot worse.

I find a blanket and pillow for him and drop them beside him on the sofa. "I guess this is where you sleep tonight."

"Thanks," he says. "For everything."

I'd like to stay and talk to him, but Lydia is waiting in the other room. I can't just ignore her. Besides, he'll be gone tomorrow and I'll probably never see him again. Better not to let anything get started in the first place.

"Well, I guess I'd better go to bed now," I tell him. "I have to get up early and go to work."

I force myself to walk away. I go in the bathroom and thoroughly wash my hands, as Lydia suggested. Time to be sensible. Then I go in the bedroom, where she's sitting in a chair beside the bed hugging her legs to her chest. She has turned on the lamp beside my bed and it throws a warm glow across the pale blue bedspread.

"Are you all right?" I ask.

"Yeah, I'm all right."

"I hope you don't mind sharing a bed."

"You know, you trust people too much. You don't know anything about him."

"I know he's hurt and he needs a place to stay," I say, sitting on the edge of the bed.

"It's that small town Midwest background of yours. You wouldn't have lasted five minutes in LA. I shudder to think what would have happened to you."

"Then it's lucky I ended up here instead of in LA," I say with a smile.

I don't see why she has taken such a dislike to Martin. I don't see how anyone could dislike him. I wonder if it's really Martin she's upset about or the pregnancy she isn't ready for.

"I just don't want you to do something stupid," she says.

"Like what?"

"You won't forget he's infected, will you?"

"I won't forget." How could I?

"It just makes my skin crawl to think I had his blood on me. Why didn't you warn me?"

Is that what this is all about? Her fear that she'll get infected? Of course she's right. I ought to be more careful.

"Sorry. I didn't think of it."

"That's what I'm saying. You've got to think about it."

I'm tired of thinking about it and I'm tired of being reminded by other people to think about it, so I don't say anything more. "Are you ready to turn in?"

"I guess so." She looks up at the ceiling. "Why is that crazy thing with feathers hanging over your bed?"

"My dreamcatcher?" I look up at it—a small circle with a web of threads interwoven with beads from which dangle a few feathers. I bought it several years ago in a little shop that has since gone out of business. Sometimes at night I lie awake and watch it. If there's a breath of air moving in the room, it slowly turns. "It's supposed to catch bad dreams," I explain.

"Does it work?" she asks skeptically.

"Not really."

She grins at me. "That's what I figured."

We climb into bed and I turn off the light.

"Do you have anyone back in LA?" I ask, looking up at the dream catcher in the dark.

"Not really. People I knew, but no family now. How about you? You got anyone?"

"No."

We're silent for a few minutes. It seems strange to be sharing my bed with Lydia, and strange too to know Martin is in the other room stretched out on my sofa.

"You really think he's going to be okay with this?" Lydia asks.

"Okay with what?"

"You know—a baby."

She means Jeff.

"It's going to be fine," I say. I want her to believe that. She said he loves her, and if he loves her, then it shouldn't matter that she's pregnant. He ought to be willing to marry her. She's lucky to have someone who loves her. Soon she'll have a husband and a baby. I feel a pang of envy. What do I have? An apartment where I eat alone and sleep alone, and that doesn't seem likely to change in the near future. Lydia is right. There can never be anything between Martin and me. To think otherwise is just a self-indulgent fantasy. No matter how charming he is, I must not forget he wears a red armband.

CHAPTER 7

I'm awoken by a noise. It's dark in my bedroom except for a pale light seeping through the window. Beside me Lydia is still sleeping soundly. I think I hear the door of the medicine cabinet in the bathroom close with a small click. I get up slowly, trying not to wake Lydia. As I come out of the bedroom, Martin is just stepping out of the bathroom cradling his arm. He smiles wryly when he sees me. I'm suddenly conscious that I'm barefoot and wearing only my old Diamondbacks T-shirt.

"Sorry if I woke you," he says. "I was looking for something to take the edge off the pain."

I step past him into the bathroom, find a bottle of Tylenol in the medicine cabinet, and hand it to him.

"I was hoping for something a little stronger," he says with a sigh.

"You need a doctor to look at that shoulder."

He shakes his head. "I'll be okay if I can just get back across the wall."

"They'll be watching for you. You said so yourself."

"It doesn't matter. Those pills in my backpack are needed on the other side."

I wonder what will happen to him if he gets caught. Thrown in jail most likely. And he would lose his job at the clinic. "Isn't there someone else who could take them?"

He looks at me. Our eyes hold for a minute.

No way. He can't expect me to take a risk like that.

"I know it's a lot to ask, but you could do it, Sarah. They're going to be looking for someone who looks like me, not like you. Half the time they don't check papers closely. All you need is a red armband."

Before I can refuse, he turns and ducks into the living room. I follow and watch as he pulls a red armband from his backpack. Just the sight of it makes me feel uncomfortable.

"They don't expect anyone who's tested negative to cross over. And I'll give you my work permit to get you back." He's talking as if he thinks this plan is reasonable. Does he really believe I would agree to this?

"No." I shake my head. I wish he'd stop looking at me all hopeful like that. He must realize I can't possibly do it. It's far too dangerous. I've survived this long by not taking risks, haven't I? Why should I start now? Does he think he can look at me with those hazel eyes and that dopey grin and I'll just agree to do whatever he asks? Do I really look that easy to manipulate?

"Please. It wouldn't be as dangerous as it sounds."

I don't believe that for a minute. "I wouldn't know where to go. What if I got caught?" Why am I arguing with him? I'm not actually considering it, am I?

"I'll draw a map. And you won't get caught."

"How can you know that?"

"Trust me. You can do this."

If I have learned nothing else in my twenty-five years, it is to be wary of young men who say trust me. It's almost always a sign that I shouldn't.

"I know you don't know me," he says. "And you probably think I have a nerve showing up here and asking you to do something like this. I wish there were time for us to get to know each other better, but there isn't. You just have to trust me."

There it is again. And why exactly should I trust him? I don't know him. How can he think I would do this? I'm not one of those women who passively do what men ask. At least I hope I'm not.

The light slowly dies out of his eyes as he realizes I'm not going to do it. "I understand. If you can't, you can't."

"I'm not like that," I tell him. "I'm not brave. I'm sure it's a very noble thing to do and it's wonderful you're willing to do it, but I can't."

"I understand," he says again, his voice dull, his eyes avoiding mine.

I look at him as he stands there cradling his injured arm. He's in no condition to cross the wall. He'll almost certainly be caught. He might as well cross holding a sign that says *Wanted*.

"You can't go across with your arm like that."

"I have to. Someone has to. I have to get those meds to the other side."

He won't make it. The guards will stop him at the checkpoint. I tell myself it's no concern of mine. He's just some guy I met. I owe him nothing. But it's no good. I don't want him to get arrested. If he gets arrested, it will be my fault. Well, not really my fault, but I'll feel guilty because I didn't go in his place.

"You really think I could get across without being caught?"

"I know it," he says, his eyes lighting up again.

"And taking these drugs across can't wait a day or two? You're sure?"

"People need them now. And the longer I wait, the more chance they may never make it across."

I sigh and decide to ignore the little voice in my head that keeps saying *no*. "All right. If it's that important, I'll do it."

"You won't regret it," he says eagerly. "You'll be helping save people's lives."

"I already regret it. I can't believe I let you talk me into this."

"I'll draw you a map. Do you have some paper?"

I get paper and a pen. We push aside the blanket and the pillow and sit down on the sofa together. The cat watches us from the armchair with mild curiosity and then stretches and yawns. Martin proceeds to sketch a map and explain the streets and how to get to the hospital. Then it's time for me to shower and get ready to go to work.

Neither of us mentions what I have agreed to do when all three of us are sitting at the kitchen table eating breakfast forty-five minutes later. I avoid looking at Martin because I'm afraid Lydia will guess something's up.

"I would have made pancakes for you if I could use both hands," Martin says. "Maybe some other time."

"I bet you don't know how to make pancakes at all." Lydia scoops a spoonful of cereal into her mouth.

"Well, you'd lose your bet. Actually I'm a pretty good cook. It was either learn to cook or starve, so I learned to cook."

"Ha," she says. "You've probably got a wife who cooks for you and half a dozen kids at home."

"No on both counts. No wife, no kids."

Our eyes meet briefly and I look away. It didn't cross my mind he could be married and have kids. I'm glad he isn't married. I hope Lydia won't ask if he has a girlfriend. If he says yes, I'm not sure how I'll feel about that when I'm about to risk my life by crossing the wall to deliver stolen drugs for him.

"So you live alone?" she asks.

"I didn't say that."

"You got family?"

"I've got a brother."

"You're lucky."

For a minute no one says anything. We are in dangerous territory. Better not to talk about family. The timer goes off and Lydia jumps to grab the coffeepot, which has now finished perking our coffee.

"So you're a teacher, Sarah?" he asks casually.

I think we are all relieved he has changed the subject.

"Yes. I teach second grade at the State School."

"And I'm her teaching assistant," Lydia says, as she pours hot coffee into the waiting mugs on the counter. "Just in case you're wondering."

Martin's eyes meet mine, and he smiles. I feel like I did as a kid when my sister Laura and I exchanged looks behind our mother's back.

Lydia plunks the three steaming mugs down on the table.

"At least we still have coffee. I could give up almost anything else but not my morning coffee."

"I'll drink to that," says Martin.

"So will I," I say.

We clink our mugs together and smile.

Even Lydia seems to call a temporary truce as we drink our coffee. It seems strange to have the two of them here but nice too. I wish I could stretch the minutes out longer. I try not to think about what I've agreed to do. Maybe it won't be so difficult after all. Maybe by this time tomorrow I'll be wondering why I was so reluctant.

I've hardly drunk half my coffee when Lydia checks her watch. "We should leave, Sarah. What about him?" She glances toward Martin.

"He's going to stay here today." I avoid Martin's eyes.

She gives me a look that says I must have lost my mind, then throws her hands up in surrender. "All right. I just hope you know what you're doing." She gulps the rest of her coffee without another word and sweeps out of the kitchen.

"I don't think she likes me very much," Martin says.

"She's got a lot on her mind right now."

"We all do." He reaches out and puts his hand over mine.

I feel the warmth of his hand, and for the moment anyway I'm glad I've agreed to help him.

CHAPTER 8

Every day on my way home I see the line of people waiting to cross the wall. It seems strange that today I'm one of them. I stand with my bike and wait for my turn to come. On my left arm is Martin's red armband, on my back his black backpack full of vials of pills. Clutched in my hand are his papers, ready to show. I wonder what the police will do to me if I'm caught trying to smuggle antiviral drugs across. It's still not too late to leave the line and go home, but if I do I may be noticed. The guards may wonder why someone with a red armband is leaving the line. I tell myself to stay calm. There are people on the other side of the wall who need the pills I'm carrying, and I promised Martin I would do this. I'm not going to let him down.

I did finally get up the nerve to tell Lydia that I was going to cross the wall with Martin's backpack. We were stopped at a red light on our way to school when I told her. I wanted her to know in case anything happened.

"Are you crazy?" she said, just as I knew she would.

My plan was to teach my class as usual. Then after school I

would cross the wall when the other workers were returning to the South Zone at the end of the workday. I would be less conspicuous that way.

Of course she did her best to talk me out of it.

"You don't know him," she said. "Maybe those pills aren't what he says they are. Maybe he's just a drug dealer. I've heard there are a lot of addicts over there. Maybe he's just using you to get his drugs across the wall. Have you thought of that?"

"I believe him," I said. "He's no drug dealer."

But that didn't stop her from trying to dissuade me.

"You don't know what it's like over there. He said himself people would kill for what you're carrying in that bag. And that's if you get past the guards."

"I'll be okay," I said, trying to sound more confident than I felt. "But just in case something happens and I don't make it back, would you look in on Mrs. Franklin?" If it hadn't been for Mrs. Franklin, I don't think I would have told her I was going to cross the wall. But if anything goes wrong, my elderly neighbor will be left stranded without anyone to bring her food. I have to make sure someone will help her.

Lydia didn't say anything for a minute. She looked as if she were about to give me a lecture but then changed her mind. Maybe she realized I was determined to go through with this.

"Of course I will," she said half angrily. "And I suppose you want someone to feed that stupid cat of yours. I'll do that too. *If* I have to. But you just better make sure nothing goes wrong. You hear me? I have no idea how to take care of cats or old ladies. And I have enough other things to worry about right now." She meant her pregnancy of course and that made me feel a twinge of guilt. I promised myself I would find a way to make it up to her when I get back.

Then the light turned green and we continued on our way. She didn't say anything more about it later when we were at school with the security camera staring down at us, just threw me dark looks from time to time and shook her head in disbelief.

To my relief the day passed without incident. I didn't get called to the office for any minor infractions. When it was time to leave, I grabbed Martin's backpack and headed for the parking lot, retrieved my bike, and rode to the checkpoint.

My watch says it's now 4:30. In another five or ten minutes I'll either be on the other side of the wall or arrested for smuggling drugs and carrying false identity papers.

The line moves so slowly. If only it would move faster. The longer it takes, the more nervous I get.

"You a secretary?" asks a man's voice behind me. I glance back. He's tall, muscular, and black, wears shades, and is dressed all in black except for his red armband. Even his bike is black. Definitely not the kind of guy you want to mess with. I could ignore him, but that might be rude.

"No, I work at the—" I remember Martin's identity papers and stop myself just in time. "Hospital."

"You new at this?"

Is it that obvious? Then I'd better be truthful. "Yes."

"Thought so. I haven't seen you before."

I turn my face toward the open gate again, not wanting to get in a conversation with him. He might be dangerous. It's never a good idea to talk to strangers, especially ones who look as if they might belong to a street gang or have spent time behind bars.

"How long?" he asks.

I try to ignore him, but he isn't easy to ignore. He raises his voice, as if he thinks I might be hard of hearing.

"How long you been on the other side—a few days? A few weeks?"

I open Martin's work papers and refold them, hoping he will give up.

"I guess you don't remember. That's okay. I don't want to remember how long I've been over there either."

The line inches forward. Now there are only about six people between me and the gate. Only one guard at the gate is checking papers. Another is in the guardhouse, and a policeman sits on his motorcycle nearby looking at a handheld device.

"You got family?" the man behind me asks. "You got a boyfriend?"

"Yes," I say, hoping that will shut him up. It doesn't.

"Which? Family or boyfriend?"

At the front of the line the guard motions for a young woman in a white nurse's uniform to step out of the line. Suddenly what I'm doing seems crazy. Why did Martin think I could get across? The guards are checking much closer than he said they would.

"They give the young pretty ones a hard time," the man behind me says. "But you knew that, didn't you? This isn't your first time to cross, is it?"

It's too late to turn back. I'll have to go through with it. The three people ahead of me—a young man in khaki shirt and pants who looks like a mechanic, an older woman wearing a business suit and tennis shoes, and a bald middle-aged man wearing a clerical collar—are waved through with hardly a glance at their papers. When my turn comes, the guard puts his hand firmly on the handlebars of my bike and stops me. He's a pudgy man with a ragged little mustache and a sneer. My stomach sinks.

"I don't remember seeing you before." He looks me up and down, ignoring the papers in my hand. "You new?"

This time I think it wouldn't be a good idea to admit to being new.

"I usually go through the next gate," I tell him.

"Is that so?" His hand stays on my handlebars. His tone of voice suggests he doesn't believe me.

"She's with me," the man behind me says loudly. "You remember me, don't you?"

The guard shoots him a wary look, then glances over his shoulder at the cop on the motorcycle. For a minute I think he's going to signal for help. I hold my breath as the seconds tick by. Evidently he decides we're not worth the hassle because he waves us both through. "Go on. Get out of here."

When we are safely on the other side of the wall, I turn and thank the man on the black bike.

He holds out his hand. "Milo's the name."

"Sarah," I say, shaking his hand. He still looks dangerous to me, but it's the least I can do. He just saved me from being arrested.

"I'm going to be your bodyguard, Sarah," he tells me.

"That's okay," I say hastily. "I don't need a bodyguard."

"Trust me. You do. So where are you going?"

I can't think of any answer to give him except the truth. I just hope I can trust him. "The hospital on Seventh Avenue. I have a map." I hold out Martin's hand-drawn map. In my head

I can hear Lydia saying, "You did what? Are you out of your mind, Sarah?"

"Yeah, I know where that is," he says, barely glancing at the map. "Let's go."

I know he might be leading me into a trap, but I follow him anyway. One look around me tells me maybe I shouldn't be riding about on my own in the South Zone. Nothing has prepared me for what lies beyond the wall. I find myself in a charred urban landscape that looks like a war zone. Many buildings have burned; in places an entire block has been reduced to rubble. Some of the fires are still smoldering and the smoke fills my nostrils and chokes my throat. Garbage lies by the curbs in black plastic bags, more often than not ripped open and spilling out, nosed by stray dogs and feral cats and pawed over by people who look homeless. The stench of rotting garbage hangs in the air. We pass dirty ragged children who stare at us curiously. On one street a small group of people carry signs announcing 'Repent' and 'The End Is Coming.' I see buildings scrawled with graffiti and dangerous looking gangs of young people in tank-tops, jeans and leather boots, some armed with guns and riding motorcycles. Because the traffic lights don't work, we have to slow down at every intersection to avoid colliding with other bikes, mopeds, and motorcycles.

We have gone about a mile when we see a man lying sprawled beside a phone booth staring up at the sky. From a dark spot on his forehead I suspect he's been shot in the head.

"Where are the police?" I ask Milo, realizing I haven't seen any since we crossed the wall.

"What police?"

The hospital is about two miles from the wall. When we get there, we find the front entrance boarded over and the boards covered by graffiti. The building looks abandoned. My heart sinks. What do I do now?

"Are you sure this is it?"

"Yeah, this is it," Milo says. "Not much to look at, is it?"

"There must be some mistake."

"You can't always judge a building by its outside. Just like people. Let's try around back."

In back is an emergency entrance guarded by a man holding a semi-automatic. We stop at a respectful distance.

"What's your business?" he demands. "We only take terminal cases here."

"Martin Jones sent me." I wave Martin's papers.

He motions for me to come closer so he can look at them. When he's satisfied, he looks from me to Milo. "What about him?"

"He's with me."

"Yeah," Milo says. "I'm with her."

The guard lets us wheel our bikes inside, where we leave them in what looks like a small waiting room and follow him down a dark hall lit only by the beam of his flashlight. It's hotter inside than it was outside. No air-conditioning. At the end of the hall, dusty windows let in the rays of the late afternoon sun. The guard takes us to an open office door where a young Caucasian woman and an older Asian-American man, both in white lab coats, are talking. They stop when they see us.

"These two say they know Martin." The guard hands the man Martin's papers.

"Is he okay?" the young woman asks, glancing from me to Milo and back again. She has blond hair pulled back in a ponytail and a brisk efficient manner.

"He's been shot," I tell her. "He's at my apartment on the other side of the wall."

"How bad is he hurt?"

"I don't think it's bad, but the bullet is still in. He won't go to a doctor."

"I'll have to go over there," she tells the man. "I can use Maria's papers."

"Are you a doctor?" I ask.

"No, but I know how to take a bullet out. Around here we need as many people as possible who can do that."

"Sandy's very remarkable," the Asian-American man says. It's hard to tell his age. His hair is graying and he has kind, intelligent eyes behind his glasses. "I don't know what I'd do without her."

"He's the doctor," she says, nodding towards him. "The only one we have left now."

He smiles at us and extends his hand. "Dr. Liu."

"Thank goodness Martin's alive and safe," Sandy says. "When he didn't show last night, we thought he'd been arrested."

"He wanted me to bring you this." I set Martin's backpack on the desk beside us. They exchange a glance, and then Dr. Liu unzips it and they both look in.

"You took a big risk bringing these across," he says. "We're very grateful to you."

I glance at Milo, wondering if he's surprised that I was carrying illegal drugs, but he's looking intently at some books on a shelf behind us on the wall and doesn't appear to have heard.

"I'll need a place to stay tonight," I tell them.

"Of course," Sandy says, looking from me to Milo. "If you and your friend will follow me, I'll give you a tour of the hospital and find you a place to sleep."

"Not me," Milo says. "I'm just the bodyguard." He turns to me. "And now since you seem to be in safe hands, I'll be on my way. I don't want to be out on the street once the sun goes down. After dark every dope fiend in the South Zone comes out to hunt for drugs or see who he can find to mug. It's bad anytime, but after dark it's open season."

"He's right," Sandy says as the guard and Milo disappear down the hall. "It's bad out there at night. And it keeps getting worse. So far we've been lucky. No one's thrown any bombs at us or tried to burn us out. Just the stray bullet or so as they shoot it out in the streets. Maybe they know they need us. But so many of them are crazy. They figure they're going to die anyway so they don't care how stoned they get or who they hurt. I don't know how much longer we'll be safe here." She sighs. "Well, never mind. Enough of that. Come on. I'll show you around."

"Do you live here?" I ask a few minutes later as she leads me up a narrow stairway by the light of her flashlight.

"Sometimes it feels like it, I'm here so much, but, no, I share an apartment with two friends in a safe house."

"A safe house?"

"Yeah, you know, heavy security. Lots of guns."

"What about Martin?"

"Martin lives with Dr. Liu, at least when he's not here or at work in the North Zone. Dr. Liu worked with Martin's father before he died. Martin's father was a doctor here at the hospital."

"Did he die of the virus?" I ask as we emerge in another dark hallway.

"No, he committed suicide." She glances at me. "Does that shock you?"

"Yes, I guess it does."

"It's funny, isn't it? All around us people who don't want to die are dying. And then someone who doesn't have to die kills himself."

"Was it very long ago?"

"Maybe five years ago."

I wonder if he was infected. He must have been if he was working in the South Zone. Maybe he just couldn't face the idea of the slow death he would have to face, a death that he would have been intimately familiar with in his profession. Or maybe he just couldn't face what he saw around him every day. Not wanting to pry, I don't ask.

We're on the second floor now. By the light of the flashlight I see a large number 2 painted next to the door. Sandy pushes it open, revealing a large room filled with forty or more beds. There's scarcely space to walk between them. She starts down one of these narrow aisles and I follow. In each bed lies an emaciated man or woman. Sometimes a husband lies next to a wife or a brother next to a brother. Sandy leads the way through this maze, moving from bed to bed, stopping to speak to people. She knows their names and asks how they are feeling and introduces me as the brave young woman who has brought more drugs until it becomes so embarrassing I beg her not to.

In the last bed a young man lies with his eyes turned toward the window as if to see the last of the daylight. He looks painfully thin in his white hospital gown, but his grey eyes are still very much alive. Sandy picks up his hand and entwines her fingers in his. "David, this is Sarah. Martin couldn't come, but he sent her with more antiviral and pain meds and he said he'll be here soon."

His eyes swivel to me. "You're a friend of Martin's?"

A friend? I hardly know him. But how can I look in his eyes and say no? So instead I say, "Yes."

He smiles. "He's my brother. My little brother. You got any brothers or sisters?"

"I had two sisters, but they're gone now."

"That's too bad."

Several beds away a girl with long brown hair sitting with a patient begins strumming a guitar and then breaks into a song in a pure sweet soprano. Something about angels.

"That's Heather," he says. "She must be part angel with a voice like that."

"Every evening she sings to her brother," Sandy says.

"It's better than a radio," David says.

"She has a beautiful voice," I agree.

He turns his eyes to me again. "So you're Martin's new girlfriend." He states it like a fact.

"Just a friend," I correct him.

"He always claims he hasn't got a girlfriend, but I know better. I could tell you some stories about Martin."

"Don't scare her off," Sandy says.

"There was the time we drove up Superstition Mountain to see the city lights. Do you remember that time, Sandy?"

"Oh, don't tell her that story. Martin will kill you for sure, and if he doesn't, I just might."

"I know lots of good stories," he says with a satisfied grin.

"I know you do," she says, patting his thin shoulder, "but it's getting dark now and I want to show Sarah some more of the hospital before it's too dark to see anything."

"You come back and see me again," David tells me. "I'll give you the lowdown on my brother. I'll tell you how he burned down our garage when he was eleven playing with a chemistry set."

"Honestly," Sandy says, rolling her eyes. "If I had a brother like you, I wouldn't bring any boyfriends around."

"How long has he got?" I ask her when we are back in the hall.

"It's hard to tell. With meds he might have months. Without them. . . ." She doesn't finish her sentence.

In the next room the patients are all children, some with a parent or brother or sister tending them.

"We let relatives stay if they want," Sandy explains. "We need the extra help. If we didn't have them, I don't know how we'd take care of everybody."

She stops beside a little boy who has his thumb in his mouth and a teddy bear clutched to his chest.

"Hi, Charlie." She brushes a curl back from his damp forehead. "How are you today?"

He regards her steadily but doesn't take his thumb out of his mouth.

"How's Mr. Muggles?"

The little boy pulls the bear closer to his chin and goes on sucking.

"It seems so unfair," I say as we move on. "Especially the children."

"The epidemic doesn't distinguish between young and old, or good and bad. Epidemics never do."

"We don't see this on the other side. Or at least not much of it. Even on the news it's usually censored. They tell about it, but they don't show pictures anymore."

"We're the lucky ones. We have Dr. Liu and we can still get our hands on medicine. But we don't know how much longer our luck will last. Some days I start feeling down and think I might as well inject myself with some tainted blood and get it over with. Of course, that's just guilt and depression. I have no right to think like that."

"You don't have the virus?" I ask, surprised.

"No."

"Then why are you here?"

"They need me."

"But I thought—"

She lays her hand on my arm. "You thought everyone in the South Zone has the virus? No, not everyone. It's not so simple as that. And not everyone in the North Zone is free of it. That's just what they want you to think."

"I never thought anyone would choose to go across the wall. Everyone is so afraid of it. I've heard of people who kill themselves rather than be sent across."

"Some of us—like Martin and I—prefer to fight it like this."

Martin and I? Does that mean he doesn't have the virus? I want to ask, but I can't, not here surrounded by all these sick children.

"You aren't afraid of catching it?"

"Of course I am. Aren't you?" She glances at me with her intelligent eyes. She's right of course. I can just as easily catch it on my side of the wall as on hers. "Come on. Let's find a bed for you before it's dark. We have oil lamps but we're trying to conserve. Everything is harder to get hold of now—batteries, candles, lamp oil, kerosene. Besides, it's better not to call attention to ourselves with lighted windows once the gangs come out at night."

We climb another stairway and walk down another dark hall to a small room with two narrow hospital beds.

"They're hard but it beats sleeping on the floor. Are you hungry?"

"No, I'm good."

"Are you sure? I could send something up."

I shake my head. I don't want to eat their food. They need it more than I do. I can eat when I get back to the North Zone.

"It's hot in here, isn't it? You're used to air-conditioning."

"Yes."

"We can open the window."

"Okay."

She pushes open the window, but the air that wafts in seems just as hot as the air in the room. In the street below a black and white striped car speeds by. A spurt of automatic fire bursts from the car, and I jump back. I hear shouts and music blaring from a radio as it rushes past.

"The wall won't hold them back much longer," she says. "They want what's on the other side. Drugs. Electricity. Air-conditioning. Food. They'll kill whoever they have to kill to get to it. Life is very cheap now."

"Have you ever thought of leaving?" I ask.

"You mean the city? I used to, back when the planes were still flying daily. But I had family here. Now they're gone, but I have . . . other reasons for not leaving. Anyway, who knows if it's any better someplace else? What about you?"

"I came here from the Midwest seven years ago."

"How was it there?"

"Better. But that was seven years ago. Now it's probably just like this."

"Yeah, maybe so." She pats my arm. "Choose a bed and get some sleep. And, hey, thanks again for helping us."

After she leaves, for a while I look out the window as the room darkens. The street below grows darker too, with only the occasional headlamp of a passing motorcycle roaring past to disturb it, while beyond the wall the lights of the North Zone wink like jewels. Just last night I was sitting over there on my balcony wondering what it was like in the South Zone. Now I know.

CHAPTER 9

I didn't sleep well last night. Maybe because of the heat or maybe because of the strange bed. Toward morning I had that dream I've had before about trying to find my way back home. In my dream it's dark and I'm in my hometown trying to find our house but everything has changed, the streets seem different, and try as I might, I can't find it. Then I wake up in a sweat.

For a while I lie in the dark thinking about my family until light begins to sift in through the window. I know I should get an early start if I'm going to get to work on time, so I get up and go in search of a restroom. I find one down the hall and splash water on my face. It's cold, of course, since there's no electricity, but I feel better afterward. There's a mirror over the sink, and I sigh when I see myself. My hair looks a mess, as of course it would after spending a night in a strange bed, tossing and turning. I regret not bringing along a brush, but yesterday it seemed better to travel light. I try to comb my hair with my fingers, which doesn't help much, so I give up on it and brush my teeth using my fingers, and rinse my mouth with water. Under the circumstances it will have to do.

Next I head downstairs in search of the cafeteria, which I find without much trouble. It's a large room with maybe twenty people scattered about the tables. No one pays much attention when I walk in. I look around, hoping to spot Sandy.

"You must be Sarah," says a young woman with long brown hair sitting alone at a table near the door. "I'm Heather." She holds out her hand and smiles. I see a guitar propped against the wall nearby.

"I heard you singing yesterday."

"Yeah, I saw you last night getting the grand tour. Sandy said to watch for you to come in and make sure you got some coffee."

"Coffee sounds good."

She leaves and a minute later is back with a Styrofoam cup of coffee, which she hands to me. "Hope you like it black. We're a little short on sugar and things like that."

"Black is fine. I'm surprised you have coffee. Hot coffee, I mean."

She grins. "We have a gas stove."

I inhale the aroma, then take a sip and feel the hot liquid flow down my throat and into my veins. It feels wonderful.

"Have you been here long?" I ask.

"You mean here at the hospital? Several months. I came with my brother Jamie when he got bad."

"Do you live here?"

"Yeah, I guess I do. Jamie's all I have left. Home is wherever he is."

"I'm sorry about your brother."

"Me too." She gathers back her long hair with both hands, then releases it in a cascade and shakes her head as if clearing her thoughts. "Sandy said you live on the other side of the wall."

"Yeah, I do."

"What's it like over there now?"

"We still have power."

She smiles. "Besides that. How about movies?"

"There aren't as many theatres as there used to be, and there aren't as many new movies, but I guess they are still making them and people still pay to go see them."

Heather sighs. "I miss movies. With no power all our theatres are closed down now. No TV either. No Internet. No computers. Without electricity we can't recharge anything. Our landline phone service is down and cell phone reception is lousy. People say the power may not come back on. I hope they're wrong. What do they say on your side of the wall?"

"No one knows."

"I hate to think what it's going to be like if it stays off. Two weeks and people are starting to act crazy. Heck, they were acting crazy at one week."

Sandy walks in wearing jeans and an orange top. Gone is the white lab coat. With her ponytail she looks like a college student. She flashes me a smile of perfect white teeth. "Here you are. I see you've had some coffee. Do you want some toast?" Before I can answer she sets a small paper plate with a slice of toast in front of me.

It seems ungrateful to refuse and I'm famished, so I eat it. As I tuck the last bite into my mouth, I glance at my watch and Sandy notices.

"You look eager to leave."

"I don't want to be late for work."

"We can go now if you're ready."

She hands me Martin's backpack. This time it contains a change of clothes and some tape and gauze to dress his wound. The rest of what she will need is in her own backpack.

"Aren't you forgetting something?" Sandy says a few minutes later as we get ready to wheel our bikes out the door. She looks down at the red band on her arm.

I pull mine out of my jeans pocket, where I stuffed it yesterday, and put it on.

When we reach the street, I'm surprised to see Milo on his black bike waiting for us.

"There's your friend," Sandy says.

Like yesterday, he's dressed all in black from his shades to his boots, except of course for the red armband.

"I think you white girls need a bodyguard."

"You think we can't take care of ourselves?" Sandy calls back cheerfully.

"It's getting ugly out here. They burned several blocks around Cactus last night."

She frowns. "Where do they think people are going to live? It's so senseless and stupid."

"I suppose a place to live isn't uppermost in their minds. You ladies planning to cross the wall?"

"That's right," says Sandy. "How did you guess?"

"Mind if I tag along?"

She shrugs. "It's up to Sarah."

"Sure," I say. "Why not?"

We retrace the route Milo and I traveled the day before.

Again I breathe in the stench of garbage and can smell smoke in the air. Dirty, half-naked children rooting in the garbage bags stop to watch us as we ride past. A little boy throws a bottle at us that hits the pavement behind us and shatters.

"Not much to look at, is it?" Sandy says.

It looks dangerous to me, and I'm glad Milo is with us.

Crossing the wall takes even more time today than it did yesterday. The line is longer and moves slower as the guards check work papers. I'm grateful I now have papers provided by Dr. Liu with my name on them instead of Martin's. All the same I feel nervous as the guards search our backpacks. The one searching mine looks at me suspiciously. He probably wonders why I have so little in it.

The one searching Sandy's backpack pulls out a first aid kit. "What's this?"

"I'm a nurse," she says calmly. "I need that on both sides of the wall."

He calls over my guard and they both peer into her backpack.

"Is there any law against carrying a few medical supplies?" she asks.

"Don't get smart," says the guard. "Maybe you'd better step aside. You've got some strange things in here."

"What's the problem?" Milo asks.

"You with her?" the guard asks.

"Yeah, I'm with her."

"Then maybe you better step aside too."

"You guys are making a mistake."

"Is that so? And why is that?"

My heart is in my mouth. I'm sure we're going to be

arrested and thrown in jail. Martin will wonder what happened to me when I fail to show up. Lydia will think I've been mugged or murdered. Strickland will wonder why I didn't show up for work.

But then Milo pulls his wallet from his pocket. He turns his back and lowers his voice as he speaks to the guard. I assume he's trying to bribe the guard. I hope he knows what he's doing. Evidently he does because seconds later the guard says, "Okay, you can go."

"Me too?" Sandy asks.

"You too, Ponytail. Go on. Get out of here before I change my mind."

Sandy grabs her backpack and we ride through the checkpoint.

"I can't believe some people go through that every day," she says when we are in the North Zone.

"I go through that every day," Milo says.

"Did you give him money?" I ask.

He shrugs. "We got through, didn't we?"

"I'd forgotten what it was like before everything got so bad," Sandy says, staring at the neat rows of apartment buildings and the bicyclists riding to work.

After seeing what the South Zone is like, it looks good to me too. It's hard to believe that everything can seem so normal here, while on the other side of the wall, things are so bad.

Milo thrusts a scrap of paper into my hand.

"What's this?" I ask, looking down. It has numbers scrawled on it—a phone number.

"In case you need a bodyguard," he says. "And now if you ladies will excuse me, I've got other things to do."

We watch as he joins the stream of traffic.

"What's he do?" Sandy asks.

"I don't know."

She gives me a funny look. "I thought he was a friend of yours."

"I just met him yesterday when I was crossing the wall. I don't know anything about him."

She looks at his rapidly receding figure. "He seems okay, but you never know. These days you have to be careful who you trust."

"I *am* careful," I say. It's true I don't know much about Milo, but I know little more about her or Martin. Milo may look like he belongs to a street gang, but he didn't pull out a knife and try to rob me. He helped me get to the hospital on Seventh Avenue, just as he said he would. Whatever he does for his day job, I trust him as much as I do anyone else.

"So where's Martin?" she says.

"It's not far from here."

Before we get to the Glenview Tower, we stop beside an abandoned building and remove our red armbands. I hope no one sees us because to be caught removing them could get us arrested. But if we are wearing them when we get back to the Glenview Tower, the security guards will probably refuse to let us in the building or, worse, turn us over to the police for questioning. It feels good to have the armband off. My arm feels lighter, although I know that has to be in my mind because it's just a piece of cloth.

By the time the Glenview Tower comes into sight, I know I'll be late for work. The ride and going through the checkpoint took more time than I thought it would. I know

Lydia can manage my class until I arrive, but Strickland is bound to notice I'm not there. Well, nothing I can do about that.

After parking our bikes in the garage, we stop by the lobby so Sandy can register. That takes more precious minutes. There are two guards on duty. One is drinking coffee and reading a newspaper, glancing up from time to time at the security monitors. The other looks at us suspiciously as Sandy signs in. She tries to be friendly, but he just glares at her.

"Are they always like that?" she asks as we ride up the elevator. She glances uncomfortably at the security camera. "Do they watch every move you make?"

"You get used to it."

She shudders. "I don't think I'd ever get used to it."

When I open the door to my apartment, the cat is there to greet me. She meows and rubs against my legs. I have to kneel and pet her before going a step farther. Martin is sprawled on the sofa with an open book in his lap and earbuds in his ears.

"It's about time," he says, pulling out the buds. "I was right, wasn't I? It was a cinch."

"I got there," I say, setting his backpack on the floor beside him, "but it was not a cinch."

"You certainly look comfortable," Sandy says. "And here I thought you were bleeding to death."

"What are you doing here?"

"I came to take that bullet out."

"Couldn't someone else have come?"

"You could say you're glad to see me." She glances at me. "Martin and I are old friends."

"Don't believe anything she said about me. I'm really a very nice guy."

She bends over him and reaches for the bandage. "Let's see it."

"You didn't tell David about this, did you?"

"No, David doesn't know."

"Good. He'd worry."

"If you don't need me, I think I'll take a quick shower," I say.

"Don't you want to watch her take the bullet out?" Martin asks. "You never know when you might need to know how."

I roll my eyes. "No, thanks."

I lose no time getting into the shower. Standing under the showerhead with the water streaming over me, I feel as if I'm washing away the heat and grime of the South Zone. It's wonderful to be able to take a warm shower. I'd stay in longer, but I need to get to work, so I dry off and dress as quickly as I can.

When I come back out, Sandy has the wound uncovered and is doing something with what looks like a large pair of tweezers. I quickly look away.

"You're leaving already?" Martin asks, looking up. "But you just got back."

"I have to go to work. I'm already late."

"Ouch, that hurts."

"Hold still and don't be such a baby," Sandy says.

"Your phone rang a lot last night," Martin says.

I stop with my hand on the doorknob. "You didn't answer it, did you?"

"No, I let it ring. But someone really wanted to get hold of you."

"It probably wasn't important."

"Is it okay if Martin stays here another night?" Sandy asks. "He should rest a little more after I take this bullet out."

I glance at Martin and our eyes meet. I hesitate a fraction of a second. It would be heartless to say no, wouldn't it?

"Sure, he can stay."

By the time I get to school, I'm almost an hour late. Lydia is showing the children a documentary about dinosaurs when I walk into the classroom. She throws me a look but doesn't ask why I'm late. While they're watching the documentary, I join her at the back of the room.

"Strickland wants to see you right away," she says in a low voice, glancing at the security camera. "I hope you've got a good story prepared for him. You're going to need one."

I expected this of course. I knew Strickland wouldn't pass up the opportunity to call me to his office. Oh, well, I'd better get it over with.

Lydia gives my arm a sympathetic pat as I leave.

I stride down the hall, determined not to let him browbeat me. When I enter the outer office, Mrs. Stevenson greets me with a warm smile.

"I hear he wants to see me," I say.

She gives a little grimace and nods. "Go on in, dear. And good luck."

"You're late," Strickland snaps as soon as I enter his office. He looks at me over his glasses with accusing eyes.

"I'm sorry. I overslept." It's a flimsy excuse and I know he won't believe it. I never oversleep. I'm never late, for that matter.

"Where were you last night?" he demands.

I meet his gaze straight on. I'm not about to tell him I crossed the wall and spent the night in the South Zone. "At home. Why?"

"Why didn't you answer your phone?"

"I didn't notice it ringing."

"Don't play games with me."

"What do you want?"

"Have you thought about my offer?"

His offer? He sounds as if we're discussing a financial transaction, like the sale of a piece of property. Which maybe we are.

"Your little Indian pupil."

"Mary?"

"Yes. Mary whatever-her-name-is."

"We don't know her last name," I say politely.

We glare at each other.

"Then I take it there is no deal?" he says coldly. "Because if there is no deal—"

I look at the monitors. There's my classroom, where Lydia is standing at the front of the room with thirty-five pairs of eyes watching her. Somewhere among them is Mary.

"What exactly do I have to do?"

"I think you know."

Yes, I know. I'm not stupid. What else would a sleaze like Strickland want? And the very idea of what he's proposing makes my skin crawl. How can he think I would ever agree? The thought of being touched by him makes me feel physically ill. I would just as soon hook up with a stranger off the street. I want to tell him to go to hell; there's no way I'll do what he wants. But then Mary will be sent to a reservation, where she'll probably die. Wouldn't I regret it later, knowing I could have saved her and didn't? He sits there watching me with narrowed calculating eyes from behind his glasses, tapping his pen on the desk in that maddening way he does, waiting. I think of Mary standing alone at the fence on the playground watching the other children play, taking my hand and running with me during the drill, looking at me so trustingly. How can I turn my back on her? If I can do this and it saves her life, shouldn't I agree to it?

"If I do, you'll let Mary stay?"

He considers this. "I think that can be arranged."

"All right then I will if you'll swear you won't send Mary away."

"Very well. You have my word. So that's settled. Now where and when? How about after school today? We can go to your place. You live alone, don't you?"

Immediately I remember Martin is recuperating on my sofa. And even if he weren't there, I wouldn't want Strickland to come to my apartment. It's my private space, and I don't want him invading it.

"My cousin is staying with me," I tell him.

His eyes narrow. "Your cousin?"

"We'll just have to go someplace else."

"Where?"

I can't think of any place. Where do people go for illegal assignations? He won't suggest his own house because his wife will be there. There are few hotels anymore and anyone registering at them would be closely watched. We would be asked for ID's and proof of marriage. No, a hotel room is out of the question.

"You're not really going to do this, are you?" he says.

I glance again at the monitor that shows my class. I have to do this, for Mary's sake. "Tomorrow might be okay. But it will have to be here." I expect him to object. Maybe he'll even change his mind about our sordid little arrangement.

He taps his pen on his desk as he considers this. "All right, but if you don't cooperate, your Mary will go to a reservation. Remember that."

"I'll cooperate. But just this once. And if you don't keep your part of the bargain, I'll make sure everyone knows what you did. That includes the police."

"Is that a threat?"

"Maybe."

"Well, I think we understand each other. Now shouldn't you be getting back to your class?"

Mrs. Stevenson looks up as I emerge from his office. "Is everything all right?"

"Yes, everything is fine." I wonder what she would say if I told her the truth about Strickland. I can imagine the look of shock and disbelief that would spread across her face. But what could she do? What can any of us do? It isn't like in the past when one could lodge a harassment complaint. Even if I went through the motions, I doubt anything would come of it. In the face of the enormity of the epidemic, small injustices are barely noticed.

CHAPTER 10

"So what was it like?" Lydia asks.

It's the end of the school day and she's walking with me to the parking lot so we can talk without being overheard by Strickland on the intercom.

"Not good." I tell her about the garbage in the streets and the lawlessness.

"You didn't have trouble crossing with all those drugs?"

I hesitate, uncertain how much I want to tell her. "This guy I met helped me."

She rolls her eyes. "Another guy? And I suppose this one was infected too?"

"I guess he is. He was wearing a red armband. But then I was wearing a red armband too."

"You listen to me. You have to stay away from guys who wear red armbands. Next thing you know, you'll be wearing one too, and it will be for real."

"You worry too much."

"And you don't worry enough."

I kneel to unlock the chain on my bike.

"What about that guy Martin?" she asks. "Is he still hanging out at your apartment?"

"He'll be gone tomorrow."

"You just make sure nothing happens *tonight*. You want me to come over and keep you company?"

"No." I squint up at her against the sunlight. "I think I can manage."

She grins and shakes her head. "I guess you think I've got a nerve offering advice when I couldn't keep from getting knocked up."

"Did you talk to Jeff?" I ask her.

"Yeah, I did."

"Did you tell him you're pregnant?"

"Yeah, I told him."

"Well?"

She breaks into a smile. "He wants to marry me. He doesn't care what his parents think."

"That's great."

"He'll get his blood test tomorrow and I'll get mine the day after. We'll get married on Saturday."

"I'm so happy for you."

I think we both have tears in our eyes. Everything is going to be okay. She and Jeff will marry and have their baby. She's young for marriage, but what does that matter when life seems so tenuous? Better to grab what she can of happiness while she can. None of us knows what the future holds.

As I ride back to the Glenview Tower, I feel optimistic for once. Things are working out for Lydia. I wonder if it's possible for them to work out for me as well. Martin is waiting for me at my apartment and the thought of him makes my heart beat faster. I know that after tomorrow I may never see him again, that he could walk out of my life just as suddenly as he walked in. I know this, but I push those thoughts aside. I'm tired of never letting myself feel.

When I get to the Glenview Tower, I resist the urge to rush up to my apartment to see Martin. First I stop by the lobby to see if I have any mail in my box. The security guard at the desk watches me suspiciously. He's the guard who knocked on my door the night Martin arrived.

"Is your *cousin* still here?" he asks. He looks pointedly at the register. "What did you say his name was?"

I hesitate. I used a name with Martin's initials, didn't I? Then I remember. "Michael Johnson." I meet the guard's eyes evenly. Has he checked and found there is no such person? It's a common name. There should be lots of Michael Johnsons in the city.

He frowns and writes something in his register.

"Is anything wrong?" I ask.

"What do you think?" He smirks, as if we have shared a dirty joke. He knows Martin isn't my cousin. Is he going to report him? At that moment his phone rings. He answers it and while he's talking, I slip away.

When I let myself into my apartment, I find Martin watching news on my small portable TV, his left arm in a sling.

"Hey," I say.

"Hey," he answers, smiling.

"So the bullet is out?"

"It's out. Sandy says I'll be back to my old self in no time."

"Anything on the news?"

He points the remote at the TV and turns it off. "Nothing about the power outage in the South Zone. I thought there might be."

"Security didn't come up, did they?"

"No, why?"

I tell him about the security guard downstairs. "I'm not sure it's safe for you to stay here."

"I'll leave first thing tomorrow. Unless of course you want me to go sooner. I don't want to cause any trouble for you."

"It's okay. Nothing I can't handle."

My phone rings and we both look at it. It rings again.

"Aren't you going to answer it?" Martin asks.

Reluctantly I pick up. "Hello?" There's silence at the other end. It's probably Strickland. "What do you want?"

"Is your cousin there? Do you really have a cousin?"

I turn my back to Martin and speak in a low voice. "Stop calling me. I told you I'd do it." I hang up before he can say anything else.

Martin is watching me when I turn around. "Is anything wrong?"

Just then the cat meows and rubs against my ankles for attention, so I bend down to pet her. "No, it wasn't important."

I avoid looking at him. I don't want him to know about Strickland. I'm afraid he wouldn't understand.

"All right," he says, holding up his hand. "So it's none of my business. Let's talk about something else. Why don't you tell me about yourself. Where are you from?"

"The Midwest."

"So why did you leave?"

"Nothing to stay for."

He picks up the small framed photograph of my family from the end table. "Is this your family?"

I sigh. It seems as if it was taken many years ago, in another lifetime. A summer day, the sun shining. My mother, father, Laura, Emily, and me. Everyone gone now except for me, the sole survivor. The pain is blunted now, seven years later, but the emptiness remains. I'm alone in the world. I'll never see any of them again. I want to tell Martin he's lucky—he at least has a brother. But I can't say that. His brother is dying. Soon he'll be alone in the world too.

"I met your brother."

Martin sets the photograph back on the table. "It's funny, isn't it? When we were kids, we used to fight. I always thought my parents liked David better than me. He was bigger, stronger, smarter, faster, harder working. You name it, he was better at it than I was. And he wanted to be a doctor, just like my dad. I'm sure my dad loved that. All I ever wanted to do was dig up dinosaur bones."

I try to imagine him as a boy. It isn't difficult. I can see the boy in him. "And now you smuggle drugs."

"That and other things. I'm no hero. If I were a hero, I'd find a way to stop this epidemic before we're all dead."

"Maybe it can't be stopped."

"I don't buy that. In fact, I think our government knows how to stop it."

He sounds like a conspiracy buff—one of those people who think the government has a cure and is keeping it from us.

This is a side of him I didn't suspect. "A cure, you mean?" I ask cautiously.

"No, a vaccine."

Just as elusive as a cure. "I thought a vaccine wouldn't work. There are too many different strains, and the virus mutates too fast."

"I believe they have a vaccine. Don't you remember when they used to say they were very close? They were testing a vaccine on animals."

I do remember. It was early in the epidemic. But nothing came of it. Could he be right? Surely there's no vaccine. Everyone would know about it. It would be in the news. "If they have a vaccine, where is it?"

"Closely guarded. They choose who gets it. They sell it to the highest bidder. They play God."

Now he really does sound like a conspiracy buff. I don't want to believe the government could have a cure but would keep it secret. He has to be wrong. "You don't know that. If they had it, they'd make it available."

"Would they? Does the North Zone share its drugs with the South Zone?"

A few days ago I would have answered yes, but now I know better.

"In fact, I think they have a cure. But it costs so much that only the most wealthy and powerful have access to it. Everyone else who is unlucky enough to get the virus will die. We can use drugs to hold it off, for years even, but in the end it's fatal."

"Seriously, you really believe there's a cure?"

He shrugs. "I don't know. Maybe I just want it to be true."

Yes, we all want it to be true. We want the dying to stop. We want life to be hopeful and good again. We want our families around us. We want to love and be loved, not to fear the touch of friends and strangers. But that world is gone. We have to deal with things the way they are now.

"What happened to your family?" he asks.

"They died."

"I'm sorry."

I nod. I don't want to talk about it. "Are you hungry?"

"You can't hear my stomach rumbling?"

"I'll make some dinner for us."

He follows me into the kitchen and watches as I rummage in the refrigerator for lettuce, carrots, radishes, and a tomato to make a salad.

"Maybe I could help," he suggests.

I look skeptically at his arm in a sling. "With one hand?"

He grins. "Why not?"

"Accidents," I say, picking up a paring knife.

"I suppose you have a point there." He sits down at the table grinning. "You don't have a boyfriend?"

"No," I say carefully, slicing up the tomato.

"You just live alone here?"

"Yes."

"Doesn't it get lonely?"

"There are a lot of other people in the building. I'm hardly alone. And during the day I'm surrounded by my students. Actually it's kind of nice to come home, put on some music, and relax with a good book."

"And your cat," he says as the cat leaps onto the table. He deftly scoops her up and places her in his lap, where she sits blinking as he strokes her.

"She's not my cat."

"No? Whose cat is she?"

"I don't know. She's just a stray I'm taking care of until I can find somebody to give her to."

The cat leaps from his lap to the floor and begins meowing.

"She knows we're talking about her," he says. "Smart cat."

"She probably wants to be fed. She knows if she follows me into the kitchen, chances are I'll feed her."

"What's her name?"

I glance down at the cat as she brushes against my legs. "I have absolutely no idea."

"You must call her something."

I sigh. "If I give her a name, I'm afraid I'll get too attached to her and then how will I give her away? I just call her Cat."

"That's a hell of a name, isn't it?" he says, presumably to the cat, which keeps meowing until I give up on the salad and open a tin of cat food for her.

"What about you?" I ask. "I take it you don't live alone?"

"I live with a friend of my father's, Dr. Liu. He's like a second father to me. Of course lots of times I just sleep at the hospital so I can be near David as much as I can."

"I met Dr. Liu."

"He hardly stops to sleep. He's the only one left of our doctors. He's the backbone of the hospital now."

"Sandy seems pretty knowledgeable."

"Yeah, Sandy's great, but she's not a doctor."

"You two seem to be good friends."

"Yeah, we go way back."

"An old girlfriend?" I hint.

"Yes, once upon a time. But now we're just good friends. She's in love, but not with me."

Good to know. "Who's she in love with?"

"Dr. Liu."

This surprises me. I remember how they were standing together the first time I saw them, deep in a conversation Milo and I interrupted by our arrival. They just looked like two colleagues, junior colleague and senior. There was nothing to suggest something more.

"It's mutual?"

He shrugs. "Sandy says this isn't the time for personal feelings and that she'll never speak to me again if I tell him."

"He doesn't know?"

"I don't think so."

"Do you think he cares for her?"

Martin shrugs again. "Who knows? He's always praising her. Sandy can set that broken bone. Sandy can tell you what to do for your stomach pain. Ask Sandy what she recommends for jaundice. But if it's more than just appreciation, I can't tell. He's a very private person. I live with him, but I wouldn't dream of prying into his feelings. It's a sort of understanding we have. We're there for each other, but we don't pry into each other's personal life. He knows when to just leave me alone with my black moods and I do the same for him."

"Black moods? You?" I glance at him. I can't picture him in a black mood. I remember my first impression of him at the hospital. He looked like he didn't have a care in the world. Maybe that was one of the things that attracted me to him. He seemed so untouched by the tragedy around us, in spite of his red armband. He reminded me of the past, before everything began to fall apart.

"Yeah," he says, grinning. "Now you know one of my secrets."

I smile and push a plate of salad toward him.

That's when the lights go off.

CHAPTER 11

"**T**here goes the power," Martin says, stating the obvious.

"I'll get a flashlight." I grope my way to the bedroom and find the flashlight I keep by my bed. When I come back, Martin is out on the balcony. I go out and stand beside him. My hand finds his, or his finds mine. All around us the city has been plunged into darkness. The dark void of the South Zone has expanded like a black hole and swallowed everything on this side of the wall. Nearby buildings loom like black shadows. Streetlights and traffic lights are out, and only a few crawling headlights break the darkness. It's incredibly eerie, like we've been transported to another dimension.

"Looks like a total blackout," Martin says.

"Maybe it'll come back on in a few minutes."

"And if it doesn't?"

"I have some candles."

He snorts. "I meant, will the wall hold?"

I look out at the blackness and shiver. It's what everyone has been dreading. If the gangs of the South Zone use the opportunity to swarm across the wall, they might be able to do a lot of damage before the police can stop them. I wonder how safe we are in the Glenview Tower. We are only a few blocks from the wall. At least it would take anyone a while to climb the fifteen flights. That's some comfort.

"I have to check on someone," I tell Martin. "I'll be back in a few minutes."

"Wait. I'll go with you."

We make our way back through the apartment by the light of my flashlight. At the door we're careful not to let the cat slip out with us. We follow my flashlight beam down the hall to Mrs. Franklin's apartment. You would think we're the only people left on the floor, the silence is so complete. No doors open, no heads pop out to ask who's there. Everyone is sitting tight, waiting for the lights to come back on.

"Is that you, Sarah?" Mrs. Franklin calls out when we let ourselves in. She's sitting in the dark in front of her TV.

"Yes, it's me. And I have a friend with me."

"I was watching an old Judy Garland movie when the electricity went off."

"We came to see if you're okay."

"I thought I'd just sit here and wait for the power to come back on."

"That sounds like a good idea. Would you like us to wait with you?"

"That's very thoughtful of you, Sarah. I'm sure they'll have it back on in no time. Who's your friend?"

"This is Martin. Martin Jones."

"You look as if you've been in an accident, young man."

"I fell off my bike."

She turns to me. "Sarah, there are candles in the drawer next to the refrigerator. And you'd better open some windows. With the air-conditioning off, it'll get hot in here fast."

After I find and light candles and open all the windows, we sit in the flickering candlelight and talk.

"I wish Albert were still alive," Mrs. Franklin says, "but maybe it's just as well he didn't live to see what's happened. He had a stroke. I think that's a much better way to die than of this terrible epidemic."

"I'm sure you're right," Martin says.

"Back then who could ever have imagined it would be like this one day? Everyone used to worry about overpopulation. Now we wonder if anyone will be left."

"The virus isn't going to kill us off," he says. "It's ourselves we have to worry about."

I glance at his face in the candlelight. Already he seems so familiar. Already I feel as if I've known him all my life.

"You sound like a philosopher, young man. You remind me of my son. That's just the sort of thing he'd say. You should meet him sometime. He'd like you."

"Where is he?"

"Los Angeles."

No one says anything for an awkward minute.

"You probably don't hear from him much now that mail isn't getting through and phone service is down," Martin says.

"That's right. It's been a while. But Sarah takes care of me. I don't know how I'd get by without her."

"It's no trouble to pick up a few extra things when I'm at the grocery," I assure her.

"Well, I'm glad she's found a nice young man like you. What's your name again?"

"Martin."

"Ah, yes, Martin." She nods and smiles. "So nice of both you young people to spend time with an old lady like me."

Thirty minutes pass and still the power has not come back on. Martin goes back to my apartment and retrieves the two salads I made, and we eat them. Mrs. Franklin says she ate before the power went off. After we eat our salads, Martin and I go out on her balcony to look at the city. This side of the building looks out on the North Zone, now ominously dark except for an occasional light where some building has its own generator. In the distance I can hear the wail of police sirens.

"I don't see any fires," Martin says. "That's a good sign."

"So you don't think any gangs have broken through?"

"No, it looks quiet out there."

"What will they do if they get across?"

"Set fires, loot, turn over cars. . . ."

I know what they will do. Martin is right—it's not the virus, it's ourselves we have to worry about. How can I ever forget? Too many nights I've woken from bad dreams with the sound of my family's screams in my head. I didn't hear them scream the night our house burned down, but in my dreams I hear them. In my dreams I feel the heat of the flames and hear the gunfire. I traveled so far to get away from these memories, but they are still with me. I don't think they will ever go away.

"You're shivering," Martin says.

"It's nothing."

He puts his good arm around me and pulls me close. I can smell the clean smell of soap on his skin. It feels good to have his arm around me. When was the last time I had a man's arm around me? Not since I went out with Brian, the red-haired accountant I met in a bar I went to with Roberta and another teacher from school, and that was more than a year ago. We only went out a couple of times before I started finding excuses not to see him anymore. I just couldn't go through the motions. There didn't seem to be any point.

"Do you think about your family much?" Martin asks.

"I dream about them at night."

"Did they die of the virus?"

"No."

"How did they die?"

Roberta once said I should just look forward, not back. She was right of course. It does no good to dwell on the past. I can't bring them back. And yet I can't let go of them either. All I have left are memories. If I give them up, what will I have then? Nothing.

"They were murdered," I say with effort.

He holds me a little tighter, waiting. I have told almost no one the story since I left the Midwest. I just let people think they died of the virus. It's easier that way. But now I want to tell Martin.

"A gang broke in one night and killed them. The gangs from the cities were getting worse around that time. A lot of them were infected and they were high on drugs. They had guns. They set fire to the house afterward."

"Where were you?" he asks, his breath warm against my ear. I feel safe with him holding me like this. I feel I can tell him.

"I was out with a friend. When I got back, the fire department was fighting the fire, but it was too late."

I went to a movie with my boyfriend Rick that night, and

afterward we had a quarrel. Neither of us said much as he drove me home. A song was playing on the radio, something you heard nearly every time the radio was on that summer. We passed a gang of bikers going the other way. There were almost a dozen of them. They were whooping and their motorcycles were loud.

"What was that?" Rick said when they were past.

"I don't think they were from here," I said.

"They're probably just passing through."

A few minutes later we heard a siren and pulled over to let a police car and a fire truck race past.

"Must be a fire somewhere," Rick said.

I think I knew right then, but I didn't want to believe it. I couldn't say anything, just held my breath and hoped my family was safe. We were almost to my house before we saw the fire and the people standing around watching. It was like a bad dream. We had to stop several houses away because of the cars and the fire truck. I jumped out of the car without waiting for Rick and started running. I recognized some of our neighbors, but most of the people I had never seen before.

"Is anyone still inside?" I asked frantically. "Did everyone get out?" I looked all around, desperately hoping to see my family. Surely they weren't still in the house. They must have had time to get out.

Rick came up beside me and tried to put his arms around me, but I broke away. I had to know. I ran to a fireman who stood beside the fire truck. "Where are the people?" I had to shout to be heard above all the noise.

"Stand back," he said.

"I live here," I shouted as if he were hard of hearing.

"Where are the people who were inside? Where's my family?"

"How many people?" he said.

"Four. They must have gotten out. They must be here somewhere." I started shouting their names. People were staring at me as if I were crazy. A policeman came up. "People are still in there," I cried. "You've got to rescue them."

"I'm sorry," he said. "It's too late. It was too late when we got here."

I didn't want to believe it. What if they were huddled in a corner of one of the rooms just waiting to be rescued? Why wasn't someone doing something? Why was everyone just standing around watching? Even the firemen seemed half-hearted in their efforts. It seemed to me they were hardly trying to put the fire out. The flames were devouring the house. No one could survive a fire like that. They should have escaped right in the beginning. Why hadn't they? If they couldn't get to a door, they could have climbed out a window. Every room had windows. Later I would know. According to the police report, they may have already been dead at the time of the fire. The motorcycle gang we had passed had been seen parked in the driveway. They had set the fire before leaving.

For a long time afterward I felt as if a part of me had died that night. It was never the same with Rick after that. I knew the fire wasn't his fault, but somehow I blamed him because I hadn't been home that night. And of course I blamed myself. I finished out my senior year in a daze, living with the family of one of my friends who had taken me in. But when I graduated, I knew it was time to leave. I couldn't bear staying there any longer.

"So you came here," Martin says.

"Yes, and I went to college and became a teacher."

"And you tried to forget."

"Yes, I tried to forget."

"But you couldn't."

"No, I couldn't. I can't."

"It's hard to let go of the past. Too bad we can't just have it cut out of us like an appendix."

"What about your family?" I ask.

"My mother was a nurse. She was attacked by a patient with an infected needle."

I don't say anything. I know he will tell me the rest if he wants to. He didn't pressure me to talk and I won't pressure him. A moment later he continues.

"That was before David was infected. Sometimes I think he deliberately took risks, picked up guys in gay bars, total strangers. After Mom got sick, the family fell apart. My father took care of her, but he lost interest in everything else. Toward the end he couldn't bear to see her suffering. I think he helped her to die. You know, gave her a lethal dose of morphine or something. And then he shot himself in the head with a gun we had at home."

I press closer to Martin, wanting to comfort him. All these old wounds. Will they ever heal?

"The hell of it is he didn't have to die. He had a choice. My mom didn't have a choice. Maybe David didn't either, I don't know. But my dad had a choice."

I don't say anything because there isn't anything I can say. For a while we just stand there, holding each other.

When we go back inside, Mrs. Franklin is still sitting where we left her. Her head is thrown back, as if she has been sleeping. "Do you know the time, Sarah?" she asks, rousing herself.

I tilt my watch toward a candle. "Ten o'clock."

"I think I'll go to bed. It's late."

"Would you like us to stay until the power comes back on?" I ask, reluctant to leave her alone.

"That would be very good of you young people."

After she has gone to bed, Martin and I blow out the candles and curl up together on the sofa. I try to be careful of his injured arm.

"Comfortable?" he asks.

"Mmm."

"So you don't have a boyfriend?" His chin rests on top of my head.

"No."

He's quiet a moment. Should I ask if he has a girlfriend? Maybe not. I don't want anything to spoil this moment.

"What about those phone calls? Are you in some kind of trouble?"

"No." Silently I curse Strickland.

"Then who's calling you?"

I sigh. "My principal."

"What does he want?"

"I can't tell you that."

"Why not? Why can't you tell me?"

"I just can't. Look, can we talk about something else?"

"You don't let anyone get very close, do you?"

"What do you mean?" I ask, hurt.

"You know what I mean. You shut other people out. You don't let people get close."

116

"We're close right now, aren't we?" I say. "I can hear your heart beat." I don't want to talk about Strickland. He has nothing to do with Martin and me.

"Is he married?" Martin asks quietly.

"Who?"

"Your principal."

"Yes, he's married."

"So why is he calling you?"

"I can't tell you that."

"Are you having an affair with him?"

"Of course not. If you knew what he's like, you wouldn't ask."

"What's he like?"

"An ogre."

"So what's he threatening to do—fire you?"

I don't want to tell him, but I also don't want a wall of misunderstanding between us, so I try to explain. I tell him about Mary and how Strickland knows I feel sorry for her and has threatened to send her to a reservation unless I. . . .

"What? Sleep with him?"

"Yes."

"You're not going to do it, are you?"

"I have to."

"But it's not safe. You know that."

"I'm sure he gets tested, just like the rest of us."

"Are you crazy?"

"I shouldn't have told you. Just forget I said anything about it."

"When is this supposed to happen?"

"Tomorrow after school." I close my eyes and can hear

him breathing. "I shouldn't have told you. This has nothing to do with you."

"Doesn't it?"

We are both quiet a minute. I can hear a clock ticking somewhere in the dark.

"I have to do this," I tell him. "I wish I didn't but I do."

"Just tell me one thing. What's his name? I'll check his medical file in the computer system at the hospital."

I think it over. "Okay, but I don't want you interfering. I'm not letting him send Mary to a reservation."

He strokes my hair then and we just lie quietly together listening to the silent building and the faraway wail of sirens.

When I wake the next morning, Martin's good arm is around me and my head is on his shoulder. We fell asleep on Mrs. Franklin's sofa. The power has just come back on. The cheery voice of a woman newscaster bursts forth from the TV as the screen springs to life. At the same time the hum of the air-conditioning starts up. Sunlight is seeping through the windows.

"Good morning," Martin says.

"Good morning," I say, smiling at him. I wonder how long he's been awake. Has he been waiting for me to wake up?

"The power's back on," he says.

"So I notice."

"I suppose we should get up."

"Sounds like a good idea," I agree and try to do just that without jostling his injured arm.

He turns the TV off, and I close the windows. Mrs. Franklin is still sleeping, and we don't want to wake her, so we quietly let ourselves out.

When I open the door of my apartment, the cat runs to greet me and meows until I stoop to give her some attention. As I stand up, I notice the window by my bookcase is open. I stare at it, trying to remember if I opened it last night. I'm fairly certain I didn't.

"Did you open that window last night?" I ask Martin.

He looks around. "What window? No, I didn't open any windows."

"Someone's been here." I go to the window and close it.

"Are you sure? Who has a key?"

"No one. Except the security guards of course."

We look at each other.

"Why would they have come in here when the power was off?" he asks.

"I don't know."

"You think they might have been looking for me?"

Our eyes meet again. I bite my lip. "Maybe."

"In that case I'd better leave before they come back."

"What about breakfast?" I don't want him to go, not yet.

"I'd better not hang around."

I know he's right, but I feel disappointed. "Where will you go?"

"The hospital. It's time I got back to work."

This seems dangerous to me. "But won't the police be looking for you?"

"It's a chance I'll have to take. They don't know I'm the one who stole the drugs."

"What about your arm?"

"I'll say I fell off my bike."

"Wait—" I dash into the kitchen and fling open the

refrigerator door. What can I give him to eat? I grab an apple from the crisper.

"Thanks," he says, grinning when I hand it to him. "I hope there weren't any snakes where this came from."

I grin back. "I don't think there were."

I wish I had something more to give him. One apple doesn't seem like much.

"Your security may be suspicious about who I am, but if I'm gone, they shouldn't bother you, and since you gave them a phony name, they can't trace me."

"Be careful," I tell him. I don't want him to be arrested. I hate to see him go, but I know if security comes back, he could be taken into custody.

"Is there a stairway?" he asks as he reaches for his backpack.

"Yes, but it's fifteen flights down."

"That's okay. There are probably no security cameras in the stairwell." He turns toward the door.

"When will I see you again?" I ask.

He takes my face in his hands and kisses me. "I'll call. I promise."

CHAPTER 12

All day I watch the clock, dreading the end of the school day. Knowing what's coming makes it difficult to concentrate on lessons. Lydia asks if anything is wrong, but I don't want to tell her. Bad enough that I told Martin. I try not to think about what will happen after classes are done. It's not too late to change my mind, but then I'll have to find another job, and Mary will be shipped off to a reservation. For her sake, I have to go through with it. If I don't, I'll have her on my conscience for the rest of my life. But I hate Strickland for demanding this of me. As I eat lunch in the noisy cafeteria, I look around the room and wonder who else he has caught in his net. Next to me Roberta is raving about a fitness club she just joined.

"You should all join," she tells the rest of us sitting at the table. "It's important to be as healthy as possible, especially nowadays."

"Who has the time?" says Ellen, a first grade teacher hired just last month, straight out of her sophomore year of college.

She munches on carrot sticks and frowns at her nails. Maybe she has chipped one?

"I make time," Roberta says. "It's a matter of priorities."

I envy her confidence and wonder what she would do if Strickland tried to pressure her into an after-hours meeting in his office. She'd probably laugh in his face and tell him to go to hell. Why couldn't I be like her? But I know the answer to that. Because of Mary, and because I'm not her. As she said, it's a matter of priorities, and my priority is Mary. It's as simple as that. Besides, it isn't like I'm a virgin. I've slept with men before. Just not recently. That was in another life, back in the days when it wasn't a crime for which you could be arrested, and I had a boyfriend I thought I might marry. Later there were others as I tried to forget about the night my family was murdered, but sleeping with someone never managed to obliterate old memories and so eventually I gave it up. Besides, by then it was too risky, and it was hard to find comfort or take pleasure in an act that might lead to death. This business with Strickland is different. I expect no comfort or pleasure from it. I will treat it like a visit to a dentist, something on a par with a root canal. Every day people have to do things they don't like. Why should I be any different? I'll just steel myself, get it over with, and that will be that.

The afternoon drags by. I watch the clock as the minutes tick relentlessly by. When at last the bell rings and the children pour out of the building, it's time to report to Strickland's office. I postpone the moment as long as I can, erasing blackboards, clearing the papers from my desk, watering the plants on the windowsill. Then I take a deep breath and force myself to leave my classroom. As I walk down the empty hall, my heels clicking on the tile floor, I feel as if I'm on my way to an execution—*my* execution.

In the outer office Mrs. Stevenson is working on her computer. "Go right in, Sarah," she says and gives me an encouraging smile. I wonder if she knows why I'm here. Probably not. I don't think she would sit there so casually if she knew what Strickland has planned.

When I enter his office, he's standing at one of the windows looking out. He has taken off his jacket and loosened his tie.

"So you've come," he says and points at the chair in front of his desk. "Sit down, Sarah." It sounds strange for him to call me Sarah, not Miss Davis. I don't like it, but under the circumstances there doesn't seem to be much point in objecting.

Reluctantly I sit down on the chair facing his desk where I have sat often enough before. I'm not sure what I expected, but so far this is no different from a usual meeting. I glance at the security monitors. Only a few teachers are still in their rooms. In the cafeteria half a dozen children have been kept after school for detention. In the outer office Mrs. Stevenson taps away at her computer keyboard. Knowing she is just outside the door makes me feel better. I'm not utterly alone with Strickland. I wonder what's going through his mind. Perhaps this is just a bad joke. Perhaps he doesn't intend for anything to happen. Maybe he's just testing me. Maybe I misunderstood.

"Would you care for a drink?" he asks.

"No," I say quickly. At least this is different. He has never before offered me a drink.

"Are you sure? No? Well, I think I'd like a drink." He goes to his desk and takes a bottle of vodka and a glass from a drawer.

I'm surprised. Who would have guessed old Strychnine kept a bottle of vodka in his desk?

"I believe in enjoying the pleasures of life while you can," he says. "Don't you?"

"It depends on what the pleasures are," I answer warily.

"Well, there are many pleasures, yes. There are pleasures of the mind and pleasures of the body. Take me, for example. I'm forty-six years old. I think I've sadly neglected the pleasures of the body. In fact, I think it was my biggest mistake."

"You could go to jail for this."

He smiles. "Yes, I could. We both could. So if you know what's good for you, you will say nothing about this after you leave here today. Remember, you came here of your own free will. Mrs. Stevenson can testify to that."

I glance again at the security monitor which shows Mrs. Stevenson diligently tapping at her keyboard. Would she testify to that?

I wonder how long this will take. It's all I can do to keep from jumping up and running out of the room. I ask myself how I can possibly go through with it. I detest the man. The thought of being touched by him makes me nauseous. Why did I think I could do this?

"You don't mind if I put on some music, do you?" he says. "I've recently acquired a taste for opera. It's ironic actually. Back when there used to be operas and ballets and concerts, I hated it when my wife dragged me to them. I thought they were a waste of time. But now that they're gone, I find I miss them. Isn't that odd? If someone had told me one day I would love opera, I wouldn't have believed it. But I do. I can think of few pleasures more exquisite than to listen to the aria from *Madame Butterfly*. Do you know it?"

I've never been to an opera, but I do know the famous aria he's talking about. Like everyone else, I've heard it in movies and TV commercials often enough.

"But this isn't *Madame Butterfly*. This is from *Tosca*. Do you know *Tosca*?"

As a clear soprano voice bursts into song from the speakers on his desk, I feel as if I'm caught up in a surreal nightmare. Yes, it's beautiful, but it doesn't belong here in this office under these circumstances. Does he intend to have that playing while he assaults me? Does he expect me to be moved by the power of the music and to overlook the sordidness of what is about to occur? Or is he just trying to cover up any inconvenient sounds we might make? In the next room can Mrs. Stevenson hear the music, and if so, what does she think is happening behind the closed door of his office?

Strickland seems unperturbed, his head tilted to one side, eyes closed, as he listens to the music. "Do you know the story? It's about a woman who is desired by two men. She has a choice—surrender herself to the one she doesn't love in order to save the one she does or let him die. It's such a simple choice. But of course she doesn't keep it simple and so it turns into a tragedy. I love the perfect symmetry of it—love and death." He sips his drink thoughtfully. "Do you ever think about death, Sarah?"

I see no reason to answer his questions. Does he care what I think? With so many lives already claimed by the epidemic, does anyone *not* think about death?

"No, maybe not. You're young, you're healthy, you probably think you'll live forever." He takes off his tie and frowns at it as if he doesn't recognize it. It's a red tie. "Young people always think they're going to live forever. But it's a mistake to think that. The truth is we're all going to die."

I glance at my watch. It's 3:50. I've been in his office for five minutes. How long until this ordeal is over? Half an hour? An hour? Longer? Surely he'll let me go before dark? I don't want to ride home after dark. It's far too risky. Yeah, right, is that any riskier than what I'm about to do?

"Look, can we just get this over?" I say, anxious to be done and on my way. If he keeps drawing this out, I'm going to lose my nerve.

"Such impatience. You need to learn self-control. You should savor the moment."

Not this moment, I think. This moment is one I want to get through as quickly as possible and forget.

"Tell me," he says, nursing his drink. "What would you most regret having left undone if you died now—tonight?"

I feel a prickle of fear. Until this moment I hated him, I felt repelled by him, I saw him as loathsome, but now it occurs to me that he might also be dangerous.

He seems to read my mind. "Don't worry. I'm not going to kill you. I'm not a monster."

"Why are you doing this?" I ask.

"Why? I thought that would have been obvious. Because I can. Isn't this what every man fantasizes? Don't I have a right to grab whatever pleasure I can while I can still enjoy it? Tomorrow may be too late. Tomorrow may never come. We're all going to die. Don't you understand that? Even you, though you probably think being young makes you exempt."

This is so not good. Is he mentally unbalanced? The thought never crossed my mind before, but it does now. He always seemed so staid, so conventional. Sadistic maybe, but conventional. This is a side of him I have never seen before, a side that frightens me. I'll have to be careful.

He grins. It's a cruel grin that sends chills running up and down my spine. "You don't believe me, do you? You think because you're young you'll live forever. You think everyone else will catch the virus but not you. But you're wrong. You're going to catch it too. One day you'll look in the mirror and see the signs. Even before that you'll know. You'll know when you wake in the night in a sweat. You'll know when the nightmares come. And there won't be anything you can do."

He twists his red tie in his hand as if it's a piece of rope. What is he going to do? Every nerve in my body says *run*, but yet I sit here because if I don't, what will happen to Mary?

He walks slowly and deliberately around his desk until he stands so close I can smell the cloying scent of his cologne. I stare hard at the monitor which shows Mrs. Stevenson sitting at her computer. I tell myself as long as I can see her, I will be okay. I grip the arms of the chair the way I do when a dentist is about to start drilling. It will all soon be over, I promise myself. It isn't as if he's going to kill me. He can't, not with Mrs. Stevenson sitting right outside. He's only trying to frighten me. It probably gives him pleasure to frighten me.

"Hold out your hands," he says. "Hold them together, as if you are praying."

"Why?" I ask, watching the red tie with mounting alarm. This was not part of the deal.

"I'm going to tie them together," he says with a kind of weary patience as if explaining something to a child.

127

I can feel the panic rising within me. "Why?"

"Think of it as a little game we're going to play."

"No." I jump to my feet and get the chair between us. There is no way I'm going to let him tie my hands.

"Sit down," he says coldly.

At that moment there is a knock at the door. We both look at it. Strickland swears under his breath. "What is it?" he calls.

The door opens part way, and Mrs. Stevenson looks in timidly. "Excuse me for interrupting. There's a phone call for Miss Davis. An emergency of some kind."

"Can't you take a message?" he says irritably.

"They said they had to talk to her. They said it was urgent." She smiles apologetically.

He glares at her and then at me.

"We aren't finished," he snarls in a low voice. "I don't know what this is all about, but I swear if you leave now, you'll regret it."

Tosca is still playing. He still holds the red tie in his hands. Mrs. Stevenson looks at us curiously. Has she guessed what was about to happen? Is it really an accident that she intervened when she did? As I bolt from the room, I almost expect the phone call to be a ruse.

But it isn't. Martin's frantic voice greets me when I pick up the phone on her desk.

"You haven't done anything, have you?" he asks. "You didn't—?"

"No, I didn't."

Mrs. Stevenson, who has sat down again at her desk, busies herself with some papers.

"Thank god," Martin says. "I was afraid I was too late. Listen, I used the hospital computer to access Strickland's medical records. He's got the virus."

"What?" I clutch the phone tighter to my ear and glance again at Mrs. Stevenson.

"He's infected."

"That's not possible."

"It is possible. I told you before—it's a mistake to think everyone who has it is on the other side of the wall."

"You're not just saying this to—"

"Would you get out of there?" Martin says, his voice rising. "Don't you get it? He has the virus and he's trying to give it to you."

"Why?" Suddenly I feel sick. I think of stories in the news of people deliberately trying to infect others. They do it out of a warped idea of revenge or out of bitterness against their fate. Some expose others out of simple callousness. That's why a special law was passed: to knowingly expose others to the virus is a capital offense.

"He's sick," Martin says. "He knows he's going to die."

Strickland appears in the doorway of his office and glares at me. He doesn't look like a man who knows he's going to die. He looks like a man very much bent on getting his way.

"All right. I understand." I hang up the phone and take a deep breath. "I have to go now." I look straight at Strickland. "I've just received word that someone I know has the virus."

"I'm so sorry," Mrs. Stevenson murmurs sympathetically.

Strickland just glares. He can't say anything in front of her.

As soon as I'm in the corridor, I start running. I want to get away from there as fast as I can. My footsteps echo on the tile floor. I feel as if I'm running through a deserted building. I don't stop running until I get to my classroom. Just as I grab my backpack, Strickland's voice comes over the intercom: "Miss Davis, return to my office at once. If you leave this building, you're fired. Do you understand?"

I know he's watching me on the surveillance camera. I ignore it and head for the door.

"Think very carefully about what you're doing," he says.

I give one last look around the room where I've been teaching for almost three years, taking in the neat rows of desks, the green blackboard, the students' artwork displayed on the bulletin boards, the TV monitor suspended from the ceiling, the plants I water every morning on the windowsill, my desk with the Snoopy mug sprouting pencils and pens. It seems strange to think I may never see this room again. I have no idea what I'll do, but I doubt I'll be back.

"You're making a big mistake," Strickland warns. "You'll regret this."

"Will I?" I say under my breath.

"I'll put her on that bus. I swear it."

I know what I have to do as I walk out of the classroom, and I know I have to do it before he can stop me.

When I leave the building, I turn toward the student dorm. I've been there several times to visit Lydia, who shares a suite on the first floor with several other young assistants at the school. The children live on the second and third floors. In this building too there are surveillance cameras, but Strickland doesn't have access to them in his office. They are monitored by the security guards.

Lydia looks surprised when she opens her door and sees me standing there. "Sarah. What are you doing here?"

"I need to see Mary right away."

"Why? Is something wrong?"

"There's no time to explain. Just take me to her."

She glances over her shoulder, then steps into the hall. "What's this all about?"

"I have to get Mary out of here. Please. Every minute we stand here talking puts her into more danger."

"What do you mean?"

"Strickland wants to send her away."

"Send her away where? You're not making any sense."

I can't waste time explaining. I turn and head towards the stairs that leads to the second floor.

"Hey, wait a minute," she says, running after me. "You can't just walk in and take one of the kids away."

"No? Just watch me."

"Okay, I'll take you up to see Mary, but there's no way you can take her out of here unless you've got a pass for her. Do you have a pass?"

"No."

She sighs. "The guards won't let her past the gate without one, you know."

"I'll think of something. Now would you please just take me to her?"

"Okay, I'm going to assume you know what you're doing. But if you get in trouble, don't say I didn't warn you."

She leads me up the stairs and along the second floor hallway. We pass several rooms crowded with beds, then come to a room where a group of children are watching an old episode of *Sesame Street* on TV. Mary sits cross-legged on the floor at the back of the group with a doll in her lap. She looks up as we enter the room. A few of the others look up too, then go back to watching the TV screen.

I go to Mary and kneel beside her. "How would you like to come home with me?" I ask in a low voice.

She stands up without asking any questions, clutching her doll to her chest with one hand. The other she gives to me.

"We don't have much time," I tell her. "We have to pack your things fast."

Lydia is outside the door. "Maybe you should think about this," she says nervously when we come out.

I shake my head. "There's no time. If I leave her here, Strickland will send her to a reservation."

"You could lose your job. Have you thought about that?"

"I already lost my job. Please, there's no time to explain. I have to get Mary out of here."

Lydia looks from me to Mary. I can see she wants to ask more questions. "I just hope you know what you're doing," she says, and then without another word she leads the way to the room Mary shares with nine other children.

The beds all have navy blue coverlets and are neatly made with a green blanket folded at the foot. Against the wall stand several small bureaus. The walls are starkly bare except for a single pale green stripe that runs around the room at about eye level. It's all neat and clean, but it looks more like a detention center than a home for children.

"Where are your things?" I ask Mary while Lydia stands guard at the door.

Mary walks to one of the bureaus and pulls open a drawer. I empty the contents onto the nearest bed: pants, T-shirts, jeans, and socks. She watches as I stuff everything into my backpack.

132

"Anything else?" I ask when it's all in.

She looks down at her doll, a rag doll with black braids. I wonder if her mother made it.

"Of course," I say. "Put her in too."

She hesitates, then pushes her doll into the bag and watches as I zip it up.

"How are you going to get her past the guard without a pass?" Lydia asks as we scope out the hall.

"I don't know. I'll think of something." I slip my arms through the straps of my backpack and pull it on. As I step into the hall, I notice a fire alarm mounted on the wall across from us.

Lydia just has time to say, "Don't—" before I pull it. Instantly the air is filled with loud ringing.

"I hope you know what you're doing," she shouts in my ear.

Children swarm into the hall. They are used to drills and don't push or panic. I hold tightly to Mary's hand, and we let ourselves be swept along by the tide of children, down the hall, down the stairway, and out through the double doors onto the pavement in the late afternoon heat. Once outside, the children mill restlessly around the fenced-in enclosure of the school grounds.

"I still don't see how you're going to get her out," says Lydia, who has managed to stay with us.

Across the grounds I see Strickland stride out of the school. I crouch, so he won't see me, and Mary crouches with me.

"What now?" Lydia says.

"I don't know."

Within minutes we hear the siren of a fire truck. When it pulls up in front of the dorm, the children cheer and surge toward the chain-link fence to see it better. I know this is my chance to escape with Mary.

"Wish us luck," I tell Lydia. She gives me a quick hug. Then, holding Mary's hand and still crouching, I weave my way through the crowd of children toward the parking lot. I know the firemen will have to search the building to see if there's a fire. We wait, and when the guard on duty leaves his post to talk to them, we run into the parking lot, where I unchain my bike as quickly as I can. Once I'm on, Mary climbs on behind me and wraps her arms around my waist. I'm not accustomed to the extra weight and feel awkward and unbalanced at first, but there's no time to lose. No one tries to stop us as we ride out through the open gate, now unguarded, and once we are in the street I pedal hard and pick up speed.

CHAPTER 13

Every time a siren wails, my heart pounds. I keep glancing back, half expecting to see a police car in pursuit. With Mary on the back of my bike, I can't go very fast. Occasionally a car rushes past us, but for the most part, the streets are deserted. The distance home has never seemed so far before. At least Mary is safe, I tell myself. I can feel her holding tightly to my waist. Now Strickland won't be able to send her to a reservation. And if he reports me to the police for taking her, I'll tell them he has the virus and tried to give it to me. I don't care what they do to him. He deserves it. Has he infected any other women or was I to be the first? In my mind I see him again with the red tie in his hand and feel sick in the pit of my stomach. It was a close call. If Martin hadn't phoned to warn me, I would have been exposed to the virus by now. I was so stupid to think there was no risk. There is always a risk. I should have known that. I almost threw my life away by allowing a man I detest to get too near to me.

When the Glenview Tower looms into sight, I feel relieved. With Mary behind me, I glide silently into the deserted parking garage. It will be dark soon and the automatic lights haven't come on yet, so the garage is dim, shadowy, and cavernous. Except for us and about a dozen cars, it's also empty.

Mary climbs off the back of my bike but stays close to me, watching intently as I unzip my backpack and begin to search through her belongings.

"I'm looking for a scarf or a hat, something to put on your head," I explain.

Reaching in, she pulls out a red baseball cap. "How about this?"

"Perfect." I put it on her head and tilt it forward to hide her face. "When we go in, keep your eyes on the floor. There's a camera in the entry and another one in the elevator. Don't look up at them. Do you understand?"

She nods.

"Good girl."

I try to shield her with my body from the camera in the entry and then again from the camera on the elevator. I know the security guards will see her if they're paying attention, but I hope they won't get a good look at her. She keeps her head down, and neither of us speak. When the doors open on the fifteenth floor, we get out and walk quickly without talking down the hall to my apartment.

As soon as we step inside, the cat appears to greet us. With a small cry, Mary drops to her knees to pet her.

"Do you like cats?" I ask.

She looks up at me from under her red cap and nods. "Is she yours?"

"Not really. Just until I find a home for her."

"She likes me. What's her name?"

"She doesn't really have a name. I just call her Cat."

"Why doesn't she have a name?"

"I guess I haven't gotten around to it. You know what? Why don't you give her a name? I bet she'd like that."

Mary tilts her head and regards the cat solemnly. "What's your name?" As if in answer, the cat meows. "I know. I'll call you Beggar." She glances up at me. "If that's okay with you?"

"Why do you want to call her Beggar?" I ask, amused. "Is it because she begs to be petted?"

Mary shrugs. "She has to have a name. A real name."

"So she does," I agree. "Beggar it is."

At that moment my phone rings. I debate whether to answer it. Who would be calling? Strickland? Security? Martin? I don't want to talk to Strickland, but if it's security, I should pick up. They may have seen Mary on their monitors, and if I don't answer, they may come up. If it's Martin, I want him to know I'm safe. I reach for the phone.

"Are you all right?" Martin asks.

I feel a rush of happiness at the sound of his voice. "I'm fine."

"I called back and told your principal I know his little secret and if I ever hear again he's trying to pass the virus on to anyone, I'll report him."

"You talked to him?" I ask, surprised.

"I wanted to be sure you had left."

"Where are you?"

"About a block from the wall. I just wanted to make sure you're all right before I cross over. Once I'm on the other side, my signal will cut out."

"I'm all right," I assure him. "How about you? Was everything okay at the hospital? No one suspects you of taking . . . anything?" I don't want to say 'drugs.' Someone might be listening in.

"Not a word. I'll call you tomorrow, okay? I've got to go—it'll soon be dark. I don't want to get caught out on the streets."

"Martin—"

"What?"

I don't want to let him go. What if something happens to him and I never see him again? There's so much I want to say. But there's no time. Every second we delay makes it more dangerous for him. I have to let him go. "Be careful." It seems like so little when I want to say so much.

"Don't worry," he says. "I can take care of myself."

Right. Like that bullet in his shoulder. Next time he may not be so lucky. I hang on the phone after the connection is broken, then set it back down on the end table. Mary is still petting the cat. I'll have to think of a story to tell security to explain why she's here. Which reminds me, I should go down to the lobby and sign her in before a security guard shows up and starts asking questions.

"I have to go downstairs for a minute," I tell her. "Don't unlock the door for anyone while I'm gone and don't answer my phone if it rings. Okay?"

She nods. "Okay."

Downstairs the short man with the mustache is on duty again at the front desk. He sees me coming and his eyes harden.

"Don't tell me. Another relative, Miss Davis?"

So he saw Mary on the monitors. I'll have to put the best face on it that I can.

"Yes, my niece has come to stay with me," I say, reaching for a pen to sign the register.

"Ah, your *niece*. And how long will your *niece* be staying?"

"I don't know. That depends."

I write 'Mary Logan' on the register and a fictitious address. Even if I knew her real last name, I wouldn't give it to him. I don't trust him any more than he trusts me.

"You seem to have a great many relatives and friends, Miss Davis," he says, frowning at what I've written.

"I know a lot of people. Don't you?"

He glares at me with dislike. "We have to be careful you know. Better safe than sorry, right?"

There's something about the way he says it that makes my skin crawl. It sounds like a veiled threat. Maybe I should try to be friendly, but I can't. I want nothing to do with him. So I turn and leave without another word.

When I get back to my apartment, I search my cupboards for something to fix for dinner. My shelves are discouragingly bare. I'll have to ride to the grocery store tomorrow. I'll also have to start looking for another job right away. I have some money saved, but with the rent for the apartment and food for Mrs. Franklin, Mary, and myself, it won't last long.

I sigh and open a can of tomato soup. Soon Mary is sitting across from me at my kitchen table and we are both spooning warm soup into our mouths. I'm surprised how delicious it tastes. She smiles at me and suddenly things don't seem so bad. I smile back, determined to make her feel at home.

"Do you live here all by yourself?" she asks, looking around my little kitchen.

"Yes. Just me."

"And Beggar."

"And Beggar." I glance at the cat, which has just managed to spring onto the counter and has knocked over a plastic glass holding pens and pencils. Of course it's only until I can find someone who will take her. Beggar is not a permanent resident of my apartment. I sigh, get up from the table, and lift her off the counter. I don't know why I bother. She will just jump up again or try for the table next. Evidently she has lost interest in her own dinner, the small dish of cat food sitting on the floor near the wastebasket.

When I sit down with Mary again, I notice she seems to be thinking hard about something. I wait, expecting her to ask why I spirited her away from the school. I feel I owe her an explanation, but I'm not sure what to tell her. Clearly I can't tell her about Strickland.

"Will you miss the dorm?" I ask.

She shakes her head. "Louise didn't like it there."

"Louise?"

"My doll."

I glance at the rag doll with the black braids, which is sitting on a third chair at the table. "What about you? Did you like it there?"

She shakes her head again. That makes me feel less guilty.

"Do I have to go to school tomorrow?" she asks.

"I think it would be better if you stayed here. Is that okay?"

"Yes, it's okay." She sips another spoonful of her soup, and neither of us says anything for a few moments.

"Can I ask you a question?" she says after a bit.

I brace myself. Here it comes. I try to smile. "Sure. What do you want to know?"

She looks at me solemnly. "Are you going to get into trouble for bringing me here?"

Not the question I was expecting. "Maybe a little."

She nods. "I thought so."

Just then the cat makes a graceful leap up onto the table, and Mary lets out a small gasp of delight. I have to stop eating and lift Beggar off. Mary would share the rest of her soup with Beggar if I let her. I suggest she can pour some milk into a saucer instead. When we finish, I put our dishes in the sink, set the red baseball cap on Mary's head again, and take her down the hall to meet Mrs. Franklin. With luck the cap will help hide her face from the security camera in the hall.

When we let ourselves in, Mrs. Franklin is sitting in her favorite armchair in the semi-dark in front of the TV watching a quiz show.

"Who's this?" she asks.

I introduce them.

"I'm pleased to meet you, Mary." She holds out a gnarled hand for Mary to shake.

"She's going to stay with me a while," I explain.

"You'll have to come visit me," she tells Mary, who is pressing shyly against me. "I'm sure we'll be great friends."

Mary looks at the TV and doesn't answer. Apparently she has lost her voice again.

"Oh, what a nice doll," Mrs. Franklin says.

"Her name's Louise," Mary whispers, looking down at the doll she's cradling in one arm.

"What do you think of my dolls?" Mrs. Franklin points to her collection of Hopi dolls on the wall shelf.

Mary studies them. "They're very nice," she says politely in a nearly inaudible voice.

"Would you like one to take with you?"

She hesitates, then shakes her head.

"Why not? Don't you like them?"

"It might be lonesome all by itself."

"Well, being by one's self can be lonesome," agrees Mrs. Franklin. "You're right about that. Let me think. Is there something else I can give you? I know. Go in my bedroom and look in the top drawer of the dresser. See if you can find a necklace that looks like a bird."

Mary glances up at me uncertainly. I nod to let her know it's all right. Gathering up her courage, she ventures into the bedroom.

"She's very shy, isn't she?" Mrs. Franklin says. "Is she Navajo?"

"No, Havasupai."

"Will she be staying with you long?"

"Just until I can figure out what to do with her. I'll try to find someone who can take her in."

"No family?"

"Not as far as I know."

"Poor thing."

I glance at the TV. "Anything happening in the news today?"

"Oh my, you didn't hear?"

"Hear what? I got home late."

"A bomb went off at the White House. It did quite a lot of damage, and several people were killed, but the President is okay. He wasn't there at the time. They're urging people to stay calm. I'm surprised you didn't hear."

A bomb at the White House? "Did they say who did it?"

"A terrorist group."

There are so many of them now. The virus has had an impact on governments, economies, and law enforcement. If Washington descends into chaos, what will happen to the rest of the country? Will every city be on its own?

"Let me know if you hear anything more," I tell her.

"Is this it?" Mary asks, emerging from the bedroom with a small pendant on a thin silver chain cupped in her hand. "Is this the bird?" She holds it out for Mrs. Franklin to see.

"Yes, that's it. You found it. What a clever girl you are."

"What kind of bird is it?"

"A phoenix. Do you know anything about the phoenix?"

Mary shakes her head, her eyes large and solemn.

"It's a mythical bird that sets itself on fire and burns to death, then rises again from the ashes. Would you like to have it? Since there's only one, he won't feel lonesome."

Mary looks at me, clearly tempted by the offer. I smile at her. "Okay," she says, breaking into a smile. "Will you put it on me?" she asks, handing the necklace to me. She stands very still while I fasten it around her neck.

"That looks as if it belongs on you," says Mrs. Franklin. "I do believe it was just waiting in my drawer for you to come and claim it."

Mary feels the phoenix with her fingers. "I can keep it? Really?"

"Of course you may. I gave it to you," says Mrs. Franklin. "You'll take good care of it, won't you?"

Mary nods eagerly. I can tell she really likes the necklace. From time to time as we talk, she reaches up and touches it, as if to assure herself it's still there. Her eyes roam back to the Hopi dolls and then to the rock collection and the Navajo rug hanging on the wall and the framed family photos sitting on the mantel. I'm glad she says nothing about the fire alarm and how I whisked her away from the school. I don't want to explain to Mrs. Franklin what happened. Fortunately she asks no awkward questions, but just accepts that Mary has come to live with me.

"Can I live with you always, Miss Davis?" Mary asks later when we're sitting on my balcony. The cat is curled up contentedly in her lap. I'm writing in my journal, but it's almost too dark to see what I'm writing.

"Call me Sarah," I tell her. "I don't know about always. We need to find a safe place for you."

"Isn't it safe here?"

I hesitate, not certain how to answer. I don't want to make her feel anxious.

"Please can I stay here with you and Beggar?"

I reach out and lay my hand against the side of her face. I can't keep her of course. It's a temporary arrangement, just like with the cat. When things are so uncertain, who knows what will happen tomorrow or the next day? The police could come pounding on my door and take her away. But I can't tell her that. I don't want to frighten her.

"Are you afraid to die?" she asks suddenly.

Her question startles me. "Why do you ask that?"

"Some of the kids at school say we're all going to die. Do you think that's true?" She watches me, waiting for my answer.

"Everybody dies sometime," I tell her. "But you're very young. You have your whole life ahead of you." It doesn't seem right for an eight-year-old to be thinking about death. Yet how can she not think about it when it's all around her? The fact that she was at the State School means that her parents are dead or at least have disappeared.

"Mr. Reed said everybody is going to die from the virus."

Ted Reed, a third grade teacher, is a hypochondriac whose favorite topic is illness.

"He shouldn't have said that."

"I'm not afraid to die." Mary touches the silver phoenix at her throat.

"You're not going to die," I tell her firmly. "Don't even think that."

"But I don't ever want to be sent to the other side of the wall. Mr. Reed says it's terrible there. He says they kill children."

"They don't kill children. He was probably trying to scare you kids so you wouldn't want to go there." Whatever he was trying to do, it showed appalling insensitivity to talk of dying to children who have lost their families to the epidemic. If I were going back to work tomorrow, I would give him a piece of my mind. Things are bad enough without frightening children by telling them such horror stories. "Did he really say that?"

She nods. "He said everybody who goes to the South Zone dies."

I look out at the wall. The red glow of fires can be seen again. I hope Martin is safe, and that none of those fires is the hospital where his brother David lies dying. Then I look at Mary beside me petting the cat. I saved her from being sent to a reservation, but can I save her from the world we're living in? I reach out and gently push her hair out of her eyes. I'm not sorry I took her away from the school. As long as she's with me, Strickland can't harm her.

"Is it true?" she persists. "Does everybody who goes to the South Zone die?"

I think of what Sandy told me about choosing to be in the South Zone. "No," I say. "It's not true."

She lays her cheek against Beggar's fur and closes her eyes for a moment. For now she is safe. And she is not alone—she has me.

In the middle of the night I'm awoken by the doorbell ringing and someone pounding on the door. I look at my alarm clock. 2:00 a.m. Who could it be at this hour? Have the police come to take Mary away? The pounding continues. I have to answer it. If it's the police, they will get security to open my door if they have to, or break it down. Even if it's someone else, I must stop them before they wake other tenants. I slip out of bed, trying not to disturb Mary, who is asleep beside me with her doll clutched in one arm.

When I look through the peephole, I see Lydia. I can't imagine why she's ringing my doorbell at two in the morning, but I open the door for her. She rushes in with her hair wild and her mascara smeared. Once inside she closes the door quickly behind her and secures the chain again.

"Something's happened to Jeff," she bursts out. "I don't know what to do."

"What do you mean?"

"He's disappeared. He's gone." Her hand shakes as she unzips her backpack.

"Calm down," I tell her. "Everything's going to be okay."

"I didn't know where to go. You're the only one I could think of. I couldn't stay at the dorm. They came there looking for me."

"Who did?"

"The police."

I stare at her. "What did they want?"

"I don't know. I hid. Irene—do you know her? She's a new first grade assistant. She told them I was out. But I was afraid they'd be back."

"You rode here on your bike in the dark?" I know she must be really scared to risk going out after dark. The streets may be safer on this side of the wall, but you do hear about people being attacked and robbed at night. There's more crime than there used to be. Better to stay off the streets at night.

"I got a ride on the back of some guy's motorcycle."

"What guy?"

"Just a guy."

"Oh, Lydia!" She must have been desperate.

"I know. I know. I could have been raped or murdered." She runs one hand distractedly through her hair. "But I didn't want to stay there and get arrested."

"How'd you get in the building?"

"A janitor downstairs let me in. I told him it was a matter of life and death." She sits down on the sofa as if her knees have just given way. "Sarah, what am I going to do?"

The night security guards will have seen her on their monitors. "I'd better go down and sign you in."

"Don't bother. I already signed myself in. I told them I was your sister."

"My sister?"

She smiles through her tears. "Yeah, your sister. They didn't say a word."

They may not have said a word, but I doubt they believed her. First a cousin, then a Native American niece, and now an African-American sister. Do other people at the Glenview Tower have such a diverse family as I do? But there's no time to worry about it now. If the police are looking for her, that's a bigger problem.

"Maybe they wanted to question you about what happened this afternoon," I suggest. "Maybe they're really after Mary or me."

She shakes her head. "I don't think so. I was supposed to see Jeff tonight and he never showed up. That's not like him."

"Maybe something came up."

She shakes her head again. "He would have phoned." She begins to rock back and forth, hugging herself. "I just know something bad has happened. I feel it in my bones. Oh, if anything's happened to him, I don't know how I'll bear it."

I put my hand on her arm. "We can't do anything tonight. Let's make a bed on the sofa for you, and you try to get some sleep. Tomorrow we'll find out about Jeff. I promise."

Once she is settled on the sofa, I go back to the bedroom. Mary is still sleeping peacefully in my bed clutching her doll. In the dark I see the glint of silver at her throat—the phoenix. I climb into bed as carefully as I can, trying not to disturb her.

Although I tried to sound strong for Lydia, I don't feel strong. I feel as if the ground is slipping away under me. I've lost my job. I have Mary to take care of and old Mrs. Franklin depending on me. Now Lydia expects me to help her too. I wish Martin were here, so I could talk to him. I wonder what he would have to say about the bomb that went off at the White House. I suppose he's one more person I'm going to worry about. He walked into my life less than a week ago, but now he's never far from my thoughts. How would I bear it if he were to suddenly disappear? Who could I turn to for help? I think of Lydia in the next room. If our roles were reversed, I know she would help me. I would be sick with worry if Martin were to disappear, just as Lydia is sick with worry about Jeff. I wonder if she will be able to sleep or if she will lie there thinking about him until morning. Tomorrow I'll have to help her find him. We all have to help each other now. If we don't, there will be no hope for any of us.

CHAPTER 14

Jeff's parents live in the North Zone in a pink suburban house in a tract where all the houses look alike. With the help of a map I located it, but it takes almost an hour to get there on my bike, and by the time I do, I'm sweating. I take a long swig from my bottle of water and look the house over from across the street to see if it looks safe to approach. You can tell this neighborhood still has people living in it even though the houses have a shuttered look. The sprinkler system is spouting in one front yard, the shrubbery is freshly trimmed. There are no doors standing open or windows broken as in the areas where people have fled.

I wheel my bike up to the door, hoping no one shoots at me. There have been incidents of people being shot by nervous homeowners. I wanted to phone first, but Lydia insisted it was too risky—their phone might be tapped. When I ring the doorbell, a dog inside begins to bark—a big one from the sound of it. The McAllisters will look at me through the peephole first of course. I take off my sunglasses and try to look harmless. At last the door opens a few inches with the chain on.

"What do you want?" a gruff voice demands through the narrow opening.

"Mr. McAllister? I'm a friend of Lydia Hogue. She's worried that something's happened to Jeff." I just hope he knows about Lydia. If not, this is going to be even more difficult than I anticipated.

"Do you have the virus?"

"No." I can't blame him for being suspicious. He doesn't know me. But he can see I'm not wearing a red armband.

"How do I know you're telling the truth? Do you have your clearance paper on you?"

I pull my paper out of my pocket and hold it up for him to see the date and the large N stamped on it.

"How do I know that's genuine? You could have forged it."

"I didn't forge it."

"It's just a piece of paper."

"Well, it's all I've got," I say. "I've come a long way in the heat to talk to you about your son, but if you don't want to hear what I have to say, I'll go."

"This is about Jeff?"

"Yes, this is about Jeff."

"And you're alone?"

"I'm alone."

"All right," he says, unchaining the door. "You can come in. But I warn you, you'd better not try anything funny. We've got a guard dog in here that'll chew you up if I tell him to."

If I hadn't promised Lydia I would do this, I would turn

around right now and leave. I don't like the idea of entering a strange house with a dangerous dog, especially if I'm not welcome. But I promised Lydia, and I don't want to let her down. As I step into the dark interior, I feel the rush of cool air from the air-conditioning system. It feels good after being out in the sweltering heat. My eyes take a minute to adjust after the bright sunlight. Mr. McAllister lays down the handgun he has been clutching on a polished end table. He's a tall dignified-looking man in his fifties, white-haired, well-tanned and fit. His wife, equally tanned and fit, peers nervously at me from a shadowy hall doorway. A Great Dane regards me from a few feet away, ears alert, a low growl rumbling in its throat.

"Duke, stop that," Mr. McAllister says sternly.

At once the growling stops, and the Great Dane turns and trots ahead of us down the hall. The living room Mr. McAllister leads me to is thickly carpeted and furnished with a beige sofa, a couple of recliners, a large screen TV, and a breakfront full of china. On the walls hang paintings of cowboy scenes. I sit down on the sofa, sinking into its cushions, and the Great Dane trots over to sniff me. When it's finished, it lies down beside Mr. McAllister's recliner and puts its head on its paws. Mrs. McAllister seats herself next to her husband in the other recliner.

"You say you're a friend of . . . Lydia's?" Mr. McAllister asks, pausing before he says her name.

"Yes." At least they know who she is. I'm relieved I don't have to explain.

"Did she send you here to ask for money?"

It seems a strange question. Why does he think Lydia would ask them for money? "No, she's worried about Jeff. She was supposed to see him last night and he didn't show up."

"Jeff is dead."

"Dead?" I look from one to the other. I thought maybe they would say he was sick or had been injured in an accident, but despite Lydia's fears I didn't expect to hear he was dead.

"He was killed in a police shootout Wednesday night," Mr. McAllister says in a carefully neutral voice, staring at the carpet, his fingers pressed together in a steeple.

"We know he was planning to marry . . . Lydia," Mrs. McAllister says, hesitating in the same way her husband had, "but you might as well know we weren't in favor of the marriage. We thought he was making a mistake."

"Did Jeff tell you that she's pregnant?" I ask.

They glance quickly at each other. Mr. McAllister clears his throat. "Jeff told us she thought she might be pregnant. Of course, if she is there's no way to be certain it's Jeff's child unless they were to get blood tests. And now obviously that's not going to happen."

Mrs. McAllister begins to cry. "Oh, what does it matter now? What does anything matter now?"

"As you can imagine, this has been very hard on us," Mr. McAllister says, patting his wife's hand. "Jeff was our only child."

"Tell . . . Lydia . . . we're truly sorry, but we can't help her," Mrs. McAllister says, dabbing her eyes with a tissue. "I suppose she'll want to get an abortion. I know they're hard to get now, but there must be doctors around still willing to do them. And besides, she shouldn't have taken such a risk if she wasn't prepared to face the consequences. She must have known something like this could happen."

I've heard enough. I've found out what I need to know,

and I see no point in staying longer and prolonging this distasteful conversation. It's clear they don't care what happens to Lydia. I stand, and the Great Dane lifts his head, alert. We eye each other warily.

"Will there be a funeral?" I ask.

Again the McAllisters exchange quick glances.

"Just a small one," Mrs. McAllister says. "Just family and close friends. I'm sure Lydia wouldn't want to come. It would be awkward."

"She loved your son."

"No one knew about her." She dabs at her eyes again.

I should probably stop but I don't. "She's carrying your son's child. She has a right to be at his funeral. I think she would want to be there."

Mrs. McAllister looks at her husband. "Should we tell her?"

Her husband looks stonily at the floor. "She probably gave it to him," he says angrily. "She probably already knows."

"Knows what?" I say, my stomach knotting.

"They did an autopsy," Mrs. McAllister explains. "Jeff had the virus. He was infected." Tears begin to course down her cheeks again. She struggles to control her feelings. "So in a way maybe it's a blessing he died the way he did. Maybe that was better than a slow terrible death."

"You tell Lydia she'd better not come around here expecting any handouts," Mr. McAllister says. "There's no proof that's Jeff's child. It could be anybody's. She comes around here, she'll have the police to deal with. You tell her that."

I don't stay to hear more. The Great Dane trots behind me

as I find my way back down the hall to the front door and let myself out. Outside I am again surrounded by blinding sunlight and burning heat, but I'm relieved to have escaped from the McAllisters. I ask myself if they would have told me Jeff had the virus if they hadn't feared Lydia's presence at the funeral. It even crosses my mind that they could be lying about him, but, no, I believe them. I don't think they would lie about that. It's the daily horror creeping closer to everyone's life. I understand now why the police came looking for Lydia at the dorm—not to break the news of Jeff's death, but to take her into custody as a suspected carrier and have her tested for the virus. Someone told them about Lydia, and I have a pretty good idea who.

All the way home I dread breaking the news to Lydia about Jeff's death. I know it will be hard, and it is. When I tell her, she cries and storms and paces and moans.

"He can't be dead," she says again and again.

I put my arms around her and try to comfort her, but what can I say? She wants Jeff back, alive, and I can't give her that. Anything else is meaningless.

When she begins to calm down, I tell her the rest—that his parents don't want her to attend the funeral, that he was infected by the virus, that Mrs. McAllister has recommended she get an abortion.

"I won't," Lydia declares fiercely. "This is Jeff's child. And mine. It's all I have left of him." She has stopped crying now. We sit facing each other across the kitchen table. "I'm going to have this baby even if we both have the virus."

"You may not have the virus," I remind her. "Unless you get tested, you can't be sure you've got it."

"I can't get tested," Lydia snaps. "If they find out I'm pregnant and not married, they'll put me in jail. If I've got the virus, they'll wait until the baby's born, and then if the baby tests negative, they'll keep it and send me across the wall to die. If the baby tests positive, they'll send us both across the wall to die."

I know she's right. She'll have to hide from the authorities if she wants to have her baby. In any case she can't go back to the State School.

"Do you have any place to go?" I ask. "Someone who could take you in?"

She shakes her head.

"Then you'll have to stay here."

She shakes her head. "No, the police will come looking for me. We both know that. And I don't trust your security guards."

I don't trust them either. And she's right about the police. Strickland will tell them where I live and they'll come looking for her. We'll have to find somewhere else for her to stay, and we'll have to find it fast.

"I know a place where the police wouldn't look for you," I say as a plan begins to form in my mind.

She looks at me with tears still brimming in her eyes. "Where?"

"The South Zone."

"You're not serious."

"Think about it. The police don't cross the wall."

"The police don't cross the wall for a very good reason. They want to stay alive."

"It's dangerous, yes. But there are safe places. Like the

hospital where Martin's brother is. I bet you could stay there. And if there isn't room, they could find someplace else for you to stay. They'll help us."

"Everybody knows it's awful in the South Zone," she says. "People sick, people dying. People getting shot. The place is crawling with drug fiends, rapists, pyromaniacs, and god knows what else. Nobody wants to go over there. We're all terrified that *they're* going to come over *here*."

"Then stay with me."

"I can't. I'd be putting you and Mary in danger." The tears start to flow again. "Why did Jeff have to get himself shot?" She jumps up and resumes pacing. "He didn't know he had the virus. He would have told me. He wouldn't ever have put me at risk. Jeff wasn't like that." She wipes her eyes with the back of her hand and stands straighter. "I'm going to have this baby, Sarah. No one's going to stop me. I'm going to do it for Jeff. I owe this to him."

"We'll figure out a way," I tell her. "We'll find a place for you to hide."

"Okay, let's just suppose I decide to cross the wall. I'm not saying I will, but let's just suppose. How would I do that?"

"I could call Martin. He'd help you."

She paces some more, then stops. "Okay, call him. Do it now before I change my mind."

I find the number for the hospital and punch it into the phone. I ask for the blood lab. When a young woman answers, I ask for Martin Jones. She is polite but firm. He is not at the hospital. She has no idea how I can contact him. "He lives in the South Zone," she says, "which means you can't phone him, and even if you could, I couldn't give you his number because we're not allowed to give out personal information about our staff."

"What's the matter?" Lydia asks when I hang up.

"Martin's not there."

"So what do we do now?"

"We could wait until tomorrow. Try again then."

"And if you can't get hold of him tomorrow?"

She's right. I can't be sure of contacting him tomorrow. He could be sick. He could have been arrested. If we wait too long, it may be too late. Lydia should get out of the North Zone right away. Every hour that we delay increases the likelihood of her being arrested.

"We could try to cross by ourselves," I suggest.

"Don't we need papers?"

Of course we need papers. I forgot that. Then I remember Milo. I take out my wallet and find the scrap of paper on which he scribbled his phone number.

"What's that?" she asks.

"The number of a guy I met when I was crossing the wall. He helped me get to the hospital. He said if I need help, he'll help me."

"A guy? Who?"

"His name's Milo."

She looks skeptical. "Do you know anything about him? Where he lives? Where he works? His last name?"

I shake my head. "But I trust him."

She rolls her eyes. "Of course you do." She heaves a big sigh. "Let me get this straight. You want to put our lives in the hands of some guy whose last name you don't even know?"

"Lydia, please. We have to take a chance. We can't just sit here and wait for the police to show up."

She closes her eyes tightly and takes a deep breath. "This is completely crazy, but okay, call him."

When I dial Milo's number, I get his voice mail. "You want to talk to me, you've got to leave a message," it says. That's all.

"This is Sarah," I say after the beep and leave my phone number. I hesitate and then add, "I need a bodyguard."

CHAPTER 15

An hour later I'm waiting in the parking garage when Milo swoops in on his black bike. As before, he's dressed all in black with his red armband tied around one thick biceps. He's also got some heavy chain jewelry hanging from his thick neck. Without doubt he is a scary-looking guy, not someone you would want to meet alone on a dark street at night. And yet here I am meeting him alone in a deserted parking garage.

"What's this all about?" he asks, taking off his shades.

He didn't let me explain anything on the phone. The phone isn't safe he said when he called back. You don't know who's listening. If I'd give him my address, he'd be there in half an hour.

"I have a friend who needs to cross the wall," I tell him. "She's in trouble. Her boyfriend was a policeman who was killed two days ago. It turns out he was infected."

His eyes sweep around the garage. It's empty except for a few cars, trucks, and vans, plus the rack of bikes near the door. "A cop, huh?"

"Yes." Surely he won't refuse because Jeff was a policeman?

"Is she infected?"

"We don't know."

"If she's not infected, she's got nothing to worry about."

"She's also pregnant."

He sighs and shakes his head. "So she's in trouble either way. I get it."

"Will you help her?"

He looks around the garage again. I wonder if he's calculating how much he could get for some of the cars. "Yeah, sure. Why not?"

He chains his bike with the others, and then I let him into the building with my key card. I decide to skip the security desk in the lobby. Even if he weren't wearing a red armband, one look at him and the guards will probably refuse to let him in.

However, my plan to bypass security is dashed when the elevator doors open and a security guard is standing there. He looks at us with a startled expression and his hand moves automatically to his holster. Milo just gives him a cool nod and puts his shades back on. I wonder what's going through the guard's mind. Milo is a head taller and looks like a weight lifter. The guard's eyes keep traveling nervously to the red armband. I expect him to challenge us, but he doesn't. He's still on the elevator when we get off at the fifteenth floor. He and Milo exchange polite nods, like two boxers acknowledging each other's prowess, and then the doors close and he's gone.

"I can't believe he didn't stop you," I say.

Milo shrugs. "Why should he? It's a free country, isn't it?"

I could answer that but don't. I doubt people exiled to the South Zone would agree.

When I open the door of my apartment, Lydia is sitting in a lotus position in the middle of the room meditating. She too looks startled when she sees Milo. I don't know what she was expecting, but clearly it wasn't Milo. Like the security guard, she stares at his red armband.

Milo doesn't seem to notice but stands there looking around my apartment. There isn't much to see. Books, my small portable TV, a print of Van Gogh's *Starry Night* on one wall, the sliding glass doors leading to the balcony. The cat opens her eyes and regards him with mild interest from the back of the sofa, where she's been napping. I wonder what Milo is thinking. There isn't anything worth stealing if that's what's going through his mind. After he has checked out the room, he looks at Lydia, who is now standing, staring at him.

"Are you Sarah's friend who wants to cross the wall?" he asks.

"That's right," she says cautiously. "You must be Milo."

"She says you're in trouble."

"Could be."

"You know what it's like over there?"

"I know it's pretty bad. I also know I don't have a lot of options."

"If you were really smart, you'd get the hell out of this city. Both of you." He looks pointedly at me.

"Yeah, how—on a bicycle?" she says.

"Any damned way you can."

"And go where?"

"Anywhere. This place is going to blow. And when it does, a lot of innocent people are going to get hurt."

"Then why don't you get out?"

"I still have things to do."

She turns to me. "I thought you said he'd help."

"I'll help," Milo says. "I wouldn't be here otherwise."

"Can you take us across today?" I ask. "As long as she's on this side of the wall, she's not safe."

"She may not be safe over there either."

"That's a chance we have to take."

He removes his shades. "What's this 'us'? You don't have to go. I can get her there okay."

"I want to go with her."

"Why?"

"I want to see she gets there safely."

It's not quite the truth. The fact is ever since I found out Martin was not at work, I have worried that something may have happened to him. I want to cross the wall to find out if he's all right.

"This is no game," Milo says. "Every time you cross, you take a chance. Something could go wrong."

"I know that."

He looks as if he's going to argue. Then he shakes his head in resignation. "All right. If that's what you want, I'll take you both across. But I have some things to do first. Here's the plan. If we're going to do this, we have to cross the wall by 5:30. It gets harder once the rush is over. Two females—you might be detained."

"What about papers?" I ask.

"Just use what you have. Keep them folded and just wave them."

Lydia groans. I can tell she doesn't think much of his plan.

I have to agree. I remember how the guard at the checkpoint was harassing young women when I crossed the wall before.

"And she doesn't have a bike," I add.

"Okay, I'll take care of it." He stops. Mary is standing in the doorway from the balcony staring at him. "Hey, there," he says. "Who's this?"

"That's Mary," I tell him. "She's staying with me."

"She's not crossing the wall too, is she?"

"No."

"Good. Taking a kid across could really complicate things." He checks his watch. "Okay, I'll be back in an hour. Be ready."

When he leaves, the room suddenly seems deserted.

"Who was that?" Mary asks.

"A friend."

"What did he want?"

"He's going to help Lydia and me cross the wall."

Her face looks anxious. "Why?"

"She's not safe here."

"What about me?"

"You're going to stay with Mrs. Franklin while I'm gone."

Her eyes dart to the cat, perched on the back of the sofa. "What about Beggar?"

"Beggar can stay here. She'll be okay."

"I don't want you to go."

I cross the room and put my arms around her. She feels so small and vulnerable. "I have to, sweetie. But I'll be back. I promise. Now go get what you need to spend the night at Mrs. Franklin's."

"I don't like this," Lydia says when we are alone. "Are you sure we can trust this guy?"

"Do you have a better idea?" I ask.

"Look, where I come from, guys like him kill each other over a pair of sneakers."

"You're not in LA anymore."

"Yeah, but it's sure as hell not the small town Midwest either."

I reach out and touch her arm. "You can't stay here. You said so yourself."

"Yeah, I did." She brushes a tear from the corner of her eye. "You know he's going to steal a bike, don't you? Oh, hell, let's just hope he doesn't come back with a police squad behind him."

And with that she drops to the floor and resumes her lotus position, hands cupped palms up, eyes closed.

Two hours later we're still waiting for Milo to show up. I've taken Mary down the hall to Mrs. Franklin and fed the cat. Lydia is pacing back and forth like a caged animal in my small living room.

"What's taking so long? It's almost five. He said we have to cross the wall by 5:30."

"He'll be here." I want to reassure her, although I'm far from feeling reassured myself. It's true I don't really know anything about Milo. I'm putting my trust in a complete stranger. If I turn out to be wrong about him, I could be placing both of us in danger.

Finally at 5:30 the phone rings.

"I'm in the garage," Milo says. "Meet me here."

Lydia and I ride down the elevator in silence. I hope this is not a mistake. If we get caught crossing the wall, it will be a lot worse for her than for me. I could be arrested and temporarily tossed in jail, but she could be in a lot worse trouble than that.

When we reach the garage, we find Milo straddling a motorcycle, the engine idling. The rumble is deafening; it fills the cavernous garage.

"What's this?" Lydia asks, staring at the motorcycle. She has to raise her voice to be heard.

"Put this on," Milo says, thrusting a helmet at her.

"I thought you were going to get me a bike."

"Couldn't find one."

"You *stole* a motorcycle? Seriously?"

"Do you want a ride or not?"

"Yeah, yeah." She puts on the helmet and climbs on behind him. "It's not like I've got a choice, is it?"

"I'll go slow," he tells me as I unchain my bike. "Don't worry."

If he doesn't go slow, I won't be able to keep up. As I follow him into the street, I wonder if he did steal the motorcycle. It seems like a bike would be less conspicuous. The motorcycle rumbles and roars. Heads turn as we ride down the street. I just hope we don't run into any police. One look at Milo and they will be on our tail with a blinking blue light.

Several blocks from the wall he pulls into an alley and hands us red armbands to put on.

Lydia looks at hers with obvious distaste. "Guess I better get used to this."

"That's your personal pass to cross the wall," he says. "You can't cross over without it."

I look at the red armband I have just slipped on. It doesn't bother me so much this time. After all, it's just a piece of cloth. If it gets me past the checkpoint, that's all that matters.

"You sure this is going to work?" she asks.

"You got a better plan?"

"I'm working on it."

Milo turns to me. "Stay close when we get to the gate. Once we're on the other side, we better keep together. It could get dicey."

"Don't worry," I say. "I'll be right behind you."

There is still a line of people at the gate when we get there, but it's short. Only one guard is on duty. As before, he waves some people through nonchalantly without checking their papers. Maybe he knows them. Others he stops and examines their papers more closely. Milo and Lydia are in front of me. When it's their turn, the guard looks at Milo's papers, then holds his hand out for Lydia's. She hesitates before handing them over. He looks at them and then at her. "These are your papers?"

"What's wrong?" Milo asks.

"Stay out of this." The guard lays his hand on Lydia's arm. "Please get off the motorcycle. You have to come with me, Miss."

"Why?" Lydia looks scared.

"She's not going anywhere," says Milo.

"If necessary, I'll use force," says the guard.

"So will I." Suddenly Milo has a gun in his hand. He shoots the guard in the leg. A woman in line behind me screams. Then Milo and Lydia roar off on his motorcycle, speeding through the gate before anyone can stop them.

I stand there with my bike and stare after them. It all happened so fast. The guard lies on the pavement clutching his leg and shouting for help. A policeman jumps out of a squad car parked close by and sprints toward him.

Then a man from behind me in line passes me on his bike, riding toward the gate. Others follow. Suddenly everyone is rushing toward the gate. I join in, hoping the policeman won't start shooting at us. After I'm through the gate, I keep going. Not until I'm at least a block away do I stop to look around for Milo and Lydia. Other bicyclists streak past me, quickly disappearing. Around me are the scorched and graffiti-covered buildings of the South Zone, but no sign of Milo and Lydia. With my heart still pounding, I realize I'll have to find my way to the hospital by myself. I just hope I remember how to get there and won't run into trouble on the way.

CHAPTER 16

Only a few blocks into the South Zone I come to a street blocked on one side by an overturned car and on the other by a burning trash can. To continue, I'll have to pass between them. I slow as I approach and have almost reached the narrow gap between them when I notice several teenaged boys lurking on the sidewalk in front of a graffiti-covered wall. I don't like the look of them. They are dirty, rough-looking, and armed with knives and pipes. I try to turn back, but it's already too late to retreat. Three more boys are close behind me. It's a trap, and I've ridden straight into it. Frantically I look around for a way to escape. On my left is an old church with its stained glass windows partially boarded up. I have no way of knowing what might be inside. It could be deserted or hiding even worse dangers, but there is no place else to go and I have to act quick.

I turn my bike toward it. The boys, seeing what I'm doing, shout and run after me. When I get to the church, I jump off my bike and race up the steps. I try to pull open the doors but they're locked. In desperation, I pound on them with my fists.

Behind me I can hear my pursuers. They are closing in slower now that they have me cornered. "Chickie, chickie, chickie," they call and make crowing sounds.

Just when I think there's no escape, one of the double doors swings open. A man with a worn face, a priest, stands in the shadowy doorway.

"Please help me!" I plead.

He looks past me at the gang of boys, who are now on the steps.

"Inside, quick," he says.

Gratefully I dart through the narrow opening. Once I'm in, he stands boldly barring the way to the boys.

"What are you doing?" he demands. "This is the House of the Lord. You can't come in here unless you're going to behave yourselves. Angel, Mike, TJ, Ramirez—you ought to be ashamed of yourselves."

"You better be careful, old man," says a boy with curly black hair and a red sweatband. "We can come inside anytime we want."

"What would your mother think if she could see you now, Angel? She was a good woman, and she raised you to know right from wrong."

"What did being good ever get anyone?" The boy spits on the steps. "What did it get my mother?"

I can see them beyond the priest. They are younger than I thought, maybe only fourteen or fifteen years old, a dirty ragged band of children. But they still look dangerous.

"Blessed are the meek, for they shall inherit the earth," the priest says.

"Come on," one boy says to another. "Let's get out of here before he gets started."

"One of these days you'll get yours, old man," the other says.

They turn away sullenly and drift back down the steps.

The priest closes the door and turns to me. "You're safe now. They didn't hurt you, did they?"

"No, I'm okay," I tell him. "Thank you for letting me in."

"They get a little wilder every day. So far they still don't come charging in here. They've got a little respect left for the church. But who knows how much longer that will last."

He opens the door again and looks out to see if the boys have left. "Is that your bike?"

I move up beside him and see the boys picking up my bike. They argue about who will get it, and the boy with the red sweatband apparently wins.

"Yes, it's my bike."

"I'm afraid I can't help you there." The priest closes the door and bolts it. "Do you have far to go?"

"To the hospital on Seventh Avenue."

"That's a ways. You'd better wait here until morning. It's almost dark now. It won't be safe out there."

I know Lydia and Milo will worry when I don't show up, but the priest is right. I should wait for morning.

"I'm Father Chavez." He holds out his hand, which I shake.

"Sarah Davis."

He's a tall thin man with hollow cheeks and shaggy hair. His black robe looks dusty and his white collar is soiled. I guess him to be in his forties, but he could be older or younger.

"Do you live here?" I ask.

"Yes, I live here. That way anyone who needs me can find me."

"How long have you been here?"

"Since I first came to the South Zone three years ago." He sits down in one of the pews and I sit down beside him. His face is pale and he's sweating. He takes out a handkerchief and mops his face.

"Are you all right?" I ask. He doesn't look well.

"I'll be okay in a minute. It will pass."

"Is it the virus?"

"In full bloom. I bear the marks. The stigmata."

"What do you mean?"

"You don't know?" He pulls open his robe and bares his chest, revealing ugly purple sores. I quickly look away.

"Surely you've seen them before?"

I shake my head. "No, I haven't."

"One day you will have them too. We will all be punished."

"Punished for what?"

"Punished for being the sinners that we are." He puts his hand on mine. He has a large hand with long tapering fingers and dirt under the nails. "You should pray. The Day of Judgment is near."

While I'm relieved to have found a sanctuary, I'm not happy at the prospect of spending all night in the company of Father Chavez, who appears to be a little crazy. It is, however, preferable to going back outside where the gang of teenage boys is prowling about. Father Chavez gives me an old blanket, which I fold up and use for a pillow in the front pew. At least it's better than nothing. Then he disappears through a side door and I'm all alone in the shadowy nave. I can hear an occasional motorcycle race by outside, shouts, screams, and sporadic gunfire. Around me is the profound silence of the church. The wooden pew I lay on is hard, and for a long time I can't sleep. I wonder where Martin is and if he's safe. I tell myself that tomorrow I'll find the hospital and Martin will be there and he'll explain why he hasn't been to work. There will be some perfectly reasonable explanation and my worry will look silly.

I don't think I can sleep, but eventually I do. Around midnight I'm awoken by someone pounding on the church doors. Father Chavez stumbles out of the side room with a flashlight and hurries down the aisle mumbling to himself.

"Yes, yes, I'm coming," he shouts. "What is it?"

He unbolts the doors and opens one. I hear a boy's voice, excited: "Father, the Rats are coming. They burned down the gas station on Buckeye and now they're on their way here."

Father Chavez comes hurrying back down the aisle toward me with his flashlight bobbing. At his side trots a boy of about nine.

"Wake up," Father Chavez says. "You have to leave."

"What's happened?"

"Isadore says the Rats are on their way here. They're a motorcycle gang—one of the worst. You've got to leave right away. I can't protect you."

"But isn't it safer here than outside?" I ask, reluctant to leave the safety of the church.

"They'll be high on drugs and alcohol. Even when they're sober, they're bad news."

"I could hide."

"It's too risky. They might find you. I'm sure they know you're here. That's why they're coming."

"What about you?"

"I have to stay here. This is my church. It's all I have left." Again there is loud banging on the doors. "Go quickly—before it's too late. Isadore will show you the way."

The boy runs toward the side door and I hurry after him. When I look back, Father Chavez is walking back up the aisle to unbolt the doors. Isadore grabs my hand and tugs me into a dark room. This one leads to another. I bump into bulky pieces of furniture several times. Then he opens a door that leads outside and we emerge into the night air. His mission accomplished, he drops my hand and starts running. I try to follow him, but he turns a corner and disappears as completely as if he'd gone down a rabbit hole. Crouching in the shadow of an apartment building, I look back at the church. I can hear gunfire and wild cheers. I tell myself if I wait, maybe I can sneak back into the church when the gang is gone.

Ten minutes pass. The stained glass windows of the church begin to flicker and glow. I realize with horror that the church is on fire. The gang is racing up and down the street on their motorcycles, firing guns. No one else comes out to see what's happening. All the buildings around me are so dark and silent they might be deserted.

When the gang finally rides away, I creep around to the front of the church. Father Chavez lies on the steps in a crumpled heap, his robe wet with blood. I try to feel for a pulse in his thin wrist, but my hands are shaking too badly to find it even if there is one. It occurs to me that he might still be alive if I hadn't sought shelter in his church. The Rats came, he said, because they knew I was there. Not finding me, they killed him instead. I feel overwhelmed by guilt. It's like the awful night I came home to find our house in flames and my family dead. My worst nightmare sprung to life again. Only this time there are no firefighters, no police, and no kind neighbors to comfort me.

I push that old memory away. I must concentrate on the present. I must try to get help. Maybe Father Chavez is still alive. I run to the nearest apartment building and bang desperately on the first door I come to. There's no sign of life.

"Help," I shout. "Someone's been shot." People must be hiding behind those doors. They surely could not have slept through all the rumble of motorcycles, whooping, and gunfire. I shout again. "Please help! Father Chavez has been shot."

I try two more doors with the same results, and then, sobbing in frustration, I run back to where Father Chavez lies on the steps of the church. I pull his limp and lifeless body farther down the steps, away from the burning church. "I'm so sorry," I tell him, just in case he can hear, but I don't think he can.

Then I hear the roar of motorcycles again. The Rats are coming back. After saying a quick prayer for Father Chavez, I hurry away in the direction I suppose the hospital to be, trying to stay in the shadows of the buildings. A whooping band of young people on bikes sweeps by, passing close enough for me to see their painted faces. Fortunately they don't see me.

Before long I realize making my way to the hospital in the dark is a futile endeavor. It's too far and I'm not sure which direction to go. If I run into any of the roving gangs, I could end up like Father Chavez.

I slowly move farther away from the church, darting across streets when I think no one will see me. There are no streetlights, but the full moon illumines the pavement enough for me to see and also be seen if I'm not careful. I've gone several blocks when I accidentally kick a beer can. It clatters as it rolls off the curb and into the gutter. In the nearest building a dog starts barking. A door opens. I duck behind a trash can and hope the dog won't be loosed on me.

"Who's there?" a man demands. "Come out or I'll shoot."

I wonder if he knows where I am. Then he fires and I hear the bullet strike the ground only a few feet away. That answers my question. Hoping he won't shoot, I stand up with my hands raised.

Down the street a motorcycle gang roars around the corner, their headlights aimed at me.

"Quick—inside," the man calls, lowering his rifle.

I have no desire to have another encounter with one of the local gangs, so I sprint toward the door he's holding open.

"Keep Pete quiet," he orders someone in the dark room.

I guess Pete is the dog because I can hear movement in the background and the dog doesn't bark. Outside the motorcycles roar past and then fade down the street. When they are gone, my captor—or rescuer—lights a candle. By its light I see half a dozen adults and at least five children in the room. One of the children—a boy of about twelve—is holding tight to a black Labrador retriever. As soon as he lets go, the dog rushes over to sniff me, wagging its tail.

"Who are you?" the man demands. Now that there is some light I can see him, an angular, unshaven man with piercing eyes, perhaps in his thirties.

"My name is Sarah Davis," I tell him.

"What are you doing out at this time of night?"

"I'm lost. I was at a church several blocks from here, but a gang showed up. They set it on fire and shot the priest."

"Father Chavez?" asks a woman in the background.

"Yes. I think he may be dead."

"You're not sure?"

"I tried to feel his pulse. . . . I don't know."

"It's all right," the woman says. I think she feels sorry for me. Maybe she can see I'm on the verge of tears.

"Sounds like the Rats," a man says.

"Yes, that's what he called them."

"You're not one of them, are you?" asks another man suspiciously. "This isn't some kind of trick, is it?"

"Of course, it isn't," says one of the women. "Look at her. Does she look like a Rat to you?"

I hope I don't, but how much can they see by the light of a single candle?

"Shouldn't we send someone to see if Father Chavez is still alive?" asks another woman.

"It's too dangerous," says the man who brought me in. "It'll have to wait for morning. Besides, by now someone who lives in that block will have checked on him."

"Where do you live?" asks one of the women in a kind voice. She's young with stringy blond hair and pale skin.

I hesitate, wondering if they will turn me out if they know I'm not infected. It's a risk I decide to take. "The Glenview Tower."

"That's in the North Zone," a woman says.

"Yes, I crossed over late yesterday with some friends," I

explain. "We were on our way to the hospital on Seventh Avenue when we got separated. Maybe you can tell me how to get there." I look from one face to another.

For a minute no one says anything.

"You don't have the virus?" asks the woman with stringy blond hair.

I hesitate again, conscious of the red band on my arm. I'm an impostor who has no right to wear that badge. "No," I admit. "I don't have it."

There's another minute of silence. Will they refuse to help me?

"You better stay here until morning," says the man who brought me in. "It's not safe out there, especially if you're not one of them."

They are going to let me stay. I feel a wave of gratitude. They give me a narrow cot to sleep on and the candle is blown out. It's hot in the room, and I doubt I'll be able to sleep, especially after all that has happened and surrounded as I am by strangers in a strange place, but the events of the evening have exhausted me, and before I know it, I fall asleep.

CHAPTER 17

In the morning I'm able to see my surroundings better. The room is larger than I thought with lots of cots scattered about. There are about nine children. As nearly as I can make out, some of them are with their biological parents, but others have been rescued from the streets. Now that there is light coming in the windows, I can see the young woman with the stringy blond hair is pregnant. I also notice a young man on a cot against the wall appears to be dying. Life and death are going on side by side in this room.

They invite me to share some breakfast with them before I set out for the hospital. I hesitate, wondering if they can spare the food when there are so many mouths to feed of their own, but they assure me there is enough, and having eaten nothing since the previous afternoon, I'm hungry, so I accept.

We eat breakfast at a long table made of boards laid across sawhorses. On either side of me sit two little girls who have vied for this privilege. The one on my right is a little redhead with freckles who is given to fits of giggles.

"Are you going to stay with us?" she asks.

"No, I have to find my friends," I tell her.

"Do you really live in the North Zone?" asks the little black girl on my left, who is shyer than the redhead but equally inquisitive.

"Yes."

"Then how come you're here?" asks the redhead.

"I'm helping a friend."

"Where's your friend?" asks my other interrogator. They are taking turns now.

"Waiting for me at the place I'm going to, I hope."

"Where are you going to?" asks the redhead.

"The hospital on Seventh Avenue."

"Is that very far from here?" asks the little black girl, shyly proud of herself for coming up with the question.

"I don't think so."

Throughout breakfast they keep up a steady barrage of questions. I don't think they are really interested in my answers. It's more like a game of ping pong with the object being to keep the ball bouncing.

Breakfast consists of dry cereal and canned grapefruit juice. For the youngest children there is canned milk. Nothing is cold because there's no electricity. In the corner of the room is a hot plate used for cooking when the power was still on and a refrigerator which now serves as a cupboard. All of the windows are open and the air inside is still bearable, but I know that later in the day it will be sweltering hot in this room.

After breakfast a tall long-haired man called Sam by the adults and Dad by several of the children in the group, although they don't look enough alike to be related by blood, volunteers to guide me to the hospital. The man who brought me in the night before has gone out even earlier to inquire about Father Chavez.

Getting to the hospital on foot takes longer than when I covered the distance by bike. On the way we see juvenile gangs but no older gangs like the Rats. Maybe they sleep by day and only come out at night. We see smoking buildings, including the burned-out ruins of a mini-mall. People are warily emerging from hiding to assess the damage done during the night. My companion appears to be well known in the area. People call out to him as we pass.

"It seems very different in the daytime," I tell him.

"Don't judge us by the Rats. There are a lot of decent people on this side of the wall. They wouldn't be here if they had a choice, but they've got no choice."

"I'm very grateful to you and your friends for taking me in."

Sam shrugs. "Don't mention it. We haven't got much, but we've got each other. That's more than some people can say."

"Is there anything I can do for you?"

He shakes his head. "We can take care of ourselves."

"Maybe I could get some supplies for you," I suggest. "Food, batteries, things like that."

"It's kind of you to offer, but, no, it's too dangerous. Look what happened to Father Chavez last night. The same thing could have happened to you. You're lucky you got out of there when you did."

I don't say anything for a minute. I'm thinking about Father Chavez. If only he hadn't opened the door . . . maybe they would have gone away.

"You shouldn't be crossing the wall if you don't have to," Sam tells me. "It isn't safe. Get back on the other side where you belong and stay there. Things are going to get worse."

"What about your people?" I ask. "Are they safe?"

"As safe as anybody else. We just take things day by day."

When we finally get to the hospital, it looks boarded up and abandoned, just as on my previous visit.

Sam sticks out a big hand for me to shake. "Remember what I said. Don't take foolish chances."

I shake his hand and then cross the street. When I look back, he waves and I wave back. He stands there until I turn the corner of the building and disappear from his sight. It's the sort of thing my father did when I was growing up. I have one of those moments when a memory flashes back so vivid it's like a physical blow. I remember my father dropping me off at a friend's house for a birthday party. When I looked back from the door as it opened, he was still sitting there in his car. Resolutely I push this image aside. No use dwelling on the past.

The young guard on duty remembers me. He nods and opens the door without asking to see my papers. "Are you all right, Miss?"

"I just had something in my eye for a minute. I'm fine now."

"Do you know your way?"

I tell him I do and set off down the corridor to find Sandy's office.

Her door is open and she's sitting at her desk with lots of papers spread out before her. She looks up in surprise.

"Sarah! Thank god you're safe."

"Are Milo and Lydia here?" I ask.

"Milo is out looking for you. He's been out since dawn. Lydia is here."

"And Martin?"

She shakes her head. "We haven't heard from him for two days."

It's what I feared she would say. "I talked to him on the phone two nights ago. He was about to cross the wall."

"We haven't seen him. He never showed up." She reaches across the desk and puts her hand on mine. "Sorry I don't have better news."

He's only missing, I tell myself. That doesn't mean he's dead.

"I heard what happened at the checkpoint. Lydia didn't know if you got through. She thought maybe you went back."

"No, I came through right after them. There was a lot of confusion and everyone just started riding through so I did too."

"Good for you." She looks at me, waiting for me to tell the rest of it. So I tell her how I got lost and how Father Chavez rescued me from a street gang and let me shelter at his church, how the Rats shot him and set fire to his church, and how I was taken in by a group of people who live nearby. When I finish, I ask if someone could be sent to see if Father Chavez is alive.

"He was brought in about an hour ago. He was already dead. He was probably dead when you saw him last night."

Poor Father Chavez. I still can't help feeling it was my fault.

"There was nothing you could do," she says.

I nod, but it doesn't make me feel any better. I remember how I held his wrist and tried to find a pulse. I try to blink back the tears.

"Lydia will want to know you're okay. I think she's in the kitchen."

I find Lydia making sandwiches for lunch. In fact, she appears to be in charge, giving advice to a girl a few years younger than herself. When she sees me, she stops what she's doing and hugs me.

"Sarah! Thank god you're all right. I've been imagining you lying dead in some alley. I would never have forgiven myself if anything had happened to you. Where have you been?"

"It's a long story."

"Well, tell me."

I quickly run through the events of the previous night again.

"Milo shouldn't have just left you there like that," she says. "I tried to make him go back, but he wouldn't until he got me here."

"He was looking out for you. And anyway everything turned out all right."

"Almost all right, you mean." She turns away.

"What do you mean? What's wrong?"

She draws me apart from the others who are helping in the kitchen. "Sandy did the test last night. I have the virus."

"Oh, no." I wrap my arms around her. It isn't fair. She's only eighteen. She should have her whole life ahead of her. "And your baby?"

"The baby may be okay. They can give me something which should keep me from infecting it—at least they'll give it to me as long as they can get hold of it." She blinks back her tears. "Hey, it's not like I'm sick yet. Sandy says it could be a long time before I start feeling sick."

I hoped by some miracle Lydia wouldn't have the virus. She doesn't deserve this. But then no one does.

"Hey, none of that. You start crying, and then I will too, and then we'll end up with soggy sandwiches. What about Martin? Any word?"

"No, nothing."

"Well, he'll turn up. Don't you worry."

She wants to make me feel better, but after last night, it seems all too possible that something bad could have happened to him. I picture him crumpled on the ground and bleeding like Father Chavez.

"He'll be okay," she says.

I nod and look at a calendar on the wall with a picture of a waterfall. It's a narrow stream of water falling from a high cliff to a pool below and reminds me of the picture of Havasu Falls, only this place looks tropical. I'm afraid if I stand here another minute I may burst into tears.

"Look, I think I'll go see his brother while I'm here," I tell her.

"Sarah?" she says as I start toward the door.

"What?"

"What Martin was doing—smuggling those drugs across the wall—that was a good thing. Maybe he's not such a bad guy after all. I just wanted you to know that."

"Thanks." We smile at each other.

As I leave the kitchen, I see Sandy and Dr. Liu in the hall standing close together, talking in low voices. I remember what Martin said about Sandy being secretly in love with him.

I don't want to interrupt, but as I'm about to pass them she lays her hand on my arm and stops me. "What do you know about Milo?"

"Not much. Not anything really. Why?"

"He told us we ought to have an evacuation plan. But do you know how hard it would be to evacuate the hospital? Many of our patients are too sick to move. And even if they could be moved, where would we take them?"

"What does Milo think is going to happen?"

"He says the violence will get a lot worse soon."

"The man who brought me here today said that too."

"They may be right," Dr. Liu says. "Maybe we should start thinking about how we could move patients if we have to."

"But where?" Sandy says, frowning. "Where could we possibly go? And how could we move everybody?"

"Maybe we couldn't move everybody," he says quietly.

"You mean, leave some of them behind? No, absolutely not." Her ponytail swings as she shakes her head. "What if they're wrong? What if it's just another rumor? Who is this Milo anyway? Why should we listen to him? He could be wrong. I'm not going to just walk away and leave some of our patients to die. We're not animals." She turns and strides down the hall away from us. We watch as she disappears into her office and slams the door behind her.

"She's been under a lot of strain," Dr. Liu says. "We all have. Too many people to take care of, too few drugs, too little sleep."

"Do you think Milo's right?" I ask. "Is the hospital in danger?"

"He might be right. Things do seem to be getting worse out there. We have no way of knowing if the power will come back on. If it doesn't, what do we do?"

I don't have an answer to that. It seems like the world around us is crumbling. I wonder if I'll ever see Martin again.

Then I remember he lives with Dr. Liu. I could leave a message. "If you see Martin—" I begin.

Dr. Liu pats my arm. "If I see Martin, I'll tell him you were here looking for him."

"Thank you." I like Dr. Liu. I don't have to explain to him. He seems to understand exactly what I want to say.

I climb the stairs to the large room crowded with forty odd beds where men and women lie slowly dying and make my way through the maze to where David lies near an open window. His eyes are closed when I reach him, his face shiny with sweat. He looks so painfully thin. I wonder how much longer he has. Not wanting to wake him, I start to turn away, but then he opens his eyes.

"Oh, it's Martin's girlfriend." He smiles. "Is my wastrel brother here too?" He pushes himself up on his elbows and looks around the room.

"No," I say.

"Do you know where he is?" He slumps back on his pillow again, looking as if he's in pain.

I hesitate, unsure what he has been told. "I think he's in the North Zone."

David grimaces. "Working."

"Yes, working." I can't very well tell him Martin is missing, but my conscience pricks me for lying to him and I have to look away when I say it.

"Why hasn't he come to see me?"

"I don't know."

"Listen, I know something is wrong." He turns his grey eyes toward me. "Has something happened to him? If it has, I want to know."

It must be awful to lie there and wonder what's happening to someone you care about. I decide to be truthful. "I don't know."

"At least you're honest."

"I'd tell you if I knew."

"I believe you would. Well, if you don't know where Martin is, he's probably got himself into some trouble. That would be just like Martin."

I smile. "Does it happen often?"

"Are you kidding? Martin attracts trouble. Didn't he tell you that?"

"No, I think he forgot to mention that."

"Did he tell you anything about me?"

"A little. I know he's very fond of you."

"We used to fight. Did he tell you that?"

"Yes, he did."

David smiles again. "I usually won. That was because I was bigger than he was. But Martin was a scrapper. It didn't matter how many times I beat him, he always figured he could take me."

I lay my hand over his where it's lying on the sheet. I feel so sorry for him. This terrible epidemic that has robbed us of our pasts, our loved ones, our lives.

"I didn't think I'd end up like this."

"Is there anything I can do?"

"Yeah, you can put another pillow behind me. I'm tired of lying here like I'm a corpse already. There's an extra pillow over there. He nods at a nearby stand on which a plump pillow sits.

I hesitate. Maybe he isn't supposed to be propped higher. What if I make him worse by doing it?

"It's not going to kill me," he says flatly.

I imagine he's right so I get the pillow and help wedge it behind him. "Is that better?"

"Yeah, that's better. What about you? Didn't you say you had two sisters?"

"That's right."

"Did you fight with them?"

"I guess sometimes I did."

"Tell me about them."

"What do you want to know?"

"Anything. It gets awfully boring just lying here waiting to die. Look, you don't have to talk about your sisters if you don't want. I've got no business prying into your life. I guess I'm just nosy because you're Martin's girlfriend. Watching out for my younger brother sort of. I'm not going to be around forever to do it, you know."

"We used to make up stories and act them out," I tell him.

"What kind of stories?"

"Like Narnia."

He nods and smiles. "With us it was Lord of the Rings. Sword fighting mostly. Were you the oldest?"

"Yes. Laura was two years younger than me, and Emily was five years younger."

"Did they die of the virus?"

I have to swallow the lump in my throat. "No, they died in a fire."

"And your parents?"

I take a deep breath. "They all died in a fire."

"I'm sorry. That must have been awful."

I don't say anything. I don't want to talk about it. I look around the room. I'm surrounded by people who are slowly dying. Was my suffering any more terrible than theirs?

"You told Martin about your family?"

"Yes."

"Did he tell you about our parents?"

"Yes."

"It's a hell of a world, isn't it?"

I squeeze his hand. "Yes, it is."

"You know, you're lucky not to have it. You don't have it, right?"

"No, I don't." I feel the guilt of the healthy surrounded by the sick. Why should I escape the virus and not them?

"Well, if my little brother turns up, tell him I want to talk to him. Would you do that?"

"Of course."

"He'd better have a damn good excuse for staying away. If you see him, you can tell him I said that."

"All right, I will."

"Will you come see me again, Sarah?"

"I'll try to."

"Let me know if you find out something. Even if it's bad. He's my brother. I want to know."

"I promise I'll let you know if I hear anything."

He nods, satisfied. "Maybe you could get rid of this extra pillow before you leave. I think I'll take a nap. Nothing else to do."

It's noon when Milo shows up. Lydia and I are sitting in the cafeteria talking when he comes striding in with a fair-skinned African-American boy of about six years old holding tightly to his hand.

"About time you got here," he says, as if I'm the one who just arrived.

"Who's your friend?" Lydia asks.

"This is Henry. I found him a couple of miles from here. He needs a place to stay. Don't you, Henry?"

Henry looks at us with big dark eyes and doesn't say a word.

Lydia smiles at him. "Are you hungry, Henry?"

The boy nods.

"Then come on. Let's find you something to eat." She holds out her hand.

He looks up at Milo to see if it's all right.

"Go on. I'll be here when you come back. I'm not going anywhere."

Lydia leads the boy away, and Milo takes a seat across from me at the table.

"An orphan?" I ask.

"Aren't they all? I found him wandering around outside a burned-out mini-mall. He said his aunt went out to find food several days ago and never came back. What about you? What took you so long to get here?"

"I ran into some trouble."

"What kind of trouble?"

"Some kids chased me."

He shakes his head. "Sorry we ditched you like that. We didn't have a whole lot of choice after that guard tried to stop us from crossing."

"It's okay. Although I wasn't expecting you to shoot someone."

"It was just a flesh wound. I figured you'd be right behind us. Lydia wanted me to stop and go back, but I thought I'd better get her here in one piece first."

"I'm glad you did."

"I went back but I couldn't find you."

"I got lost."

"I thought I might just find your body out there."

"You might have if it hadn't been for Father Chavez."

He goes very still. "What about Father Chavez?"

"He saved me from those kids who chased me. Did you know him?"

"Yeah, I knew him. Stubborn old coot. Refused to leave that church."

"They killed him."

"Yeah, I know."

"I feel like it was my fault."

"It wasn't your fault."

"If I hadn't gone there, he'd still be alive."

"It would have happened even if you hadn't showed up. It was bound to happen sooner or later."

Before I can argue this point, Lydia returns with a couple of tuna sandwiches on a paper plate and sets it in front of

Milo. "I thought you might be hungry too. Henry's eating like he hasn't been fed for a week. I'm surprised someone so small can eat so much."

"I'm going to have to leave him here," Milo says. "Think you can watch out for him?"

"Yeah, I suppose I could do that."

"You going to be okay here?"

She nods and looks away. "I've got it, you know. The virus. I tested positive."

"Welcome to the club."

"Yeah, well, it's one club I'd have preferred not to join."

"Sit down here a minute."

"I've got to get back to the kitchen," she says but then sits down tentatively beside him.

"You aren't dying," he says. "You've got the virus, but you aren't dying. Do you understand that?"

"Yeah, tell that to the people upstairs."

"They're sick, but you—you aren't sick. You got a baby to think about. You concentrate on taking care of yourself. That baby needs you."

Lydia's eyes well with tears and she bites her lip. I reach across and hold her hand. "He's right. You've got to think about the baby."

"I'll be okay. Just give me some time to get used to it. And now I'd better get back to the kitchen to check on Henry before he eats everything that's back there."

"Thanks," I say to Milo after she leaves.

"What for?"

"For what you said to her."

He picks up a sandwich. "This boyfriend of hers—the cop. I suppose she was in love with him?"

"They were planning to get married. Why?"

"I just wondered, that's all." He chomps into the sandwich. "What about this guy Martin?"

"What do you mean?"

"That's why you're here, isn't it?"

I start to deny it, then stop. It is why I'm here. "I only met him a week ago."

"And now he's got you crossing the wall."

"He's missing. No one knows where he is."

"You know anything about him?"

It's funny. That's what people keep asking me about Milo. "I know he cares about what's happening here, and he's trying to do something about it."

"Smuggling drugs, you mean."

That seems unfair to me. "What do I know about you? What do I know about anyone?"

"You could have got yourself killed last night," he says. "I shouldn't have let you come."

"If you hadn't helped me cross the wall, I'd have crossed it on my own."

We glare at each other for a minute.

"You care about him that much? You're willing to risk your life? Are you so sure he's worth it?"

"I wanted to know if he was safe."

"But you still don't know."

He's right. I still don't know.

He takes a large bite of his sandwich, chews it thoughtfully, and swallows. "So what are you going to do? You staying here or going back?"

"I have to go back."

He takes another bite. "You want a bodyguard?"

"Yes, I could use a bodyguard. And a lift would help too. I lost my bike."

"It figures." He stuffs the last bite of sandwich into his mouth.

CHAPTER 18

I know the police might be on the lookout for Milo at the checkpoint after the shooting the day before, but we make it through without any problem. After crossing the wall, we see a convoy of army trucks headed toward the freeway and some cars and pickups loaded with belongings going north. Evidently Milo isn't the only one who thinks things are about to get worse.

When I climb off the back of his motorcycle in front of the Glenview Tower, I try to thank him for all he's done.

"Listen," he says, "there's a plane leaving tomorrow for Vancouver. I might be able to get you on it. Things aren't as bad there."

"Why don't you go?" I ask.

"I can't leave yet. I have unfinished business."

"I can't leave either," I tell him.

He scowls. "Why not? Because of this guy Martin? If he cares about you, he'd want you to get out while you still can."

"It's not just Martin."

"What then? You don't have family here, do you?"

"No." I glance at a bicyclist riding by.

"Lydia said you lost your job."

"Yeah, I did."

"So why can't you leave?"

I sigh. "There are people who depend on me. I can't just leave them."

"What people? That kid I saw at your place?"

"Yes, Mary, and there's an old lady who lives down the hall who needs me to get groceries for her."

"Sometimes you have to think about yourself. Anyone ever tell you that? You can't save the whole goddamn world."

"I'm not trying to save the whole world," I tell him, "just two people I happen to care about."

He shakes his head as if I'm hopeless.

"What about you?" I ask. "What's keeping you here?"

"I told you. Unfinished business."

Now it's my turn to guess. "Family?"

He shakes his head again.

"Girlfriend?"

He grins. "Lots of those."

"Job?"

He shrugs. "Yeah, that too."

I see my chance to find out more about him. "What kind of job?"

"What's it matter?"

"I don't even know what you do."

"Why do you have to know what I do?"

"I'm curious."

"All right, I'll tell you," he says. "I'm a trouble-shooter. When there's trouble, there I am. Satisfied? Now I have to go. If you need me, you know how to get hold of me."

I watch him roar off down the street on his motorcycle. He gives the impression of being a tough guy, but I know he has a softer side. I saw him with Henry. Lydia too. And in spite of his pose of being a loner, he is just as tied to other people as I am. If he were really the tough guy he pretends to be, he wouldn't have helped Lydia or me. He would have been looking out for number one.

When he's out of sight, I turn to the heavy plate glass doors of the lobby and wait for a security guard to let me in. The Glenview Tower is turning into Fort Knox. The guard who comes to the door is new—a clean-cut kid I haven't seen before. He's so young I wonder if he's still in high school.

"Papers?" he asks.

I hand him my papers. He seems embarrassed as he gives them back to me.

"Sorry. We're supposed to check everyone. We've been told to increase security."

"Why?"

"Just taking precautions. You know, better safe than sorry."

I roll my eyes.

So, like Milo, the Glenview Tower is also expecting something to happen, something bad. The question is how bad is it going to be?

I ride the elevator up to the fifteenth floor and let myself into Mrs. Franklin's apartment. Mary and Mrs. Franklin are playing checkers when I walk in. The TV is on in the background, but they aren't paying any attention to it. They don't notice me either for a few moments.

"Beggar likes to wake me up in the mornings," Mary tells

Mrs. Franklin. "She comes around to my side of the bed and meows good-morning and then jumps up on the bed with me and I pet her. And when I'm eating breakfast, she jumps on the table to see what I'm having, although she's not supposed to."

It's more words than I have heard her say all at one time before. I can see she and Mrs. Franklin have gotten to know each other better in my absence.

Then Mary catches sight of me standing in the doorway and runs over to hug me. "Sarah, you're back! I was scared you wouldn't come back."

"I told you I would, didn't I?" I bend down and kiss the top of her head. She smells of shampoo and peppermint.

"Why don't you get Sarah some lemonade?" Mrs. Franklin says. "I'll bet she's thirsty. In fact, why don't you get lemonade for everybody?"

Mary releases me. "I made it myself. I read the directions on the package."

"Well, I'd love to have some," I tell her.

"She's such a sweet child," Mrs. Franklin says after Mary has gone to the kitchen. "And smart too. She nearly always beats me at checkers."

"Did she tell you anything about her family?" I ask.

"No, should she have?"

"No, I just thought. . . . She hasn't said a word about her family. I thought she might have said something to you. I can't help wondering. . . ."

"When she's ready to talk about them, she will," says Mrs. Franklin. "Did Lydia get to her destination safely?"

"Yes, she did."

"Good. I hope she'll be safe."

Mary returns from the kitchen carrying three glasses of lemonade on a small tray. "Have you heard about the fires?" she asks.

"What fires?" I reach for one of the glasses. The cold lemonade tastes wonderful as it slides down my dry throat.

"They said on TV there are fires everywhere."

"Maybe not everywhere," Mrs. Franklin amends, "but throughout the Southwest."

"It's because of the drought," Mary explains. "There hasn't been much rain. They think some of the fires were started on purpose."

"There aren't enough firefighters to keep them from spreading," Mrs. Franklin adds. "The situation is so bad that the President has signed an emergency law making it possible to imprison anyone suspected of setting a fire."

"Suspected?" I raise an eyebrow. "What happened to being innocent until proven guilty?"

"What indeed."

For the rest of the day I keep thinking about the fires burning in the Southwest. One more bad sign. Milo thinks I should leave, but I can't. Without me to buy groceries for her, what would Mrs. Franklin do for food? And what about Mary? If I hadn't taken her away from the school, she might be on her way to a reservation by now, and in fact if the city is about to turn violent, that might be a safer place for her than here with me.

By bedtime I've decided to find out if I can still get her on that bus going to a reservation. Of course, after what happened with Strickland, he won't be inclined to do me any favors. But I could offer to return Mary to the State School, and then maybe he'll carry out his threat to put her on a bus leaving the city. I can let him think he's getting revenge against me and will just have to hope he doesn't guess that I want her on the bus because then he might keep her off just to spite me.

The next morning I'm up early and, after leaving Mary with Mrs. Franklin, I head for a bike rental shop six blocks away. Having lost my bike in the South Zone, I need another, and renting one for a few days seems the simplest solution. Later when I have more time, I can search for a bike to buy.

I arrive just as the shop is opening, but several other people have gotten there first so I have to wait.

The big burly man with a beard ahead of me is angry when he hears what the shop is charging to rent bikes.

"You've got to be kidding. That's highway robbery. For that I could buy a new one."

The tall thin balding clerk behind the counter shrugs. "Then do it."

The customer swears under his breath but pulls out his wallet and slaps five $100 bills on the counter. "I haven't got the time."

The clerk unlocks a bike and the man wheels it out of the store, still grumbling.

"Why does it cost so much?" I ask when it's my turn. Five hundred dollars is a lot more than I expected to pay. The man before me was right. For that I could buy a new bike. However, I don't want to spend the whole morning hunting for one or to have to walk miles looking for a bike shop. If I'm going to persuade Strickland to put Mary on the bus, I need to act fast.

"We have no way of knowing if it will come back," the clerk says wearily. "Do you want one or not?"

Reluctantly I pull my debit card out of my billfold.

"Cash only."

"I haven't got that much on me," I protest.

"Then I can't rent you a bike. Next!"

I leave the rental shop feeling frustrated. I'll have to find an ATM to get cash. There's one a few blocks up the street, and so I start walking in that direction. Every time a bicyclist passes, I curse my bad luck for having lost my bike. I hope the boys who took it enjoy their spoils. Then I think of poor Father Chavez and feel guilty for moaning about the loss of a bike. It was only a bike after all. What is that compared to a man's life?

As I near the ATM, I'm surprised to see a long line of people waiting to use it. I've never seen more than three or four people here before. However, if I want money, I'll have to get in line and wait my turn, just like at the bike rental shop, so that's what I do. In front of me is a plump middle-aged woman with platinum blond hair and large sunglasses with jewels at the corners that sparkle in the sunlight. She keeps looking at her silver bracelet watch, as if she's late for an appointment.

"Why are there so many people here?" I ask her.

"To get cash of course," she replies, barely glancing at me.

"But why are there so many?"

She looks at me more closely over her sunglasses. "Everyone's afraid the banks are going to close. Haven't you heard?"

"Why would they close?"

She sighs. "Don't you ever turn your TV on, honey?"

I don't want to confess that I seldom do. Maybe it was in the morning news. If it was in yesterday's news, Mrs. Franklin would have told me.

I hope it isn't true, but obviously the rest of the people in line must have heard the same rumor. Another bad sign.

In the end I have to wait almost thirty minutes before getting my turn at the ATM. And then the machine only lets me take out $600, but at least that will rent me a bike and give me a little extra cash. As I walk back to the bike rental shop, I notice that there is a line of cars, pickups, and vans waiting their turn at the pumps at the corner gas station. For months the streets have been nearly deserted, and now suddenly there are vehicles again. People evidently think it's going to be hard to get gas in the coming days or they are getting gassed up to flee the city. There is panic in the air, and I'm beginning to catch it.

At the bike rental shop, I have to wait in line again. The rental bikes are rapidly disappearing. When it's my turn, the clerk pulls out a battered-looking bike with worn tires. It looks like something left over from a yard sale.

"Don't you have anything else?" I ask.

He shrugs. "Take it or leave it."

It's not worth the money, but I have to have a bike, and so I give him the five hundred dollars and wheel it out of the shop without arguing.

In the afternoon I ride my rental bike to the State School to see if I can get Mary on that bus to Tucson. As I approach the compound, I'm surprised to see the gate unguarded and the bike rack empty. I feel uneasy as I cross the playground. Where is everybody? When I push the main doors open, I know for certain something is wrong. The air conditioning system isn't running and it's even hotter inside than out. I hurry down the hall past empty classrooms. At the end of the hall the outer office is empty, and the door to Strickland's office is locked.

I go back outside and cross the playground to the dormitory, looking for someone who can tell me why the school is deserted, but the dormitory too is empty and the air conditioning off. I brave the heat and climb the stairs to the second floor, where the children were, but there's no one there. The beds are all neatly made, the toys put away. In the hall I see a small red ribbon lying on the carpet and pick it up. It's all that's left of the horde of children who lived here. The silence is eerie. It's as if they've been spirited away by the Pied Piper or abducted by a UFO. I have the odd sensation of being the last person alive after a mysterious catastrophe and hurry back down the stairs and out into the sunlight to reassure myself that the world is still there.

Where has everyone gone? I decide to ride to Roberta's apartment in search of an answer. By the time I get there, I expect to find her gone too, but instead the door is standing open and her brother Victor and another man are carrying out a small sofa.

"Hey, Sarah," Victor calls out. "You're just in time."

"In time for what?"

"The farewell party."

"You're leaving?"

"As soon as we finish packing." He and the other man heave the sofa into the back of a pickup.

"Where are you going?"

"Mehico. Dear old Mehico. Want to come?"

"What's there?"

"Tequila." He flashes me a smile. "Lots of tequila."

Inside, the living room is nearly bare. Roberta emerges from a bedroom speaking Spanish to Victor's wife. When she sees me, she gives a wild shriek of joy. "Sarah! Where have you been? I heard what happened. So Strickland canned you, did he? I hope you told him where to go. Well, it doesn't matter now. No more school." She hugs me. "I'm so glad you came. I thought I wouldn't get a chance to say good-bye."

"Victor says you're going to Mexico."

"That's right."

"Why Mexico?"

She shrugs. "Why not? It can't be any worse than here."

I'm not sure that's true. "I thought things were rough down there."

"Things are rough all over. Or hadn't you noticed?"

"Will you be okay?"

We've been hearing for a long time about the food shortage in Mexico. There are fires there too as a result of the drought. But why mention these things? She knows all of this as well as I do.

"We have relatives in Puerto Penasco," she says, pushing a stray lock of hair back with the back of her hand. "We'll be okay. It'll be better than here."

I find that hard to believe but don't say anything. She's probably wise to get out of the city before it implodes.

"Why don't you come with us?" she says. "We're taking a pickup and a car. We could squeeze you in. And after we get there, I'll find you a nice Mexican boyfriend."

"Tempting, but I have to pass."

"Seriously, you should get out."

"It seems like everyone is leaving," I admit. "Can you believe I had to pay five hundred dollars just to rent a bike? And it's not worth ten."

"Sarah, listen to me." She grasps my arm. "You want to stick around until the power goes off? You know what's going to happen when all those infecteds in the South Zone cross the wall? Without planes coming in, there won't be enough food to go around. It's going to be like *Mad Max*."

"Is that why the school is closed?"

"Yeah, that's another reason I'm leaving. No more job. No more paychecks. No more reason to stay."

"Where did the kids go?"

"They're being evacuated to Vancouver. Things aren't supposed to be so bad there. They were shuttled to the airport this morning. It happened very fast. We just found out yesterday."

I think of Mary back at the Glenview Tower. If I hadn't taken her away from the school, she would have been with the other children about to embark for the safety of Vancouver. But now, because of me, she's trapped in a city about to fall into chaos. Somehow I have to get her out.

"When does the plane leave?" I ask, wondering if there's still time to get her on it.

"I'm not sure. Later this afternoon I think. Why?"

"Mary is at my place. She wasn't with the others."

Roberta frowns. "The little Havasupai girl? Why is she at your place? Well, never mind. I guess you're stuck with her—unless you can get her to the airport in time to put her on the plane."

"You think there's time?"

"A couple of hours maybe."

I hastily say good-bye and wish her well. Then I ride back to the Glenview Tower as fast as I can. But when I try to phone the airport to find out when the plane is scheduled to leave, I keep getting the busy signal. Mary watches me with worried eyes from the sofa as she pets Beggar.

"I don't want to leave," she says.

"You have to," I tell her. "You can't stay here. It isn't safe."

"Please let me stay. I don't want to go. I promise I'll be very good. Please don't send me away."

I take her in my arms and try to explain. "I want you to go where you're safe, sweetie. It isn't safe to stay here anymore. Now, hurry. Pack your things into my backpack. We don't have much time."

The airport is in the southernmost part of the city, which means we'll have to go through the South Zone to get to it. It's much too far to travel by bike and too dangerous to travel by ourselves through the South Zone. We'll have to go by the Freeway; however, only official travel is permitted on the Freeway, which is controlled by a military checkpoint. We'll have to get permission to travel with a military convoy. So with Mary on the back of my rented bike, I ride to the checkpoint where the Freeway cuts through the wall.

I'm surprised by the amount of activity going on when we get there. We aren't the only ones trying to get to the airport. A lot of other people are there with bags and backpacks. Soldiers mill about, and jeeps and trucks keep arriving. I'm sent from one soldier to another, and to each I try to explain that Mary must be on the plane. No one wants to let us through because I have no papers for her to show she's Negative. At last I stumble upon a sergeant who either believes me when I say Mary is from the State School for Homeless Children or just plain takes pity on us. In any case he finds space for us in the back of a transport truck. It's already crowded with people and luggage when we climb in. A woman is complaining loudly because she's allowed to bring only one piece of luggage. Her husband keeps trying to hush her. An old couple huddle together holding hands and two little boys bend over a hand-held game while their parents talk in low worried voices. One young woman holds a baby. We sit in two rows, facing each other across the luggage. Mary holds tightly to my hand and clutches her doll to her chest.

"It'll be all right," I tell her.

She stares at the woman with the baby but says nothing.

It's almost an hour before the truck begins to move. We are part of a convoy of large transport trucks and jeeps with artillery. The back of our truck is open and we can see the jeep behind us and the next truck behind that. The convoy travels in the middle of the road with pavement stretching away on both sides. Twice we hear gunfire, but I don't know if it's someone shooting at the convoy or just lawlessness in the South Zone.

It takes about forty-five minutes to reach the airport. When we get there, we pass electrified fences with gates guarded by soldiers. Once we are inside the perimeter, I know we'll be safe. The plane is sitting near the terminal with the passenger boarding bridge attached. It's such a relief to see it sitting there looking so large and solid and normal. All I have to do is get Mary on it.

But as soon as we enter the terminal, I realize that's going to be a lot more difficult than I thought. The terminal is packed with people. The uproar is deafening, people shouting, babies crying, voices blaring announcements in Spanish, English, and other languages over the PA system. A man in a cowboy hat pushes me so hard I lose Mary's hand and for a few minutes we are separated. When I find her again, I can see she's frightened. I thought I could explain to an airline representative that Mary should be part of the group of children from the State School for Homeless Children, but I can't get near one. All the representatives are swamped with people. I see a girl a little younger than Mary who is crying. It's bad for children caught in the crowd. At least I can see across the room and down the corridor. There are people everywhere—more than the plane can possibly hold—and they all want to leave the city before it's too late. You can feel the desperation in the air. As I look around for anyone I might know, I realize with a sinking feeling how little hope I have of getting Mary on the plane.

Then incredibly among all those people I spot Strickland standing in line waiting to board. Beside him is his wife, a pale blonde wearing a bright green jacket. I recognize her from having seen her at school functions. I don't see any of the children from the school so perhaps they have already boarded. If I can just get to Strickland, surely he'll be able to put Mary on the plane. Her lack of papers won't be a problem. He won't refuse because of what happened between us. He can't be that callous. None of that matters now. All that matters is getting Mary to safety. But how am I going to get her across that crowded room to him?

"Excuse me," I say loudly to the people in front of me. "Excuse me." Nothing happens. They can't move to let us through because there is no room for them to step aside. I have no idea how we are going to get to Strickland.

I'm trying to figure out what to do when a woman screams on the other side of the room followed by two gunshots. There are more screams and a wave of panic sweeps through the crowd as people push each other to get away from the danger. Everyone seems to be shouting at once. I hold tightly to Mary's hand, determined not to lose her. I have to get her out of here. There's too much danger of a child being trampled. It will mean giving up all hope of getting her on the plane, but that's what I have to do. Keeping her close, I struggle to go back the way we came.

When at last we're out of the crush, we walk until we come to a snack shop, where I buy a couple of cans of soda and we sit down at a small table to drink them. I feel discouraged as I watch Mary lift her soda can to her mouth and drink.

"I shouldn't have taken you away from the school," I tell her.

"But I want to be with you," she says, her lip trembling. She looks at me with those big black eyes of hers. She's my responsibility now. Somehow I have to take care of her.

I try to smile and pat her hand to reassure her. "It'll be okay, sweetie."

I feel bad that I can't get her on the plane. I wonder if there's some other way to get her out of the city. Maybe I could find someone who's leaving who could take her with them. I think of Roberta and her brother, but they're probably already on their way to Mexico, and even if it weren't too late to send her with them, I'm not sure I would. Mexico could be even worse than staying where we are. I hope Roberta and her brother will be all right. I wonder if I'll ever see them again.

After we finish our drinks, I take Mary's hand and we head for the nearest exit.

The convoy trucks are sitting where we left them. A young soldier helps us climb aboard one. "You never know," he says. "There may be another plane next week. Maybe you'll be able to get on that one." I can tell he feels sorry for us. I doubt there will be any more planes. Or if there are, next week will be too late.

CHAPTER 19

A red sun is setting as our convoy starts north on the Freeway. The truck we ride in is almost as crowded as it was on the way to the airport. The faces of the people who sit across from us look tired and disappointed. No one talks. Mary has fallen asleep against me. The convoy moves fast, intent on getting out of the South Zone before dark. Even after the sun is down, the trucks drive with their lights off, trying not to make themselves easy targets for snipers.

It's dark when we reach the North Zone. I wake Mary and the soldiers help us climb out of the truck.

"Are we going home now?" she asks, rubbing her eyes.

I tell her yes, we're going home now. It seems strange that already we think of the Glenview Tower as her home, and yet it seems right. I regret that I didn't manage to get her on a plane, but I'm also glad she's here with me. I promise myself I'll do everything in my power to keep her safe.

My rented bike is where I left it chained to a fence. All

around us other people from the convoy are getting on bikes or walking away. A lucky few have cars.

I'm getting used to Mary's extra weight on the back of my bike. As we ride back through the deserted streets, I stay in the lighted areas as much as possible. Who knows what lurks in the shadows? About a block from my apartment building, we hear a piercing whistle and someone shouts. I don't know if they are shouting at us, but I keep going, and soon the Glenview Tower looms ahead with its neat columns of lighted windows and its well-lit entry. I feel relieved knowing soon we'll be inside, where it's cool and lighted and safe, at least for now.

As we get closer, I see workmen are installing metal shields over the plate glass doors of the lobby. It's odd that they would be working at night. The place is beginning to look like a fortress.

"What are they doing?" Mary asks.

"I don't know. Making the building safer, I guess."

A security guard stops us at the entrance of the parking garage. Like the boy who stopped me the day before, this guard doesn't look more than fifteen years old and seems too young to be carrying a gun.

"Papers?" he asks.

I show him mine. "What's going on?"

"We're expecting trouble."

"What kind of trouble?"

He doesn't answer. "What about her papers?" he says, looking at Mary.

"We forgot and left them upstairs. Shall I go up and get them?" I don't think it would be wise to try to explain why we don't have papers for her. Better to bluff if I can.

"Is she your daughter?"

"Niece."

A voice crackles over his walkie-talkie and he motions us in while trying to answer it. Thank goodness he isn't going to give us trouble over Mary's lack of papers.

After I take Mary up to the apartment, I go down to the lobby to pick up my mail and find out if I have any messages. I'm hoping for some word of Martin. The security guard at the front desk looks at me oddly when I ask if there are any messages for me. When I leave, he turns to his partner and says something. They laugh. I tell myself not to be paranoid. It probably has nothing to do with me.

Beggar is glad to have us back and meows so much you'd think she's trying to tell us something. After we feed her, we go down the hall to check on Mrs. Franklin and let her know about our fruitless attempt to get Mary on a plane.

She listens sympathetically to our description of the crowded terminal and the chaotic conditions at the airport.

"Never mind," she says. "Somehow it will all work out."

Will it? She might not be so optimistic if I told her about the metal shields, but I keep that to myself.

When Mary and I get back to the apartment, I make grilled cheese sandwiches for us. She yawns several times while we're eating. I'm tired too. It's been a hectic day. I decide to skip writing in my journal and turn in early.

I have just finished washing our dishes when the doorbell rings. Mary is sitting at the table drawing on a tablet. Our eyes meet.

"Go into the bedroom," I tell her in a low voice. "Stay there until I find out who it is."

I keep the chain on when I answer the door. In the hall stand three men. The one in front is a policeman. I suspect the other two are too even though they aren't wearing uniforms. Probably they are looking for Lydia, but thankfully she's beyond their reach.

"Sarah Davis?" asks the man in uniform, his expression neutral, voice clipped.

"Yes."

"We have some questions we want to ask you."

I know a chain isn't going to keep them out, so I unhook it. As soon as it's off, they push their way in, handcuff me, and read me my rights. One of them does a quick search of the apartment, but evidently Mary has had time to hide.

"Is anyone else here?" demands the policeman.

"No," I say, not wanting them to find Mary. I know she will be all right. She can go to Mrs. Franklin after I'm gone. "Why are you arresting me? What have I done?"

"You're wanted for questioning," the policeman says.

I have no choice but to go with them. I tell myself to stay calm as we ride down the elevator and then exit through the lobby. I don't look at the security guards. Let them think what they want.

It's my first time to ride in the back of a police car. It feels strange to be handcuffed, and the wire mesh and safety glass that separate me from the two men in the front seat make me feel trapped. The third man leads the way on a motorcycle. I wonder what I'm in trouble for. Is it because I helped Lydia escape to the South Zone? Or because I took Mary from the State School? Does it have anything to do with Martin? The more I think about it, I've probably broken half a dozen laws in the past few days. I suppose it was just a matter of time until I got caught for one of my infractions.

When we reach the police station, I'm taken first to a large room with at least twenty desks in it where I have to answer questions about myself: name, address, age, how long I have lived in the city, where I work, where I lived previously, place of birth, parents' names, medical history, and more. I can hear other people being asked the same questions. I look around the crowded and noisy room. At the next desk a woman is crying. Beside another slouches a sullen teenaged boy with a shaved head, pierced brow, and tattoos covering his arms. Beyond him sits a nervous-looking man in a suit. Some of the police are in uniform, others aren't. A few are women. Then at a desk halfway across the room, I spot Milo. He's sitting at a desk, questioning a Mexican girl in a red tank top. I can't believe it. What's he doing here?

"What?" says the policeman across from me, and my eyes snap back to him. He's middle-aged, paunchy, balding, and tired-looking. The name on his desk says Cooper.

"Nothing," I answer quickly. "I thought I saw someone I know, but I guess I was mistaken."

Milo is a cop? How is that possible? He has the virus—how can he be on the force? When Cooper has his eyes on the report form, I sneak another glance. Milo isn't wearing a red armband. Could it be someone who just looks a lot like him? Someone else who is big and tough and black? A twin brother maybe? No, not likely. It's Milo all right. I don't know what to think. Why didn't he tell me he's a policeman? I asked him what he did. What was it he said? A troubleshooter. I thought maybe he was a bouncer at a bar or even a bodyguard for a businessman or a politician. I thought maybe he was mixed up in something illegal. It never crossed my mind that he could be an undercover cop. Both Sandy and Lydia warned me not to trust him. How stupid could I have been? Was he undercover when I met him? And was he in any way responsible for my arrest? I decide I'd better not say anything to the policeman about Milo. If they don't know I know him, maybe we should keep it that way.

After Cooper is done asking questions, I'm fingerprinted and photographed. As I'm led out of the room, I have to walk past Milo. He glances up, but his face shows no sign of recognition. Either he doesn't see me or he doesn't want anyone to know he knows me. I don't blame him for not wanting to get involved.

Flanked by Cooper and a young policewoman, I'm escorted through a maze of halls to a small room with a two-way mirror which gives us a view of an adjoining room, where an interrogation is under way. Walking around the table in the adjoining room is an older detective with his sleeves rolled up. Sitting at the table is a young man with his arm in a sling. With a shock I recognize Martin. His clothes are rumpled and he looks tired, but otherwise he seems well. I feel a wave of relief. He's alive—that's what matters. Whatever else happens, I no longer have to worry I might never see him again. Now I know why no one has heard from him. He was picked up by the police.

"Do you know this man?" asks Cooper, pointing his finger at Martin.

I try to think quickly. Would it be better for Martin if I say I don't know him or if I say I do? I decide to go with the truth since they may already know that I know him.

"Yes."

"What's his name?"

"Martin Jones." I figure they know this already too.

"Do you know where he works?"

"The State Hospital."

"How long have you known him?" the young policewoman asks. I heard Cooper call her Evans. She's on my left and he's on my right. I wonder how they decide who will ask which questions or if they just play it by ear.

"Not very long. Just since last week."

"How'd you meet him?"

"He did my blood test." No harm in revealing that.

"What is the nature of your relationship?" Cooper demands.

"He's a friend."

"Have you slept with him?" asks Evans.

I look at her. Young, pixie haircut, baby face. Is she married? Does she have a boyfriend? What if someone asked her a question like that?

"Do you refuse to answer?" asks Cooper. His tone suggests I could be in trouble if I don't answer. Or deeper trouble than I'm already in.

The detective in the next room bangs his fist on the table. We can't hear his fist hit the table or hear what they are saying. It's like watching TV with the sound turned off.

"What's he done?" I ask.

They ignore my question of course. I don't get to ask questions.

"Do you know his viral status?" asks Evans.

Oh, great. The question I never got around to asking. I

doubt they'll buy that. "He wears a red armband. I assume he's infected."

"We know he came to see you on the fifteenth." Cooper hands me a photograph. It's distorted by the angle and grainy, but I recognize Martin with his arm around my shoulders on the elevator of the Glenview Tower. Apparently they got it from the security camera. I wonder if this is why the security guard looked at me oddly when I picked up my mail. Did he know they were coming to arrest me? Is he the one who saw me the night I let Martin in and did he report me?

"We know he spent two nights at your apartment," says Evans. "Do you deny it?"

No, I don't deny it.

"Did you sleep with him?" she asks again. She stares straight ahead at the two-way mirror and I do too. If we slept together, they could charge Martin with attempted murder.

"We didn't do anything." It's the truth, but I have a feeling it's not truth they're after.

"You are in big trouble," Cooper says. "You knew his viral status, and that he was breaking the law by being in the North Zone after curfew and yet you let him stay with you."

There doesn't seem to be any point in denying it, so I don't. They have the security tapes to prove it.

"You registered him under a false name and claimed he was your cousin. Isn't that right?"

"Yes."

"Is he your cousin?"

"No."

"Why didn't you report him to the police?" asks Evans.

"I don't know." That isn't true, but how can I explain that

I liked Martin from the beginning? He trusted me when he came to me. If I have to choose sides, I choose to be on his side, regardless of whether it's right or wrong in the eyes of the law.

"Were you aware that he had a bullet wound in his shoulder?" Evans asks.

In the next room Martin leans back in his chair. He looks exhausted. I wish he knew I'm here on the other side of the mirror. "Yes," I say softly.

"Did he tell you how he got it?"

"Someone shot at him."

"Who?"

"I don't know."

"Were you aware that he was smuggling drugs?" Cooper asks.

This is a far more serious charge than violating curfew. And I too have smuggled drugs. Maybe it's time to stop being honest. "No, I wasn't aware."

"We believe he was," says Evans.

I glance at her and then at Cooper. Suddenly I realize. They have no proof. They only suspect Martin has been smuggling drugs. They want me to incriminate him. That's why I'm here.

"We believe he was shot running from the police," Cooper says. "And by allowing him to stay with you, you sheltered a fugitive as well as an infected."

"Then I guess you'll have to charge me."

"You bet we're going to charge you," he says. "We're going to charge you and your boyfriend with setting a fire at the First National Bank."

A fire? Martin set fire to a bank? I look at him in the next room. For a moment my faith in him wavers. How much do I really know about him? If he steals drugs, could he also be capable of arson? Have I allowed myself to fall in love with a common criminal? No, I refuse to believe it. I may not know him well, but I know he's no criminal. If he set fire to a bank, he had a reason for it. A good reason.

And then with no warning the lights go out, plunging us into darkness.

CHAPTER 20

I can see nothing. It's pitch black. Cooper swears. Someone bumps into me, knocking me against the wall.

"You stay here," Cooper says gruffly to Evans. "I'll go see what's happening." I hear the door open and close.

"I wonder if this is it," Evans says. "The big blackout everyone's been talking about—when the power goes off and stays off."

"It'll probably come back on in a minute." I don't know why I feel the need to reassure her. I guess I feel sorry for her. She's young and inexperienced, and I can tell she's scared.

"Any day now all hell is going to bust loose," she says. "You just wait and see. It won't be a pretty sight."

The door opens and a flashlight beam sweeps over us.

"Is that you, Cooper?" Evans asks, holding up an arm to shield her eyes from the light. "Get that thing out of my eyes."

"Cooper told me to take your prisoner for lock up."

I recognize Milo's voice. The flashlight turns on me, blinding me. He moves forward, grabs my arm, and pulls me roughly toward the door without waiting for Evans to respond. Outside in the hall people are shouting and flashlights throw wild crisscrossing beams.

"Come on," Milo says, still gripping my arm. I know by the tone of his voice that he isn't taking me to a jail cell. He's helping me escape.

"Wait. We've got to get Martin." I turn toward the door to the next room.

He swears and pulls me back. "Are you crazy?"

Suddenly the door swings open and the detective stands in the doorway, blinking. "What happens now?" he asks Milo.

"I can take your prisoner back to his cell," Milo says without missing a beat.

"I'll take him myself."

"Suit yourself." Milo punches him in the gut. The detective isn't expecting it and falls back into the room dazed. Milo shines his flashlight on Martin. "Well, don't just sit there."

Martin jumps up and rushes toward us.

"Sarah, what are you doing here?"

"Later," Milo growls.

People are running down the hall. No one pays any attention to us except a few who follow us because we have a flashlight. At last we tumble out of the building from a side exit. We can see better outside, where the moon gives us some light.

"This way," Milo says, walking rapidly toward the parking lot with Martin and me close on his heels. We pile into a police car, Milo behind the wheel, me in the middle, Martin against the passenger door.

"I can't believe you just broke me out of jail," Martin says.

"I didn't know you had gotten yourself arrested," I say. "And what's this about setting fire to a bank?"

"Don't believe everything you hear."

Milo snorts and starts the engine. We take off with a squeal of tires.

"Why didn't you tell me you were a policeman?" I ask Milo.

"You mean why didn't I just hang a sign on me—undercover cop?"

"You're a cop?" Martin asks.

Before Milo can answer there's a loud explosion. The car skids to a stop.

"What was that?" I ask.

As if in answer, there's another explosion, closer this time.

"The wall," Milo says grimly. "They're breaking through."

"Well, at least it ought to be easier to cross it now," Martin quips.

"You think this is some kind of joke? You want to go back to the station and take your chances there?"

"Hey, I have no problem with being rescued."

"If it were up to me, you'd still be back there."

"All I meant to say was, I need to go across the wall. If I don't have to go through a checkpoint, so much the better. By the way, I don't think we've been introduced. I'm Martin."

"I know who you are. Right now I don't much care."

"Thanks for breaking me out," Martin whispers in my ear. "Remind me to return the favor sometime."

"Maybe we all should go across," Milo says. "It's probably going to be safer over there than here."

I shake my head. "I can't. I have to go back to the Glenview Tower."

"Why? You got a death wish?"

"I have to make sure Mary and Mrs. Franklin are safe."

"Who's Mary?" asks Martin.

Milo swears under his breath as he starts the engine again. He speeds through the dark streets. There are no streetlights, no traffic signals, no lighted signs or lighted windows. In the headlights we see people running. Several times he has to jam on the brakes to keep from hitting someone.

When we get to the Glenview Tower, it looks deserted, looming dark and ominous before us, the ground floor glass now covered by metal shields. Milo stops the car at the entrance to the garage. There is no security guard, just a gaping black hole that swallows our headlights.

"I don't like this," Milo says.

"I can walk in," I offer.

"You stay put. It's too dark to see the door in there."

He drives forward slowly, our headlights casting their beams ahead of us on the concrete walls. Near the door leading into the building is an empty parking stall. He swings the police car into it. We climb out, look around nervously, then head for the door. I open it with my key card by the light of Milo's flashlight.

Inside all is silence. No hum of an air conditioner, no lights, no elevator. I'm surprised there isn't a backup generator.

"We'll have to take the stairs," Martin says.

Milo shines his flashlight at the door to the stairwell. "Look, we better make this quick. We may not have much time."

"Maybe you should go on," I suggest, suddenly worried. "It's fifteen flights up. Maybe Mary and Mrs. Franklin are safer up there. Who's going to climb fifteen flights?"

225

"They don't have to climb fifteen flights," Milo retorts. "They can just set fire to the damn building."

He's right of course. A building can burn as easily as a house. I can't leave them up there.

"Come on, Sarah," Martin says, taking my hand. "It's going to be okay."

I nod and throw him a grateful look. We start up the narrow concrete stairs by the beam of Milo's flashlight. At the fifth floor landing we pass a man coming down with a flashlight of his own who eyes us distrustfully as we sidle past each other. At the eighth floor we pass a woman clutching a bag to her chest as if she's afraid we might try to take it from her. I wonder what's in it—money? jewelry? Aside from these two we see no one else. Evidently most of the residents are sitting tight, hoping the power will come back on.

"It didn't seem like nearly so many floors when I was coming down," Martin remarks as we pass the tenth floor. "Five to go."

"We're only at the tenth?" Milo says. "Are you serious?"

"You want to wait here for us?" Martin asks cheerfully.

Milo swears but keeps climbing.

I never realized before how many stairs you have to climb to get to the fifteenth floor. It seems to take forever, but finally we are there, spilling out of the stairwell and charging down the dark hall to Mrs. Franklin's door.

I let us in without knocking. Several candles are burning in the living room. We find Mrs. Franklin and Mary on the balcony, the old woman sitting on one of two white plastic patio chairs and Mary standing at the railing looking out at the city. When Mary sees me, she gives a little cry and throws herself into my arms.

"You came back. I knew you'd come back."

"Thank goodness you're all right," Mrs. Franklin says. "We were so worried."

"I hid under the bed," Mary says.

I stroke her hair. "You were very brave."

Milo and Martin are standing behind me. We all look out at the city, which is dark except for several fires. I can hear the wail of sirens. None of us says anything. I remember what Milo said about setting fire to the Glenview Tower and pull Mary closer.

"You can't stay here," Milo says. I don't know who he's speaking to—me or all of us.

"He's right," Mrs. Franklin says, turning to me. "The fires could come this way. Get Mary to safety."

"You have to come with us," I tell her. "I can't just leave you here."

"I'll be all right," she says. "You've been very kind to me, but now you have to think about saving yourself and Mary."

"We won't go without you."

"I don't want to leave my things. And who knows, maybe tomorrow the power will come back on. Don't worry about me."

"It's not safe here," I argue. "Not for me. Not for Mary. Not for you."

"Sarah," she says, reaching for my hand. "I'm not young anymore. I've lived my life. I'm not afraid to die." Her hand feels thin and fragile in mine. The turquoise necklace her husband gave her forty years ago gleams at her throat.

"You don't have to die. Come with us."

"I'd never be able to get down the stairs. It's hard enough just to get to the bathroom."

"I could carry you," Milo says.

She looks at him in surprise, as if noticing him for the first time. "It's fifteen flights, young man."

"I know. I just came up them."

"I can't walk. I can't run. I'd be a burden."

"We have a car," Martin says. "All we have to do is get you down to it."

"*Please,*" Mary says, slipping her hand into Mrs. Franklin's and pressing it to her cheek.

Mrs. Franklin looks back at her living room in the flickering candlelight. It's too dark to see much, but no doubt in her mind she is seeing her Hopi dolls, the rocks, the Navajo rug, and all the other memorabilia she has collected over her lifetime. She touches the turquoise necklace at her throat thoughtfully. "When we were young my husband wanted to go whitewater rafting. I told him it didn't look very safe to me, and he said safety's not everything. Sometimes you have to be willing to take your chances and shoot the rapids. Maybe this is one of those times." She looks down at Mary. "I'll need my cane. And go get those pictures on the mantel."

Mary flies off to collect the items.

"All right, young man. If you think you can do it, then let's give it a try."

"Better grab some clothes for her," Milo says over his shoulder as he helps her stand and then picks her up. "Mary, you going to open doors for me?"

"Yes," she says, clutching the cane and the photos.

"We'll meet you down there," I tell him, taking the photos from Mary so her hands will be free except for the cane and the flashlight, which Milo has handed to her.

Martin follows me to the bedroom, where I find a flashlight on the stand beside her bed and pull open a dresser drawer. He goes to the closet as I start tossing underwear on the bed.

"Grab some blouses," I tell him. "Pants too. Nothing fancy. Just practical things."

"Shoes?"

"Do you see any walking shoes?"

He holds up a pair of tennis shoes. "How about these?"

"All right. Do you see anything we can put these things in?"

He rummages in the closet and pulls out a small brown leather bag. "How about this?"

"Great."

I duck into the bathroom while he fills the bag and grab soap, toothpaste, toothbrush, shampoo, deodorant, and pills from the medicine cabinet.

"We should get some things for you and Mary too," he says when I come back with my hands full.

We hurry down the hall to my apartment and quickly gather up some clothes and supplies for Mary and me and stuff them in my backpack. I regret I can't take more, but I know it will be difficult going back down the stairs if we carry too much. My journal is lying on the nightstand. I hesitate a moment, then push it into the already bulging backpack. Before we leave the apartment, I look around one last time to see if there's anything else I should take. My eye is caught by the photograph of my family on the end table. Without a word Martin picks up the photograph and hands it to me. I cram it into my backpack. When I look up again, I see Beggar watching us narrowly from the back of the sofa. I completely forgot about Beggar. We can't leave her behind. There will be nobody to feed her.

Martin must have read my mind. In one deft movement he scoops her up with his good hand. "I'll carry the cat if you'll carry the bags."

"Deal." I head toward the kitchen.

"Where are you going now?"

"Cat food," I call back.

There's no way I can fit anything more into my backpack so I grab a plastic bag and toss tins of cat food into it. No time for anything more. We head for the stairs and start down. Martin was right. Going down is easier than going up.

There are more people groping their way down the dark stairwell now. We squeeze past a man and woman struggling with a large trunk, each shouting at the other. Everyone is carrying something. Boxes, totes, luggage, plastic bags. One woman carries a plant. Evidently they have decided not to wait for the power to come back on. I wonder where they are all going.

Milo, Mrs. Franklin, and Mary are waiting for us in the parking garage.

"Where's the police car?" Martin asks, looking at the parking stall where we left it, now conspicuously empty.

"Someone borrowed it," Milo says bitterly.

"What do we do now?" I ask.

"There are bikes over there," Mary says, pointing at the bike rack near the door.

"I doubt very much that I can ride a bike," Mrs. Franklin says, leaning on her cane. "Perhaps you'll have to leave me behind after all."

"After I carried you down fifteen flights?" Milo says. "No way." He starts walking toward the ramp that leads to the next level of the parking garage. "Wait here," he calls back over his shoulder.

"Where's he going?" Mary asks.

"To find us a car, I expect," Martin says.

While we wait for Milo to return, more people come out of the building, grab bikes, and ride off. Somewhere in the garage a car alarm goes off. I wonder if that's Milo stealing a car.

Mary moves closer to me, still gripping the flashlight. She holds it pointed at the ground, giving us a small pool of light.

Soon we hear an engine roar to life, and within minutes a black Land Rover comes charging down the ramp, its headlights bouncing off the walls. It swerves wildly and screeches to a stop beside us, Milo behind the wheel.

"Don't just stand there," he shouts. "Get in."

We jump into action. I toss everything I'm carrying into the back. Martin hands Beggar to Mary. Milo hops out and lifts Mrs. Franklin into the front passenger seat. The beam of the flashlight swings erratically as Mary struggles to hold Beggar, who clearly wants no part of this.

"I can't hold her," Mary says, nearly in tears. "What should I do?"

"Just give me a second," Martin says. He walks to a nearby dumpster and rummages in it with his good hand.

"Come on," says Milo impatiently, now behind the wheel again. "We don't have time for this. Leave the goddamn cat if you have to."

"*No!*" Mary protests. "We can't leave Beggar."

"Oh, she's got a name now, does she?" Martin says. "Well, don't worry. Beggar comes with us." He pulls out a box. "Got a knife?" he calls to Milo.

Milo swears but fishes in a pocket, pulls out a jackknife, and tosses it to Martin.

"Thanks," Martin says, catching it with his good hand. He quickly punches some holes in the box, then takes the squirming Beggar from Mary's arms, drops her in the box and quickly closes the flaps. "Okay, you're in charge of her," he tells Mary.

"I don't think she'll like it in there," Mary says, picking up the box.

"She'll be all right. It's better than being left behind."

"Can we go now?" Milo asks. "Or are we going to wait for the crazies from the South Zone to show up?"

Mary carefully hands me the box and then climbs in beside me.

But before Martin can get in, the door of the building is flung open again and several more people rush out, including a big man with a handgun. He walks toward us waving his gun menacingly.

"Okay, everybody out," he bellows.

We stare at him but no one moves. I reach for Mary's hand. There's a loud bang. I duck and pull Mary down with me. The man lets out a howl, and a woman starts screaming. I see her now, crouching in the shadows by the door.

"Get his gun," Milo growls.

Martin walks warily toward the man and picks up his gun.

The woman stops screaming. "You bastards!" she shouts, taking a step forward. Her face is angry and her fists are clenched as if she wants to hit somebody. "Murderers!"

"He's not dead," Martin says, looking down at the man, who has collapsed to the floor clutching his leg and is swearing profusely.

"You had no right to shoot him!" the woman shouts. "And give us back our gun! You can't leave us here like this."

"Come on," Milo says to Martin. "Let's get out of here."

CHAPTER 21

The woman continues to swear at us as Martin hops back into the Land Rover. Our tires squeal as we speed away. The Land Rover shoots out of the parking garage and takes off down the dark street. When Milo swerves around corners, we hold on tight. People are running on the sidewalks and in the street. Again I'm afraid Milo will run someone down the reckless way he's driving. We hurtle past a store with its plate glass windows smashed and see looters carting away TV's and DVD players. It all seems so crazy. What good are TV's and DVD players if there is no power?

The night is full of wild whooping, screams, and sirens. We see buildings that are on fire and motorcyclists traveling in packs. Several blocks from the wall we spot a blockade ahead made up of overturned barrels and recycle bins. Beside them a car burns. It reminds me of the trap set by the boys in front of Father Chavez's church in the South Zone.

Milo swears.

"Turn around," Martin says.

But it's too late. Two men rush up on our right and another man and woman on our left, all armed.

"Get out with your hands up," orders one of the men on our right, who is wearing a cowboy hat and holding a rifle aimed at us. It's like we stumbled into a bad movie.

"Better do as he says," Milo says, cutting the engine.

Martin hops out on the left side of the Land Rover, one hand raised.

"Hold up your hands!" shouts the man on that side, who has a red bandana on his head, heavy metal jewelry hanging from his thick neck, and tattoos on his arms.

"I can't," Martin says. "I have an injured arm, in case you hadn't noticed."

Mary climbs out after him holding the box with Beggar. Once out, she carefully sets down the box and holds up her hands.

I get out on the right side of the Land Rover, where the man in the cowboy hat with the rifle stands. The man next to him has a shaved head and holds a sawed-off shotgun. I wonder if they're going to kill us.

"This one's got a gun," calls the man in the bandana from the other side of the Land Rover. He's referring to Milo, who is also out now.

"Well, tell him to drop it or we start shooting people," calls back the man with the rifle. He's the one giving the orders, so I assume he's the leader.

"You heard him," says the man in the bandana.

"You too, lady," says the man with the shaved head to Mrs. Franklin. "Get out of the car."

"She needs help," I tell him.

"Well, help her then."

Leaning on me, Mrs. Franklin climbs out of the Land Rover.

"Get my cane," she whispers in my ear while I'm helping her.

I turn and reach into the front seat for it.

"Hey, what are you doing?" shouts the man with the rifle.

"I'm just getting her cane."

"What's in the box?" demands the man in the bandana on the other side of the Land Rover.

"A cat," Milo says.

"Open it."

Mary kneels, opens the box, and takes Beggar up in her arms.

"See," Milo says. "Like I said, it's just a cat."

"Step away from the vehicle!" orders the man with the rifle. "All of you."

We do as he says. After all, he's holding a gun on us. Mrs. Franklin clings to my arm and leans on her cane.

"Are the keys in there?" demands the man with the rifle.

The woman, who until now has said nothing, goes to look. "Yeah, the keys are here."

"We're going to take your Rover," says the man with the rifle. "And nobody needs to get hurt."

This makes me feel relieved. I just hope no one does anything stupid.

"Okay, take it," Milo says. "Just leave us our things."

"What things?" the man with the rifle asks suspiciously.

"Clothes. They aren't of any use to you."

"You got any money in there?"

"No, just clothes, I swear."

"Show us your wallets then."

Milo and Martin pull out their wallets.

"You too," the man with the rifle says to me.

I pull out mine.

"Hand them over."

Milo and Martin hand theirs to the man with the red bandana. I hand mine to the man with the shaved head standing beside me.

"What about you?" the man with the rifle says to Mrs. Franklin.

"I didn't bring anything along," she says. "We left in such a rush I didn't think about money."

"Louise, check the SUV," the man with the rifle tells the woman.

She glances at the man beside her, the one with the red bandana, and he nods. Then she walks to the Land Rover, pulls out our backpacks and bags, and dumps them on the pavement. As we all watch, she squats down and picks among the contents. "There's nothing much here but clothes and photos."

"What about this?" the man with the rifle says.

"What?"

"Come over here."

She comes around the Land Rover to our side. "What?"

"That necklace the old gal's wearing. I bet that's worth something."

She steps closer and frowns at Mrs. Franklin's turquoise necklace. "It might be," she concedes without much enthusiasm.

"My husband gave me this forty years ago," Mrs. Franklin says. "I'm sure it's not worth as much to you as it is to me."

"We'll be the judge of that," the man with the rifle says. "Take it," he orders the woman.

She hesitates. "Aw, let her keep it. It's probably not worth much."

"I said take it."

The woman turns to us. "Sorry," she mumbles as she reaches for the necklace. She gives it a hard yank. Mrs. Franklin lets out a small gasp and totters. I grab her arm to keep her from falling.

The woman won't look at us. "Let's go. We got what we wanted."

They pile into the Land Rover, their guns still pointed at us. The engine roars to life and they take off. We watch them speed away down the dark street.

"It could have been worse," Martin says.

Milo glares at him.

"So they took our wallets and the Land Rover. The Land Rover wasn't ours and I only had a couple of dollars in my wallet."

Milo scowls at the burning car and says nothing.

"I'm so sorry about your necklace," I tell Mrs. Franklin.

"I thought I'd be buried with that necklace," she says, "but I guess I was wrong."

Mary puts Beggar back into the box with Martin's help and then we start gathering up our belongings.

"What do we do now?" I ask.

"We walk," Milo says.

"She can't walk," I say, glancing at Mrs. Franklin.

"Maybe I could just find someplace to sit down and wait," suggests Mrs. Franklin.

"Wait for what—Hell's Angels to show up?" Milo says.

"Probably not a good idea," Martin agrees.

"We're not going to leave you," I say firmly, giving Martin and Milo a warning look.

Milo mutters something under his breath. Then without another word, he goes to Mrs. Franklin, lifts her up in his arms, and starts walking. I grab my backpack and a plastic bag, Martin picks up the other bag with his good hand, Mary takes up the box with Beggar in it, and we follow him. We walk about half a block. Then Milo sets Mrs. Franklin down again on her feet.

"This isn't going to work. If we run into any trouble, we won't have time to hide. And we would have to be very lucky not to run into trouble between here and the wall."

"Well, I'm not going to leave her," I say again stubbornly.

Milo mutters under his breath again.

"How about if they wait for us at that Seven-Eleven?" Martin says. We all look at the Seven-Eleven across the street. It isn't open of course. Like every place else, it's dark. "You and I can go find some transportation or get help at the hospital and come back for them."

"Take Mary with you," I say quickly. Staying behind is risky, and I think she might be safer with them. I don't want to leave Mrs. Franklin behind, but neither do I want to put Mary in danger.

"Only if Beggar can come too," Mary says, clutching the box to her chest. "I'm not leaving Beggar behind."

"I can watch her," I say. "She'll be safe with me."

"Mary would probably be safer here with you," Martin says. "As long as you stay out of sight, you should be okay."

"All right," Milo says. "Are we all agreed?"

He picks up Mrs. Franklin again and heads for the Seven-Eleven with the rest of us close behind him. When we get there, we see the door is ajar. Inside, it's a mess. Looters have been here already. The cash register is open and empty. A cooler door stands open. Broken glass litters the floor, along with cookies, chips, and donuts.

"Stay out of sight," Martin says. "We'll be back as soon as we can."

He pulls a gun out of his sling and tries to give it to me. It's the one he picked up at the Glenview Tower.

"No, you keep it," I tell him. "You're more likely to run into trouble out there. You said so yourself."

"I'd feel better knowing you have a way to defend yourself if you need to."

"And I'd feel better knowing you have a way to defend yourself. Just be careful and hurry back."

He gives me a quick kiss on the lips and tucks my hair behind my ear. "When this is over. . . ."

"Maybe you should stay here," Milo interrupts. "I can go by myself. There's no reason for you to come along."

"No, we have a better chance if there are two of us," Martin insists. "If one gets caught, maybe the other can get through."

"Or maybe we both get caught."

"I'll be back," Martin tells me. "I promise."

"Don't do anything stupid."

He grins. "Who me?"

"Can we go now?" Milo asks, looking out the door. "Or are you going to wait for a welcome party to show up?"

Martin winks at me and then follows Milo out the door. I watch until they disappear into the shadows. Then I help Mrs. Franklin hobble to the back of the store and sit down on a packing crate. I know it won't be comfortable but at least she won't have to stand. Mary sets the box with Beggar on the floor and sits down cross-legged beside it. She opens the lid a crack and peeps in. "It's okay," she tells Beggar. "I won't let anyone hurt you." I sit down beside her and lean back against the wall. Anyone who looks through the glass door or the front windows won't be able to see us. We're safely hidden behind the last row of shelves. I check my watch. It's 10:30.

"I'm afraid I've been a lot of trouble for you," says Mrs. Franklin. "I ought to have stayed put."

"It'll be okay," I assure her. "Martin and Milo will find something."

From inside the box comes a meow. I feel sorry for Beggar cooped up in the box, but we can't let her out. If she takes off, we may lose her.

"Maybe she's hungry," Mary says, looking at the shelves of canned food in front of us.

If Beggar is, she's not the only one. I'm hungry too. Maybe it's because of all the excitement or the exertion of climbing and going back down those fifteen flights of stairs. And I could really use something to drink. I've been in this store before and I know there are cold bottles of water in one of the coolers against the adjoining wall. I see no reason why we shouldn't help ourselves to some.

"Wait here," I tell Mrs. Franklin and Mary. Then I feel my

way in the dark to the coolers. Broken glass crunches underfoot. The beer cooler has been broken into. A lot of the bottles are broken and beer is spilled on the floor. But the cooler holding water bottles and juice is intact. I pull out three water bottles and take them back with me.

The water tastes wonderful as it slides down my throat. Almost at once I start to feel better. I pour some in my cupped hand and splash it on my face. It's amazing how it revives me. Mrs. Franklin and Mary drink from their bottles too.

When Mrs. Franklin tips her head back to drink, I can't help noticing how bare her neck looks without her turquoise necklace.

"I'm really sorry about your necklace."

"I valued it, yes," she says, "but if I had to part with it, so be it. In the end it was only an object. Objects are not as important as people. My husband would understand that."

"I'm glad they didn't take mine." Mary touches the small silver phoenix at her throat.

"Even if they did, you'd still carry it in your heart," Mrs. Franklin tells her. "No one can take away the things you carry there."

I put my arm around Mary. The important thing is that we're all safe, at least for now.

Our thirst quenched, it seems natural to address our hunger. After all, we're surrounded by food. "Would you like something to eat?" I ask them.

Before they can answer, we hear a noise. The skin on the back of my neck tightens. The noise was close—not outside, but inside the store. I silently curse myself for not having been more careful. Why didn't we keep quiet? Why did I go for the bottles of water? Why didn't I search the store to see if we were alone?

"What was that?" Mary whispers.

"Ssh." I put my finger to my lips. My eyes have gradually adjusted to the dark. It's not pitch black. A little moonlight shines into the store through the glass door and the windows.

Maybe it was only a mouse, or a rat, I tell myself. It was just a movement, a small movement. I don't like the idea that a mouse or a rat might be in here with us, but neither do I like the idea that we might not be alone.

And then I hear it again, along with another sound like a low moan. No mouse would make a sound like that. That was definitely human.

We sit tensely silent, Mary holding tightly to my hand.

She leans closer to me. "I'm scared," she whispers.

Mrs. Franklin says nothing. Her eyes are closed and her lips seem to be moving silently, as if she's praying.

Whoever is in the store knows we are in it too and hasn't yet confronted us. That might mean they aren't armed. Maybe they are as frightened of us as we are of them.

I wonder if I should call out. Or should we just sit tight and wait for Martin and Milo to come back? Maybe whoever is in the store won't bother us as long as we don't bother them. But what if Martin and Milo don't come back for hours? What if we're here all night? I don't think my nerves can bear it.

"I'm going to go see," I whisper.

Mary lets go of my hand. Mrs. Franklin opens her eyes but doesn't try to stop me.

There is no way to move silently, although I try. Crunching glass underfoot gives away my every move. If this intruder has a gun, I will be at his mercy, and so will Mary and Mrs. Franklin. I doubt that I can overpower anyone if I have to fight. And yet facing whoever is lurking in here with us seems preferable to cowering for hours in fear and uncertainty.

I look down each aisle as I go and listen for a noise that will tell me where he is. I see no one. Unless he can move more silently than I can, which I doubt because of all that broken glass, there is only one place where he can be hiding— behind the counter.

I inch my way to it and listen. I think I can hear breathing, but my own heart is beating so hard I can't be sure. At last I work up my courage and peek around the counter, knowing I might find myself looking straight into the barrel of a gun.

Someone is lying on the floor behind the counter. In the dark it's hard to see much more. I crawl forward. Gradually I make out a boy, maybe sixteen or seventeen years old. He seems to be injured. There's a great deal of broken glass and his T-shirt is wet—probably with blood.

"Is he dead?" Mary asks. She has crept up behind me without my noticing.

"Go back," I tell her. This isn't something she should see.

The young man's eyes open and look up at me. They gleam in the moonlight.

"Where are you hurt?" I ask.

He doesn't answer, just looks at me, although I think his lips moved. I need a light to see how badly he's hurt.

"Find me a flashlight or matches," I tell Mary, who is still standing there staring. She turns away at once, and soon I hear her footsteps crunching around the store as she searches for something that could give us light.

"Are you in pain?" I ask the young man.

Again his lips move but no words come.

After a few minutes Mary returns with a small package of emergency candles. "How about these? We could light them."

"We don't have matches."

On the wall behind us are packs of cigarettes but no matches.

The young man's eyes close again. I reach across him and grope blindly on a shelf under the counter. I can hardly believe my luck when I find a flashlight. I snap it on. There is blood everywhere. The boy is soaked in it. The floor is wet with it. I think I'm going to throw up. Then my eye is caught by the glint of something. I bend closer to see better. A shard of broken glass juts from his side.

A small gasp tells me Mary is behind me again. I don't want her to see this, but I think she already has. And since she has seen it, maybe she can help.

"Can you hold this?" I ask, handing the flashlight to her.

She nods and takes it. The light wobbles a little, but now I can see. My fingers shake as I reach for the shard of glass. I don't know what I can do for the boy, but at least I can pull that out. I don't stop to think. I just take hold of it and tug. It's cold and smooth and sharp between my fingers. As soon as I have it out, I drop it on the floor.

The boy moans and opens his eyes. He looks up at me but doesn't speak.

"You're going to be all right," I tell him. "We'll help you. There are people coming back for us. We'll get you to a doctor."

I try to sound confident, but I know I have to stop the bleeding or he'll bleed to death.

"Get something from our bags that I can use to stop the bleeding," I tell Mary. "A blouse, a jacket, anything."

She stands up and lets out a small cry. "Someone's coming."

I jump up. Through the window I see people with bobbing flashlights approaching. There are five or six of them. I don't think it's Martin and Milo bringing help. I can hear them now. They are young and sound like they're having fun, but that doesn't mean they aren't dangerous. Probably a teen gang from the South Zone.

"What should we do?" Mary asks.

"Go back to Mrs. Franklin. Hide."

"What about you?"

I look down at the boy. His eyes are closed again. I don't want to leave him, but it's too dangerous to stay. Reluctantly I follow Mary back to our hiding place. I'll have to stop the bleeding later.

"What is it?" asks Mrs. Franklin.

I hold a finger to my lips. "Ssh, don't make a sound."

CHAPTER 22

I barely have time to crouch down before the young people burst in, their flashlight beams shooting about wildly.

"Wow, look at this place."

"God, what a mess."

"There's still some beer," says a boy who has gone straight to the coolers.

"Who wants a candy bar?"

"Me!"

"I want chips."

"Cigarettes anyone?"

There is a small chorus of me's. Then a girl's voice says, "Oh, gross! There's a dead body back here."

"Let me see," a boy says. "Are you sure he's dead?"

"If you think I'm going to feel for a pulse, you're crazy. You do it."

"Don't push," says a girl. "I don't want to get blood on my shoes."

"What's the matter? You think you might catch something you don't already have?"

"Fuck you."

"Let's get out of here."

"What's your hurry?"

"I don't like being around dead bodies."

I hope they won't look too closely and notice he's alive. You can never be sure if teens like these will show compassion or be cruel. If they're from the South Zone, that means they're infected with the virus. Life is cheap to them. They see people dying every day. I hope they'll hurry up and take what they want and leave. The longer they stay, the more blood the boy behind the counter is losing.

And then a meow comes from the box beside me. My heart stops. Beggar couldn't have chosen a worse moment. There's utter silence in the store. I tell myself maybe they didn't hear.

"What was that?" a girl asks.

"What was what?"

"That noise."

"You're hearing things."

"Am not, asshole."

Footsteps crunch on the broken glass as someone walks toward us. I squeeze Mary's hand and hold my breath. We stare toward the aisle, waiting for one of the teens to appear.

The beam of a flashlight blinds us. A moment later I can see the girl holding it. She's young, as I expected, with a nose ring that glints and heavy eye makeup that makes her look like she has two black eyes. Her red hair stands out around her head like a punk halo. We stare at each other.

"Hey, Audrey!" a boy shouts. "You see anything back there or what?"

She shines her light on Mrs. Franklin sitting on the packing crate, on Mary huddling beside me, and then on me again.

"No," she shouts back. "There's nothing here."

Then she turns away. In a flash I remember her. The girl with the red armband who rings up my groceries at the supermarket. The one who replaced Phyllis. I don't know if what she just did was a random act of kindness to strangers or if in fact she recognized me. In any case she has spared us.

"Let's *go*," says another. "This place gives me the creeps."

The girls leave first, spilling out into the street with squeals and laughter. The boys follow, lugging beer and soda with them.

We wait until we're sure they're gone before Mary and I creep back to the boy. I don't bother to tell her not to because I know she will anyway.

"It'll be okay," I tell the boy, taking his hand. "We're going to help you."

"Are you sure he's alive?" Mary asks doubtfully. "They said he was dead."

"He's not dead. You hold the flashlight, and I'll find something to stop the bleeding."

I look around with growing desperation. There has to be something I can use—a cloth, a pad. Why isn't there an emergency first aid kit? Every place should have an emergency first aid kit. I see candy, chips, pretzels, gum, cigarettes, donuts, cookies, but no first aid kit. I'm about to take off my top and rip it up when I remember there are clothes in my backpack. I hurry back to where Mrs. Franklin sits on the packing crate.

"How is he?" she asks.

"He's lost a lot of blood. I've got to stop the bleeding." I unzip my backpack and pull out a T-shirt.

She lays a gnarled hand on my arm. "No, take something of mine."

There's no time to argue. I unzip her bag and pull out the first thing I find, a cotton nightgown.

"I don't think he's alive," Mary says when I rejoin her. "He hasn't moved and I can see his eyes."

She can see his eyes because they aren't quite closed. But that doesn't mean he's dead, I tell myself. He could still have a pulse, and if he does, he's still alive. I pick up a limp hand and try to find a pulse. But I can no more find one for him than I could for Father Chavez. *Don't be dead*, I plead silently. *Please don't be dead. We'll get you to safety.* I wish I knew his name. Maybe if I said his name, he would hear it. They say people in comas may be able to hear their names. But of course he's not in a coma. I start to cry. I tell myself it doesn't mean anything if I can't find a pulse. My fingers are shaking too much, and besides what do I know about finding pulses? I'm not a nurse.

"It'll be okay," Mary says, putting her hand on my shoulder.

"I didn't want him to die."

"Let's go back."

I look at the boy lying there, his clothes soaked in blood, his eyes slightly open, unblinking. She's right. There's nothing more I can do.

She takes my hand and tugs me back down the littered aisle between the shelves to where Mrs. Franklin sits on the packing crate.

"He's dead," I tell her.

"Come sit down. The young men will be back soon."

I drop down beside Mary and put my head on my arms. I feel terrible. Mary pats me lightly on the back, trying to comfort me.

"I hate to bring this up," Mrs. Franklin says, "but do you suppose there might be a restroom here?"

I look at her blankly for a moment, not comprehending, and then start to laugh. Her question strikes me as comical, hilarious even. I laugh so hard I'm not sure if I'm laughing or crying.

She waits patiently until I stop.

"I was thinking there must be a restroom around here somewhere."

"Over there." Mary points toward a door with a sign that says 'employees only.'

She turns out to be right. There is indeed a restroom behind the door. We take turns using it by the light of our newly acquired flashlight. As I wash the blood off my hands, I see my reflection in the mirror over the sink. Lit from one side by the harsh beam of the flashlight, I hardly recognize myself. There's a smear of blood on my cheek, which makes me look like the wild teens from the South Zone. A thought flashes through my mind. What if the boy had the virus? I push it away and use a wet paper towel to wipe off the blood. Then I splash my face with cold water, which makes me feel better.

"I wonder when they'll come back," Mary says as I sit down beside her on the floor again. She has taken Beggar out of the box and is petting her. Beggar regards me with narrowed eyes. I wonder if she blames me for having been confined in the box.

I glance at my watch. 11:30. We've been here about an hour. I wonder how Milo and Martin are doing.

"I suggest we play a game," Mrs. Franklin says.

"What sort of game?" Mary asks.

I don't feel like playing a game. Milo and Martin could be in trouble. There's someone dead in the room with us who was alive only a little while ago. He had friends and people who cared about him, and now his life has been senselessly snuffed out. I don't want to pretend he isn't there. Someone has to mourn for him. Someone has to worry about Milo and Martin.

"Let's think of something beautiful," says Mrs. Franklin.

I groan. This is definitely not a game I want to play. I'm not in the mood for it. Life is not beautiful. It's vicious and terrible.

"Like my necklace?" Mary says, touching the little silver phoenix at her throat.

"Well, it could be," Mrs. Franklin says. "But it doesn't have to be an object. It could be a place, or a memory."

"How about Beggar?"

"Yes, Beggar is very beautiful."

"It's your turn," Mary says.

"My something beautiful that I remember is a sunset," Mrs. Franklin says. "I was with my husband and we were on a road trip to the Grand Canyon, and we had stopped at a lookout to watch the sunset. I think it was the most beautiful sunset I've ever seen."

"Sarah, it's your turn," Mary says.

"Oh, I can't think of anything. Skip me."

"Please!"

She looks at me so beseechingly. All right. For her sake I'll do this. Surely I can think of something to offer her. Mrs. Franklin has her sunset. What do I have? My hometown springs to mind. But what can I say about it? Will I give her Main Street with its stately old courthouse and green lawn and the row of stores that lined the street? Or how about the old brick public library where I stopped on my way home from school in the afternoon? Or walking home through leaf-strewn streets in autumn? The red and yellow leaves that carpeted the sidewalk and choked the gutters? Our street lined with maple and elm trees? Our house, not so very different from the other houses on our street, compact, neat, with tulips in the flower bed? My mother was very proud of her tulips. She planted them every spring and spent time on her knees patiently weeding them. She loved tulips.

I can't say any of these things. I'll start crying. What then? What can I give Mary? And then I remember my grandmother's farm and how I used to sit on her porch as a child and look across the road at a field of wheat rippling on a summer day. I can give her that. And the cornfields, the green cornfields, where I played hide-and-seek with cousins among the tall cornstalks.

"Cornfields," I say. "And wheat fields."

Mary doesn't ask me to explain. "Now it's my turn. I've got one. A waterfall. The most beautiful waterfall in the world."

I remember the photo I saw on the Internet of Havasu Falls.

"That was your home, wasn't it? That was where you lived."

"Yes, it's a long way from here."

"Would you like to go back sometime?"

She nods.

"I'll take you there. That's a promise. I'd like to see that waterfall too."

"What if they don't come back?" she asks suddenly. I know she means Martin and Milo.

"They will."

"I know. But what if they don't?"

"Then we'll find a way to get to the hospital by ourselves."

I have no idea how we'll do that. I can't carry Mrs. Franklin and she can't walk. I know we aren't far from the wall, but after we cross, the distance to the hospital on foot will be considerable. Maybe I'll have to leave Mary with her while I look for help.

The minutes slip by. Sometimes we hear people go by on bikes or on foot. Most of them are traveling in packs. No one else stops at the Seven-Eleven. Once a police car speeds by with its blue light flashing and siren wailing. Sometime after midnight Mary falls asleep against my shoulder while Mrs. Franklin dozes with her head leaning back against the wall.

I can't imagine why Milo and Martin have been gone so long. I'm glad now that I insisted Martin take the gun. I wonder if the Glenview Tower is still secured. Did I make a mistake taking Mrs. Franklin with us? Would it have been better for her to stay in her apartment on the fifteenth floor of the Glenview Tower than to be left sitting on a hard packing crate in a trashed Seven-Eleven with a dead body only a few yards away?

Somehow I have to get Mary and Mrs. Franklin to safety. When it's light, I'll go out and search for help. Maybe in the light of day it won't be as dangerous. I intend to stay awake, but eventually I begin to feel overwhelmingly tired and tell myself I'll close my eyes for just a few minutes and rest. The next thing I know I wake with a start, my heart racing. It's still dark.

"What's wrong?" Mary says sleepily, lifting her head.

"Ssh," I say.

Someone has come into the Seven-Eleven. Every muscle in my body tenses as I strain to listen.

"Sarah?" It's Martin's voice near the door. I can hardly believe it. He's alive and safe.

"Here," I say, springing to my feet.

Mary turns on the flashlight, and in another minute he's there in front of us, his sling gleaming palely. I'm so glad to see him that I throw my arms around his neck and kiss him.

"Wow!" he says.

"Where's Milo?" I ask. "Is he all right?"

"He's outside. Come on. We've got a jeep."

Mary and I help Mrs. Franklin to her feet and put her cane in her hand. When Mary picks up the box, Beggar meows.

"It's all right," she says softly. "They came back."

Mrs. Franklin walks between Martin and me, clinging to Martin's good arm and mine. I have my backpack on now and carry her bag in my free hand. Underfoot the broken glass crunches.

"There's someone dead back there," Mary tells him as we pass the counter. "Sarah tried to stop his bleeding."

"Did she?" he says, glancing at me.

"I couldn't save him. I tried but. . . ." I bite my lip and don't finish my sentence.

When we step out of the Seven-Eleven, I see Milo waiting for us beside a yellow jeep. "Let's go," he says, looking up and down the dark street. He sweeps Mrs. Franklin up and sets her in the front passenger seat. The rest of us climb into the back with our bags and Beggar's box.

"What took so long?" I ask as the jeep starts moving.

"It's not easy to find something on wheels out there," Martin says. "At least not something that runs. And we had to hide every time a gang came by."

"Most of the rejects from the South Zone must be over here," Milo says. "There'll be even more once it's daylight."

"How did you get the jeep?" I ask anxiously. I know we need it, but I hate to think someone was stranded because of us.

"We found it by the side of the road," Martin says. "Whoever was using it abandoned it when it ran out of gas. That's what took so long. We had to steal some gas to get it to run."

"And stealing gas wasn't exactly a piece of cake," Milo adds.

"Are we going to the South Zone now?" Mary asks.

"Yes." I pat her hand. "Don't worry. Everything will be all right."

"Miss me?" Martin whispers in my ear, his good arm around me.

I tilt my face up and our lips meet just as the jeep swings around a corner. We break apart grinning, then try again, this time more successfully.

"Look, there's the lady," Mary says as the billboard of the smiling woman comes into view. You can make out the gleam of her teeth and the whites of her eyes in the moonlight.

When we reach the wall, the gate looks as heavily guarded as ever; however, a few blocks farther we find a gap that has been blasted in it. Milo stops and turns off our headlights.

"What do you think? Can we make it?"

"I don't know," Martin says. "I wouldn't take bets on it."

"You want to check it out?"

"Sure. Why not?"

"Be careful," I say before Martin hops out.

I watch him jog across the street and disappear into the gaping hole in the wall. We duck down when a gray pickup rushes past with two motorcycles close behind. They might be pursuing it, or they might be traveling with it. The important thing is that they keep going. Then Martin reappears and gives us a thumbs-up.

Milo revs the engine. "Everyone hang on tight." He slows down as we go through the gap. The jeep lurches over rocks but makes it. When we are on the other side, Martin slides into the back again with Mary and me. "Looks like we don't have to walk the rest of the way," he says, grinning.

We race through the dark empty streets of the South Zone. The night wildness is on the other side of the wall now.

CHAPTER 23

When we get to the hospital, a yellow school bus is parked at the rear entrance with two armed men guarding it. When they see the jeep, they raise their rifles.

Martin leans forward. "What's happening?"

"It looks like they're taking my advice," Milo says.

When we get close enough for the men to see Martin, they lower their rifles.

"Where you been?" asks one, coming over to the jeep and giving Martin a high five. He's a lanky young man wearing a baseball cap.

"Around," Martin says. "What's with the bus?"

The young man shakes his head. "We were told to stand here and guard it. That's all I know."

"Looks like someone is leaving."

"That's the word."

"Where to?"

"Beats me. You better ask Sandy about that."

"Okay, I will."

"She's in the cafeteria. They're holding some kind of meeting."

"Thanks."

Milo parks the jeep and we all climb out.

"Hey, kid, want me to carry the cat?" Milo asks Mary.

She shakes her head and tightens her hold on Beggar's box. I don't think she's forgotten he suggested leaving Beggar behind.

It takes us a while to make our way to the cafeteria because Mrs. Franklin is slow, but eventually we get there. The cafeteria is crowded with people—patients, their relatives, hospital workers, people in wheelchairs, and children—everyone who is well enough to sit or walk. The room is lit by several lanterns and a dozen flickering candles. Sandy stands near one of the lanterns speaking to the group when we arrive. She looks very young as she stands there in her white lab coat in the dim light, her blond hair pulled back in a ponytail. We quietly sit down in the back of the room at a free table.

"I don't know what's going to happen," she says, looking around the room. "If the military and police pull out, the whole city may become lawless. There may be no more jobs for any of you in the North Zone. And it may become even more difficult—or impossible—to get supplies. On the other hand, things may stabilize. I'd like to be able to tell you that we have a rescue plan, but we don't. We can try to get some of you to safety. Those of you who are not infected by the virus can go to Tucson. We think things aren't as bad there, but they won't allow any infecteds in, and we can't even be sure if they will take others. It means more mouths to feed. They may shoot first. . . . I'm sorry I can't offer you a better plan."

"What about the children?" a woman shouts.

"The children who are infected are better off here with us. We can't rely on people being kind to them just because they're children."

Everyone starts talking at once.

Sandy raises her voice. "Those of you who want to leave can see Dr. Liu. He's in charge of the bus."

Evidently she saw us come in because when she's done she walks straight to our table. "I knew you'd turn up sooner or later," she tells Martin, giving him a poke on his good shoulder. "You always do."

"You know me," Martin says, grinning. "It takes more than a bullet to stop me."

"And I see you found Sarah." She smiles at me.

"It was the other way around. Sarah found me." He puts his hand on mine and we exchange quick glances. This closeness between us still feels so new.

After I've introduced Mary and Mrs. Franklin, and Mary has taken Beggar out of her box for Sandy to pet, Sandy sends someone for bottled water and cans of soda for us and milk for Beggar.

"We saw the bus outside," Martin says. "Where did you get it?"

"One of the parents used to drive it and had it stashed in a warehouse."

"Handy."

"So where have you been? I'm dying to know." She pulls up a chair and sits down with us.

"I got picked up by the cops when I was crossing the wall. They thought I started a fire."

She raises an eyebrow. "Did you?"

Martin looks shocked. "Are you kidding? Why would I start a fire? We've got enough of those as it is."

"Sorry. I didn't mean anything. It's just that David's been worried. We all have."

"Couldn't you just tell him I was okay? Make something up?"

"What was I supposed to make up? You weren't here. David's not stupid."

"What am I going to tell him?"

"Tell him the truth—that you were in jail."

"He'll never let me hear the end of it." Martin shakes his head.

Sandy grins. "He'll love it."

"I hate to interrupt this happy reunion," Milo says, "but I assume you know the wall's been breached?"

She nods. "We heard the explosions."

"You have to get these people out of here. It's not safe here anymore. The whole city is going to blow."

"You heard what I just told them. I don't know what else to do."

"Listen, there are fires in the North Zone. You know what that means if no one is trying to stop them?"

"Of course I know what it means," she says wearily. "The whole city could go up in flames."

"So do you have a plan? A real plan?"

"Take it easy," Martin says, coming to her defense. "Can't you see she's exhausted?"

Sandy presses her fingers to her temples as if her head aches. "Look, we have no place to go. I can't just walk out and leave some people to die. They can't all leave and I'm not leaving anyone behind."

"Then they'll burn," Milo says bluntly. "And so will you."

For a minute no one says anything. I put an arm around Mary, who is staring at Milo. I wish he hadn't said that, at least not in front of her.

"If you've got a better plan, let's hear it," Martin says.

"What else can we do?" Sandy asks.

"Move them."

"How? All we have is the school bus and several ambulances."

"I'll get you some more transport."

"Even if you could, where would we go? None of the cities will take in sick people. We can't just camp in the desert."

"Excuse me," Mrs. Franklin says, speaking up for the first time. "Maybe you could. I think I know a place that might work. Do you have a map?"

Soon we have a map spread out on the table and a lantern. Mrs. Franklin leans forward and studies it carefully. "Now where is it? Right about here." She points with her finger. We all lean forward, trying to see.

"What's there?" Sandy asks, frowning. "I don't see anything."

"Cliff dwellings," Mrs. Franklin says. "They're difficult to get to, but once you're there. . . . Well, you'd have walls around you and a roof over your head. And there's water nearby."

"We couldn't possibly—"

"Why not?" Milo demands.

"Cliff dwellings? Are you serious? How would we get everyone up there? Some can't walk, and others, even if they can walk, can't climb." She looks at Mrs. Franklin. "Could you make a climb like that?"

"I couldn't. Not by myself. But if we took ropes and pulleys. . . ."

"It just might work," Martin says, squeezing my hand.

"I don't know." Sandy looks at the map doubtfully.

"I say try it," Milo urges. "At least this way they have a chance."

"I agree." Dr. Liu has quietly come up behind us. "Let's try to save as many as we can."

Sandy doesn't say anything for a moment, just stares at the map and bites her lip. Then she looks around the crowded dimly lit room at all the people. Her eyes fill with tears and she blinks them back. "What do you think, Sarah? You haven't said a word."

"I think you should leave," I tell her. "It's a risk, but staying here may be a bigger risk."

She nods. "All right then. Let's do it. Cliff dwellings it is."

"Start packing," Milo shouts to the room at large. "You're all leaving. No one gets left behind."

The room bursts into cheers, followed by a cacophony of voices. There's excitement in the air.

Lydia appears, Henry in tow. "Look who's here, Henry."

The little boy looks shyly around the table, one finger in his mouth.

"Hey there, Henry." Milo reaches for the boy and sets him on his lap.

"So you're coming with us?" Lydia asks me.

I glance at Martin. "Yes, it looks that way."

"What about you?" she asks Milo.

"I haven't quite made up my mind."

I look at him. He wants the rest of us to get out because the city is going to burn, but he's going to stay? Why? What does he think he can do?

"Why not come with us?" she asks. "What's there to stay for?"

He looks at Henry sitting on his lap and then at her. "You think I should?"

"Yeah, I think you should. Henry would like that, wouldn't you, Henry?"

The boy nods, although I'm not sure he knows what he's being asked.

"And would *you* like it?" Milo asks.

She hesitates. "Yeah, sure."

"Well, then maybe I will."

"Now that that's settled," Martin says, "where do we get transport for all these people?"

"I know a place south of here, not too far away, where we should be able to find something," Milo says.

"I want to come too." I glance at Martin. I don't want to be left behind this time, wondering if he's okay. I'd rather be with him.

"Can you drive?" Milo asks.

I haven't driven a car since leaving the Midwest seven years ago, but I think it will all come back once I'm behind a wheel. They say you never forget, right? Or was that riding a bike?

* * *

Fifteen minutes later we are back in the jeep, Milo driving, Martin beside him, me in back. It's about four in the morning, and the streets are deserted. The gangs that are usually out at night are in the North Zone now, along with the crazies, the drug addicts, and the looters. Everyone else in the South Zone is apparently still sleeping.

"Where exactly are we going?" Martin asks.

"A place I know," Milo says vaguely.

"Friends?"

"Sort of."

"Are they troubleshooters too?" I ask, leaning forward.

"No," Milo says. "Most definitely not."

"Do they know what you are?"

He snorts. "What I am? What am I?"

"An undercover cop."

"*Was*, you mean. I think I'm out of a job now."

That's true. We all are for that matter. But that's not our immediate concern. We have to find a means to transport about eighty people out of the city. Sandy is depending on us.

After several miles we pull off at an industrial park surrounded by a high fence topped with barbed wire. Milo climbs out and opens the gate. Then we ride until we come to a large warehouse, where a big man with a rifle steps in our path.

"Uh-oh. Doesn't look too friendly," Martin says under his breath.

I agree, but when the man sees Milo, he lowers his rifle.

"Son-of-a-gun, if it isn't Milo the man," he says, grinning, then comes over to the jeep to give Milo a high five.

"Hey, JJ," Milo says.

"What's up?" JJ asks.

"We need a truck. You got any to spare?"

"Any particular reason?"

"Seems like a good time to hit the road."

JJ scratches his chin. He's in need of a shave. "I hear the wall was blown last night. You know anything about that?"

"You heard right."

"So what happens now?"

"I don't know. Could be bad. You want to come with us?"

"Where you going?" He glances curiously at Martin and me.

"North," Milo says.

"Out of the city?"

"That's right."

"What's up there?"

"A lot of cactus. Some snakes and lizards." Milo doesn't mention the cliff dwellings. I wonder if that's to protect us or because he thinks JJ might laugh. Then again it might just be second nature for him to be secretive about his activities.

The man laughs. "Well, you got that right."

"So you want to come?"

JJ shakes his head. "No, I'll take my chances here. I'm not partial to snakes."

Milo shrugs. "Suit yourself."

Inside the warehouse are several large delivery trucks, one of which is being repaired. A young mechanic working on it asks what we want, and Milo flashes his badge.

"You got a truck here we can borrow? There are some people over at the hospital on Seventh Avenue we need to move."

"You're taking them out of the city?" the young man asks, looking from one to another of us.

"That's the idea."

"You think those fires are coming this way?"

"Could be."

He wipes his hands on a dirty-looking rag and cocks his head to the side. "You need a driver? I could drive one of these babies for you."

"That would be great."

"Can I bring my girlfriend along?" Again he looks at each of us in turn, as if debating if he can trust us.

"Sure," Milo says. "Bring your girlfriend along."

"How about fuel?" Martin asks.

"You can fill up around back."

"Can you spare some extra?"

The man hesitates. Martin whips out a wad of bills.

"Sure. Why not? You got containers? Never mind. I'll set you up."

Soon the back of the jeep is loaded with red plastic containers of gas. Milo gives the man directions to the hospital and tells him to meet us there within half an hour if he wants to come with us.

"Be careful who you wave that money in front of," Milo tells Martin as we drive away. "You just might get our throats cut."

Martin shrugs. "He seemed like a nice enough guy."

"You never know who you can trust. And where did you get all that money anyway? I thought you said you only had a couple of dollars."

"In my wallet. I'd be stupid to put all my cash in my wallet.

What if I got robbed?" He grins. "Anyway I thought you said these guys were friends."

"That doesn't mean I'd wave money in front of them."

"He gave us the gas, didn't he?"

"Will you two stop it?" I say. "Honestly, I feel like I'm on playground duty."

Our next stop is an auto dealership. This time we have to break into the lot, which is surrounded by a tall chain-link fence with a padlocked gate. A dozen dusty cars are sitting about. Some have been stripped, but most are still in good condition. No one has bothered to steal them because without gas they can't go anywhere. Although we could hot-wire any vehicles we want, it seems simpler to break into the building and find the keys, so that's what we do. Back outside, we pour some of our gas into a black SUV and a pickup.

"Too bad we can't take more," Milo says regretfully, looking around at the other cars. "What a waste."

"We better get back," Martin says, looking to the north, where a red glow can be seen in the sky from the fires in the North Zone.

Now we have three vehicles. Martin drives the pickup, and Milo the SUV. That leaves the jeep for me. The gears make grinding sounds the first few times I shift, but gradually I get better at it. It feels good to be behind the wheel again. I like the feeling of speeding along, being in control of where I'm going. I realize I'm looking forward to leaving the city. I don't know what's waiting for us out there in the desert, but I'm ready for it.

We arrive at the hospital just as the mechanic from the warehouse pulls up in the delivery truck. It looks like he lost no time. The parking lot behind the hospital is a hive of activity with people carrying out supplies and piling them in heaps, ready to be loaded. There are more vehicles now, including several ambulances.

When I climb out of the jeep, I notice the sky to the north has grown redder. In spite of the warm night air I shiver, wondering how fast the fires will spread.

Sandy is directing people where to put things. Her eyes grow wide when she sees the delivery truck. "Where did you get it?" she exclaims in delight.

"Some friends," Milo says as the mechanic and his girlfriend jump out of the truck.

"Jon," the mechanic says, holding out his hand, "and this is Megan."

A tall gangly young woman with hair falling over one eye smiles shyly at us and ducks her head. I notice that she's pregnant.

"Glad to have you with us," Sandy says, shaking their hands. "We need every able-bodied person we can get."

"Just tell us what to do," says Megan. "It's real nice of you folks to let us come along."

"You can help load the truck. Just start putting things in. We'll take as much as we can."

"How's it going?" Milo asks as Jon and Megan walk away.

Sandy glances towards the red sky in the north. "We're going as fast as we can. How much time do you think we have?"

"Maybe only a few hours. It's hard to say."

"It's coming closer, isn't it?"

"Yeah, it is."

I stare at the red sky. In my mind I see buildings on fire—and houses. I see people trapped.

"Well, let's not stand around talking," Martin says. "Let's get to work." He tugs my arm. "Are you all right?"

"Yeah, I'm fine," I say and resolutely turn away from the red sky. He's right. We have to concentrate on the here and now, on getting people to safety.

There's no time to lose. Top priority is to get the bedridden into the ambulances and the delivery van. We lay down mattresses and bring them out one by one on stretchers. Even the children help by carrying out boxes of medical supplies and canned food. We can smell smoke in the air now and everyone is caught up by the sense of urgency. Milo borrows a moped and rides off to find out how close the fire is. Fifteen minutes later he's back.

"We should go now," he tells Sandy. "If we wait any longer, it may be too late."

"But we haven't got everything packed," she protests. "Another ten minutes."

Dr. Liu has overheard and is beside her now. "We'll just have to leave some of the supplies behind. It can't be helped. Maybe we can come back for them later. We've got all the patients in. That's what's important."

Her lip trembles but she nods. "All right." She turns to the people who are still loading the vehicles. "Okay, folks. Time to leave."

Mary runs up to me holding the box with Beggar inside. "Can I ride with you?" She looks at me with expectant eyes.

"No, sweetie," I say. "You ride with Mrs. Franklin in the school bus. She needs someone to watch out for her."

For a minute she looks as if she might argue, but then she heaves a sigh and resigns herself. "Okay. I'll take care of Beggar *and* Mrs. Franklin."

"Good girl."

I watch her run to the school bus clutching her box and climb in. I'm glad that in the end I have found a way to get her out of the city.

Martin shoves one last box of supplies in the jeep. "I guess this is it."

"I guess so."

"Listen—"

"Let's go!" Milo bellows.

Martin smiles at me. "When we get there. . . ."

The delivery truck starts up.

Martin runs a finger down the side of my face. "Catch you later, kid."

I watch as he lopes off toward the school bus and wonder what he was about to say. When did I get so attached? A week ago I didn't know him. Now if anything were to happen to him, how could I bear it? But that's how it is. It goes along with caring about people. You open yourself up to them and it makes you vulnerable to all kinds of hurt. Well, I guess I'd better get used to it.

I turn and climb behind the wheel of the jeep. There's a last-minute scramble to climb into vehicles. Then the ambulances lead off, followed by the school bus, driven by Martin, and several cars. Next come Jon and Megan in the delivery van, then Milo in the black SUV with Henry buckled in beside him, followed by one of the men from the hospital in the pickup. I'm last, driving the jeep, which is loaded with supplies. Lydia rides with me, a handgun on the floor beside her feet in case we need to protect ourselves or our cargo.

As we drive down the streets, we pass people on foot and on bikes fleeing from the fire.

"You think this is going to work?" Lydia asks as we pass a deserted amusement park, its Ferris wheel jutting up against the sky like a relic of a bygone era. "You think we're doing the right thing dragging all these people off to some ancient cliff dwellings in the middle of nowhere?"

"I don't know. But we can't stay here."

"It seems strange, doesn't it? Like civilization is moving backward."

"Maybe it is. Maybe we took a misstep and need to back up and try again."

I see her put her hand on her stomach.

"Are you all right?" I ask anxiously.

"It's too soon to feel the baby move, isn't it?"

We look at each other. Lydia's eyes brim with tears but she's smiling.

"Everything will be okay," I tell her.

"Sure."

At her throat I notice the gleam of the black onyx Mrs. Franklin gave her.

"I just wish Jeff could be here," she says wistfully. "I miss him."

"I know you do."

It's more than an hour before we are finally out of the city with the highway stretching ahead of us for miles and the desert spread out around us. The sky is growing light now. In the distance lay the mountains, but between them and the road there is nothing but cactus. In the beginning we pass people on bikes and motorcycles and see a few cars abandoned by the side of the road that have broken down or run out of gas. Soon after the sun comes up, the pickup in front of us stops to let a man, woman, and child climb into the back. I stop too and when the pickup moves forward, so do I. It isn't a place to leave people stranded, and I'm glad the pickup stopped for them.

Around midday we get our first sight of the cliff dwellings, still some distance away, carved in the side of the mountain. A paved road leads to a parking lot for tourists. From there we follow a footpath to the base of the cliff. To get up to the dwellings, we have to climb a ladder, those of us who can. Within an hour we have our pulley and winch assembled and are hoisting the first of our sickest patients to shelter.

CHAPTER 24

Mrs. Franklin was right. There's water nearby, and overhanging ledges to shade us from the sun. It's a beautiful spot, with the desert before us, and purple mountains in the distance. Every hour of the day the landscape changes as the sunlight falls across it. I look out at the view when I wake in the morning, watching the sunrise in the east. I think I'll never tire of that. And then I have the glory of a sunset to look forward to when the day is done. I feel as if I never really saw these things before.

I often find myself thinking about the people who lived here long ago, the ancient cliff dwellers. I wonder what they were like and what happened to them in the end. I like to think they moved on to another place when it was time, just as we will. But for the while that they lived here, they must have been happy. There are many rooms carved into the cliffs, and that's a sign they flourished.

Not everyone in our group lived to see this place. Heather was riding in the first ambulance with her brother Jamie when he died. We buried him in the desert below the cliff dwelling.

It isn't easy for us, but we are all safe, and that's what's important. We have cots to sleep on at night, and those who feel too confined in the cliff dwelling can sleep in the open under the stars.

For now we have enough food and water. We cook over an open fire or use a grill. Beggar seems quite at home, leaping nimbly from one rock to another, free to explore when she wants, and with many willing hands to pet her when she wants a little affection. Mary has made friends with Henry and some of the other children, and now instead of being an outcast as she was at the State School, she appears to be the leader of the pack. I haven't forgotten my promise to take her to Havasu Falls and the village of Supai. I have no idea when or how, but one day I will take her there.

Mrs. Franklin does not move quickly, but with her cane she can get around, and with the help of pulleys and winches, she can go down to the desert floor whenever she wants. More often she prefers to stay near the cots where the sickest of our group lie. She reads to them, talks to them, and tries to make them more comfortable in any way she can. Heather is frequently there too with her guitar. Sometimes when I'm writing in my journal or helping to cook the evening meal, I hear her singing and pause to listen. Her voice sounds as if it belongs in this setting, surrounded by desert and mountains. I know she misses her brother, but life doesn't stop when we lose the ones we love, and they wouldn't want it to. When she sings, I think she feels she is still singing to her brother, and somewhere he hears her. She has discovered David is partial to her singing and sometimes sings to him now that her brother is gone.

Sandy and Dr. Liu are kept busy tending to the needs of both the well and the sick. I've noticed she calls him Richard now, and when she does, it seems to hang there in the air a minute between them, as if neither is quite used to the new familiarity.

Milo and Lydia are also cautiously getting to know each other. Sometimes I've seen him watching her when he thinks she doesn't notice, and sometimes I've seen her watching him when she thinks he doesn't notice. Henry has attached himself to both, and when he's not running with the other children, he's at Lydia's side or trotting beside Milo.

What has struck me most about how we all seem to have changed since coming here is that we have hope in a way we didn't before. Against all odds people are falling in love and life is going on—not just enduring but blooming. None of us knows what the future holds, but we have hope, and that's something.

And what of Martin and me? We too are getting to know each other. We are among those who choose to sleep under the stars. His cot is next to mine, and sometimes we talk late into the night. There are so many questions to ask, so much to say. Other times we just lie together silently, holding each other, and look up at the stars.

I don't know how long we'll stay here. Unless we can find more medical supplies, those who are infected will start getting sicker and eventually die. We will need more food and water as we use up the supplies we brought with us. There is talk of sending scouts to find out if any of the communities to the north will take us in, and soon some of us will go back to the city to see how bad the damage is and if we might be able to return. At any rate we need to get more supplies if we can. We know going back could be dangerous, but we'll take that risk. I've thought about it a lot, and I know now that while we all yearn for a safe haven, sometimes we have to take risks. That's why I have volunteered to be one of the ones who go back. This time we'll be together, Martin and I, and whatever the risk, we'll face it together.

ABOUT THE AUTHOR

Deanna Madden has taught literature and creative writing at various colleges on the U.S. mainland and in Hawaii. Her previous publications include the novels *Helena Landless* and *Gaslight and Fog*, the novella *The Haunted Garden*, short stories, and essays on literature. She lives in Honolulu and is at work on her next novel.

37019685R00159

Made in the USA
Middletown, DE
21 November 2016